The Realm

JEFF WRIGHT

ISBN
979-8-88945-325-3 (Paperback)
979-8-88945-326-0 (eBook)

Brilliant Books Literary
137 Forest Park Lane Thomasville
North Carolina 27360 USA

To my beloved sister, Patty Jean, whom we called PJ -
may you rest in eternal peace in God's loving arms.

1

On a dark mountain road, Ted Barrington and his son, Gabe, were leaving Lake Tahoe, California to their plush home in San Francisco. It was just another trip the pair took since Gabe's mother passed away. Three years ago, she was killed in a horrific car accident; just a trip to the local store cost her, her life.

Gabe's depression afterward was taking affect. Even though Ted's world had collapsed as well, he needed to keep his son occupied. The trips together seemed to help.

It had rained for most of the day. By the time they had left the resort, the roads were muddy and wet. Thirty minutes into their journey, lightning lit up the night sky.

"It looks like a miserable ride home, Gabe."

"Just be careful, Dad." "I will, son."

As they proceeded down the winding mountain stretch, a beat-up truck with a camper shell rounded a steep curve coming toward them in the opposite direction. It was going fast.

"They have to be a fool traveling like that," said Ted, slowing down.

Just before the vehicles passed one another, the truck went out of control; hitting the rocky embankment then forcefully swerved back into Ted's lane.

"Dad," screamed Gabe, bracing himself.

As the truck crossed in front of Ted, it sideswiped a tree and continued downward into a ravine. Even with the windows rolled up, the sound of crushing metal was deafening.

Ted immediately pulled over. "Stay here," he ordered, switching the Jeep's emergency lights on.

"Dad!!"

"Stay here, I have to check if they're alright."

"I don't want to be alone."

"I need you to call 911. Tell 'em what happened. When they come, you show them where I went down."

Worried sick, Gabe just nodded.

Ted quickly got out, opened the tailgate and grabbed his flashlight. Crossing the road, he slid down the embankment through the thick brush where the truck had landed; upside down, one headlight still on. The air was foul with smoke and gasoline. He heard a whimpering moan coming from the driver side window.

He spotted a man hanging half-way out with blood streaming down his face. The roof was caved in; the windshield smashed.

"Are you alright?" asked Ted, kneeling before him.

"No," the man gasped, spitting up blood.

"I must have dozed off."

"Here, let me pull you out," said Ted, taking the man's shoulders.

"I can't move," he groaned; the pain was engrained on his face.

Ted reached in. The steering wheel had buckled, trapping the man.

"I feel cold, so cold," he murmured; thick red blood oozing from his mouth.

Ted knew the man was dying; there was nothing he could do.

He looked at Ted with wavering eyes. Letting go of the door, he grabbed Ted's arm. "There's a trunk in the back," he weakly spoke. "Please, I beg… take it. You're the only one who can save her. Just find the ke…"

Ted waited for more.

The man's head slumped over. Ted heard the last breath expel from his lungs.

Feeling helpless, he deeply sighed; looking at him hanging there. In that moment, he thought of the man's last words. "What trunk? Save who? Why'd you say that?"

It seemed forever that he just knelt there waiting for an answer. The gas fumes and smoke brought him full circle. He clasped his hand over his nose and mouth and hurried to the backend. The camper shell was destroyed, stuff lay everywhere.

A trunk, a trunk... where is it? he thought, scanning the area. The sky lit up; opening the forest around him. "There," he said, seeing an old steamer trunk lying half in the brush.

"Dad," shouted Gabe.

Ted spun around. "I thought I told you to wait in the Jeep!"

"The phone wouldn't work. I got scared up there."

"It's OK. I'm glad you're here. See if you can lift that side."

"What for?"

"The man told me to take it." "What's inside?"

"I don't know. You got it?" "Yes."

With the trunk safely in the back of the Jeep, Ted drove to the little town of Delmont. There, he pulled into a diner that was closed and called 911.

The dispatcher took his report, along with the mile number on Interstate 24 where the truck had left the road. Then, she asked, "Are you *thee* Ted Barrington, the one who owns the hotels?"

"Yes."

"OK, Mr. Barrington. You'll be getting a call once they retrieve the body."

"Thank you, and... I'd like to know the man's name."

"Ask... I'm sure they'll give it to you." "Thank you."

Ted sat there a moment. It had been a long, sorry night. Seeing someone die, someone you couldn't save; painful.

"You ready to go home?"

He looked over at his tired son. "Yeah, I'm ready."

It was close to 2 am when they finally reached the mansion. As Ted went around the back, his butler, James Wilmore and his housekeeper, Hazel Manning came out the back door.

Six months ago, Ted was in dire need of a good concierge to run his New York Hotel. James appeared right out of the blue. He'd never forget the day this well-groomed, distinguished black man, with an air of authority walked into his office for an interview. He landed the job before sitting down. It was James' greeting, "Welcome to the Barrington Hotel." It was simple, and yet, it wasn't; for he said it in five different languages.

During the interview, Ted found him not only extremely intelligent, but very interesting to listen to. Said he was a Yale grad, majored in history, been around the world and was astute in many subjects; ancient artifacts being one of them.

Ted's only question was why a concierge?

James replied that he found the job intriguing and loved working with the public; especially foreigners.

After just three months on the job, James had the hotel running proficiently. Ted then decided to ask him if he'd liked to oversee his three estates. His answer was quick, *yes*.

Hazel Manning on the other hand, was a tall slim woman, with short brown hair. She looked more like a school teacher and had been with Ted since Gabe's birth.

"Mr. Barrington," she belted. "What happened?" she fussed, seeing the two covered in mud.

"Sorry I did not call. I knew you two would be asleep. We witnessed a bad accident coming home. A truck went off the road up in the mountains."

"How awful," she replied.

"Did you notify the police?" asked James.

"Yes, once we reached Delmont."

"Dad tried to pull the man free. He died," added Gabe in a tone of sadness.

Hazel sighed seeing the anguish on his face. "Come now, let's get you cleaned up. It's late and you need to be in bed," she said, catching Ted's eye.

Ted gave her a tired smile.

"What about..." Gabe went to say.

"Tomorrow, son," interrupted Ted.

"Alright, you," pushed Hazel, wrapping her arm around the boy.

Gabe loved Hazel. Her mannerism was always business-like around his father, but when they were alone, she was truly fun to be with. She even played video games with him.

James followed Ted inside. They stood next to the circular staircase for a moment. He could tell that Ted was in a remorseful state. "Try and get some sleep, Mr. Barrington," he said, goading him up the stairs.

"After what I saw, I don't know if I can,

James," he replied, heading to his room.

As Ted proceeded up, James stood there leaning on the banister. *The man has been through a lot these lasts few years.* In that moment, he drifted back in time.

The wealth of one man can be extremely attractive and very powerful; especially when the name is inlaid with 18K gold on the finest hotels around the world; *Barrington.*

James had learned from Hazel that when Ted turned thirty, his father died of a heart- attack. His mother along with the CEOs knew Ted was not ready to take the helm of the hotel empire. His mother saw to the business until Ted was thirty-five.

Now running one of the most successful enterprises, just like his father, Ted was sought after by every politician, business mogul and those bigger than thou movie stars.

His handsome face had been plastered on more magazine covers and had been written about in almost every newspaper across the land; the youngest tycoon, single to boot.

The ladies, well, they flocked to ol' Ted like vultures. Ted however, was overwhelmed only by one beauty, Jennifer Dorr; daughter of Senator Kevin Dorr from Virginia. He met the Senator and Jennifer at one of his expensive parties at his other mansion in Key West, Florida.

When Senator Dorr and his daughter came over and greeted Ted. Ted found Jennifer extremely attractive. During their conversation, Ted asked the Senator, "With your permission, Sir," he said, placing his attention on Jennifer, "would you like a tour of my house."

"I'm sure my father would like me off his arm, so he can rub shoulders with the men. I'd love to."

With a pleasant nod from her father, Ted took her arm and they departed.

Over the next hour, the two found each other's company electrifying. They laughed, told jokes, and she even enjoyed his polite demeanor and his gentlemen ways. It was something you did not see often in wealthy men.

When the evening was through, she invited Ted to go sailing with her at her father's estate in Virginia. He said yes but, she figured he wouldn't come. When he did, her heart just melted.

One year into their whirlwind courtship, Ted asked Jennifer to marry him. She said *yes*. The wedding was a lavish affair. Ted made her feel like a queen. Jennifer found herself pregnant a year later. They named their son, Gabe.

A simple trip to the store destroyed the family, James sadly thought, heading to bed himself.

He took off his clothes, turned out the lights and crawled under the covers. As he closed his eyes; he imagined how terrible it must have been that day inside the Barrington household. To release his sadness, he looked upon the relationship between Ted and Gabe now. The two were inseparable. Ted even took Gabe to his business meetings in New York. Not one top adviser in the company questioned the boy sitting in on the meetings.

Losing one's mother at such a tender age had to be terrible. Everyone knew Gabe had his days and would for a long time. So, all the corporate CEOs and those who ran his hotels on a daily bases, became like aunts and uncles to the boy. Gabe seemed to warm to them too.

2

That morning around 6 am, Ted proceeded downstairs. He met James under the archway in the foyer.

"Morning, James, you have a minute?" "Yes, yes, what can I do for you, sir?"

"Let's talk in my office."

James thought it was one of the finest rooms in the house, with its big bay window, dark wood walls and black leather furniture. Books lined the back shelving; the walls decorated with photos of places Ted had visited throughout the world.

As Ted rounded his desk, he said, "The man I tried to save last night gave me something before he died."

"Really. What was it?"

"An old steamer trunk."

"Steamer trunk," repeated James intrigued.

"That's what it looks like. He begged me to take it. I thought it strange."

"What did he say?"

"He said there's a trunk in back. You're the only one who can save her."

"Wow; save whom?"

"Those were my thoughts. Right now, I'd like to get the trunk in the house without being seen."

"Heavy?"

"No, long though." "Tonight?"

"Yes," replied Ted, leaning up on his elbows. "We'll wait until Hazel retires for the night. I'm not sure where to take it."

"The basement storage room; neither Hazel nor the maids go in there."

"Good idea. Inform me when she goes to bed."

"Yes, sir, I'll get your coffee now." "Thank you."

A few minutes later, there was a knock on his door. "It's open."

In bounded Max, Gabe's beloved Irish setter, and Gabe carrying his coffee.

"What are you two doing up so early?" he asked, rubbing Max's head.

"I hardly slept thinking of what could be inside that trunk."

"Me too. Tonight, you, James, and I are going to bring it inside when Hazel goes to bed."

"You don't want her to know?"

"Not just yet. After she sees you off to bed, turn on your walkie talkie. When I say Delta One, come down to the kitchen; *quietly.*"

"Quietly?" questioned Gabe, glancing at Max.

Ted looked at the dog.

"I'll keep him quiet."

"Alright, he can come too."

The day was like any other day in the Barrington household. Hazel oversaw the maids, while James had the landscapers and pool company in. Ted spent most of his day inside his office; telephone calls and a meeting with his financial adviser. He also took one call, which he was expecting from the Sheriff's Department.

"Good afternoon, this is Sheriff Larry Biggs from Lake Tahoe. I'm calling in regards to the accident you reported on Interstate 24."

"Yes, Sheriff, do you know the man's name?"

"Yes, the license plate came back to a Ryan Wilson. The problem we're having though," he said then paused. "Mr. Wilson wasn't inside the vehicle."

"Then who was it?" "No one."

"What do you mean no one? I went down there and could not pull him free. He died right before my eyes."

"I'm sorry, Mr. Barrington. When we got to the truck, there was no one there. We searched the entire area."

"Maybe a mountain lion or a bear came and took him?"

"If an animal had, I'd suspect there would be some of his remains still inside the truck. We found no claw or drag marks, no fragile evidence, like hair, bones; not even a shoe."

The phone went silent.

"Mr. Barrington."

"I'm still here, I think."

"Look, I'm not saying that you didn't see anyone. I'm just reporting the facts to you."

"My son Gabe even saw the man. He came down when he could not call 911."

"I don't know what to tell you, Mr. Barrington. We're as baffled as you are. The truck is there but no body."

"Thank you, Sheriff Biggs." "Look."

"Yes."

"If anything comes up, I'll call you personally."

"Thanks Sheriff, I'd like to know if I'm still sane."

"No problem."

Ted got up from his desk and walked over to the bay window. *I saw the whole thing. Gabe saw it too. The man was there. I spoke with him. I watched him die,* his thoughts drifting; looking outside.

With a frustrating sigh, he shifted on the trunk. *What if it's not in the back of my jeep?* That thought disturb him. He rushed out the door through the house to the garage. When he approached the Jeep, he hesitated for a moment. Without looking through the back glass, he opened the tailgate. The trunk was sitting there.

"This is impossible; totally insane. I wouldn't have the trunk if Ryan Wilson didn't tell me to take it. What happened to him? It's like he just vanished into thin air."

"Everything OK, sir?" asked James, hearing him mumbling to himself.

Ted turned facing him. "I don't know, James," he sighed. "I just got a call from the Sheriff's Dept. They found no one inside the truck. No footprints, no drag marks, not even a shoe."

"Really?" he replied stunned.

"Do I look like a man losing his mind?" "No sir."

"If you had said *yes,* I would've then asked you - what is this?" he said, showing him the trunk.

James shook his head. "That is truly baffling, sir. However, you have the trunk. Maybe what's inside will explain all this tonight."

"I hope so," he replied, heading back to the house.

James stood there watching him leave. He gave a subtle sigh and proceeded to the men cleaning the pool.

That evening, Hazel seemed chipper than usual. She stayed up late playing Gin with James; who could not wait for her to say, *I'm done for the night.*

Ten o'clock rolled over to ten thirty, then eleven before she finally had enough. James got up and wished her a goodnight.

"It will be a goodnight when I finally beat you," she mused.

It was twenty after eleven when Gabe's walkie-talkie sounded. "Delta One."

"On my way," he whispered. "Now you be quiet. We're on a secret mission," he warned Max.

Max wagged his tail; following him downstairs.

When they gathered in the kitchen, James and Ted went out for the trunk, while Gabe held the back door open. They carefully hauled the trunk down to the basement with Max right on their heels.

Gabe opened the storage room door and turned on the lights. "It sure is dusty in here." "It sure is. Let's set it down on the floor next to the covered mirrors and dressers."

Standing back, James looked at the wooden trunk with its deer pelt top and the three straps securing it. "That's very old," he remarked.

"How old do you think?" questioned Ted. "As you can see, it is made of cedar and fastened with wooden pegs. The images carved in the trunk are from the time of Magnus Maximus, Emperor of Rome around 380 AD."

"Are you saying this trunk is over 1700 years old? How could that be?" gasped Ted.

"I don't know. Best we look inside and find out," replied James.

As Ted slowly untied the straps, James and Gabe anxiously stared at one another. Ted felt anxious himself while lifting the handle.

James peered inside. "Well now, what do we have here?"

There before them was a long object covered with a faded wool cloth. By the outline, they could not help but think it was a body.

Ted reached in and slowly pulled the cloth down to reveal a veiled face and hair. "Damn," he shrieked, jerking his hand back.

"My God, it's a dead woman!" panicked Gabe; heading for the door.

"Wait Gabe," said James.

"Wait for what? We need to call the police."

"This is an old trunk, and so is the body. It's probably a skeleton," he replied, pulling the cover off. It wasn't a skeleton. The arms and hands looked more like a doll. "Check this out," he said.

Gabe came back and looked. "Oh my God, it's a doll, a life size doll," he beamed.

"It is at that," said Ted. "James, take her legs. We'll place her in that chair."

Once the doll was seated, Ted knelt before her and removed the veil. The doll's eyes were closed. He gently lifted the lids and instantly caught his breath; staring at the most exquisite creature he had ever seen. She looked so real with her shoulder length hair, her soft pink cheeks, and perfect nose. Her sensual red lips were slightly open, as if she were saying something.

"I've never seen anything like it," he sighed, helplessly captivated by the beauty before him. Her blue eyes were as deep as the ocean, drawing him inward; ever inward. Then in a flash, he saw a tunnel on the side of an eerie looking castle with high walls sitting along a river bank. From underneath the water, something came up from the deep with razor sharp teeth. Terrified, Ted fell back on the grass; or he thought he did.

"Dad!"

Ted came out of his dream like state sitting on the basement floor.

"Sir, are you OK?" asked James, worried. "Yes, yes, I…" he replied, "I thought I saw something; something within her eyes." "Saw what?" they questioned.

"I don't know. A castle, tunnel and a dark river," he murmured, drifting. "There was something coming up from the water. Something enormous…" his voice trailed off.

Gabe looked at him then back at the doll. He stood up and walked over to her. Touching her hair, it was as soft as human hair; not some fancy wig. "Take a look at this!"

"What?" said Ted.

"This is not a wig – this feels real."

"Impossible," said Ted, getting up. He felt it too, even parted it to the scalp. "Will you check this out," he continued amazed. "You can't even tell how they wove it in. Besides that, where is her stitching?" he said, lifting the doll's arms and hands. "My God, there is no stitching anywhere on her. How can that be?" he questioned, staring at James. "If she were as old as that trunk, she'd look primitive; the stitching well defined. I don't think a company today could make such a doll as this."

"I don't think so either, sir."

"How old do you think she is?"

James shook his head thinking. "From her dress and shoes, I'd place her in the 1500, early 1600 hundreds."

"But you just said the trunk was from the Roman days," questioned Ted.

"Maybe whoever had her, Dad, changed her dress."

"You're a smart boy, aren't you?"

"Not as smart as you, James," replied Gabe.

"Why would anyone make a doll like this?" asked Ted puzzled.

"That's a good question, sir."

"Well, whoever made her had to be wealthy," added Gabe.

"True. I'd say she comes from royalty," agreed James.

"It's possible. Maybe she was made in the image of a king's daughter, who suddenly died, and he wanted her back one way or another," added Ted, looking at them with raised brow.

"You might be right, sir. I could believe such a story."

With his mind reeling, Ted stared at the doll. She was stunning, like a *Goddess*. As his eyes remained glued on her, he whispered to himself, "You're the only one who can save her. Save her from whom, from what? It doesn't add up. Why would Ryan Wilson say that to me?"

His son and James stood there listening to him.

"Maybe the loss of blood made Mr. Wilson say that without realizing what he was saying," questioned James.

"I don't know, James. He didn't sound out of his mind. He sounded more like a man making his final wish before departing this world," he replied with a thought. "Wait a minute. What if, and this may sound funny.

What if Mr. Wilson did in fact depart this world and that's why they found no body." "That's way out there, Dad."

"Yeah – way out there," agreed James.

"It could be way out there, but then again, I was just thinking. What if he just wanted me to keep the doll safe?"

James nodded. "That could have been it."

"Well, look. It's getting late. I think we should call it a night. We can work on this tomorrow."

"Tomorrow is already here, Dad."

"I know," he replied, wrapping his arm around his son. "James, turn off the light when you come up.

"I'm coming up now, sir," he replied, walking behind them. At the door, he looked back at the doll sitting there. With pleasantry in his eyes, he whispered, "very soon, very soon." With that, he shut off the lights and closed the door.

3

Through the morning mist, I see a girl. She's waving; calling out for me to come. I can't hear what she's shouting. It looks as if someone needs help.

The fog is so thick, I can't see a thing. Wait, in the misty haze, I see a faint castle wall, an opening. Is that where the girl wants me to go?

Hurry, go in. It's a dark tunnel with a dim light at the end.

"Barrington, Barrington," a female voice cried out.

"Where are you?"

"Here, I'm here. Please, I beg, save me." "I'm coming, I'm coming!"

The tunnel seems endless. Keep running, I must keep running.

"Barrington, Barrington."

"Where are you, where are you!" Ted shouted, tossing and turning. Then suddenly, he awoke, finding himself in bed. He quickly sat up, still hearing the distant voice. *It's a woman. She was in that tunnel. The same tunnel I saw in the doll's eyes.* Within his torment, he seemingly glanced over at the clock, 4:00 am.

Days after, as he and James poured over history books, web sites trying to find the date the doll's dress was made in, he could not stop thinking of her. She was in his thoughts during his conference calls, his meeting in San Fran, and the times spent with his son.

He became obsessed with the dress. It was the only thing they had to go on to find out what century *she,* the doll's image was created in. With that knowledge, they hoped to hone in on the kingdom, country, or even a village in which she may have lived.

His nights afterward were no different. He found himself tossing and turning, reliving the dream; seeing the girl waving, the fog, the tunnel, and then the soft voice desperately crying out to him.

Come Friday, when Chuck Moore, Ted's financial adviser came over. It was what he said just before he got up and left, that hit home. "You seem a little different."

"Different?"

"Yeah; you seem to have a lot on your mind."

"I always have things on my mind.

Running a hotel empire does that to a person.

Chuck laughed. "You know," he said. "Not to be nosy and all. I mean, it's really none of my business."

"Shoot."

"Are you seeing someone?" "No."

"Dating someone?" "No."

"It looks like I'm wrong. I've seen it though, in lots of men when they've met someone and can't get them out of their heads."

"Well, seeing you're my financial adviser, I'm glad you're not wrong that often."

Chuck laughed walking out. "Call you next week," he said with a wave of his hand.

Ted shut the door and stood there. He knew deep down inside that it was more than seeing someone, dating someone. He had actually fallen helplessly in love with a doll… a doll now sitting down inside his storage room. The one Ryan Wilson gave him; then *he*, Ryan simply vanished. The whole thing seemed so crazy, so unbelievable… which in reality, Chuck was right. He did have a lot on his mind but, how do you tell a close associate that you've fallen helpless in love with a doll. That's insanity at its finest.

On Saturday night, Ted decided to drink more then he usually drank before going to bed. He thought it would help him sleep. One can only wish. When he awoke with the same dream, he had had enough. There was only one thing to do. Go down and sit with her, talk to her, and keep losing his mind; the part that was left anyways.

Slipping quietly downstairs, he walked through the kitchen to the basement door. Down he went. At the end of the hall, he entered the dusty storage room filled with his old furniture. The trunk lay open on the floor; the doll sitting next to the covered mirrors and dressers.

Kneeling before her, she was like Cleopatra; perfect in every way. He wasn't there however, to just gaze upon her beauty. He could do that for all eternity. What he wanted the most was to know all about her. His questions seemed random.

"In whose likeness were you created?" "What is the woman's name?"

"Please tell me, in what century are you from?"

No reply. Just that mesmerizing stare, as if she was helplessly trying to speak. It wasn't only in her eyes; it was there on her parted lips, as if she were talking when she was frozen in place. The only thing that came to mind was one minute the Tin Man was chopping wood, the next minute he was rusted solid from the rain. That's what she looked like; helpless.

With a heavy sigh, he lifted her soft velvet hand. "Never in my life would I have dreamt of falling madly in love with such an exquisite creature as you. Even if you were a painting, I would sit for hours in your company."

After those words, he looked upon her; taking in every detail of her gorgeous face.

"Do you know a Ryan Wilson?"

No response.

"I suppose not. Before he died, he begged me to watch over you; keep you safe. I will do that with all my heart, and hopefully one day, I'll discover who you are."

As he went to stand, the reflection of the trunk sat within her eyes behind him. He stared at the reflection then slowly looked back at the trunk. A thought appeared. *Is it possible that somewhere on that trunk is the answer I'm seeking?*

There was nothing inside that he could see. He closed the lid and turned the trunk this way and that; nothing. He flipped it over; nothing but two small holes on the back. As he placed the trunk upright; looking at the deer skin lid, there was padding underneath. *Hmmm,* he thought, checking the underside. The deer hide was pegged to the wood.

He looked for something to pry them out. Under his late wife's sewing machine was a pair of scissors, alongside some needles and thread.

He used the sharp point to remove the pegs and pull back the fur. Goose feathers flew everywhere. To his disbelief, there in the center was a compartment with what looked like a binder; a book of sorts. On the cover was a symbol. It looked like a family crest; A lion's head on a banner with two crossed swords over it.

The book was secured with two strands of rope; brittle with age – easy to break. The front and back covers were made of thin wood, bound together with twine. The paper was parchment. It looked as old as the Pharaohs.

Taking a seat on the floor next to her, he opened it. The first page was the same symbol. When he turned the page, at the top was written, The Royal Kings of Ur.

The first king was King Hess, his wife, and the names of their children. Each one had something written about them.

As Ted read down the list, he stopped and read the story of each of the king's daughters; hoping to find the daughter the doll's image was possibly made in.

When he came to King William Tyrus' family, an unimaginable tale unfolded before him.

King William of Ur, ruler of the Northern Kingdom betrothed his youngest daughter, Juliette Tyrus, Countess of Lyon Head Castle to Richard Lennard, son of King Fredrick Lennard, ruler of the Southern Kingdom. The wedding was to stop the wars between the two empires once and for all.

This arrangement was unsettling to the sisters of Black Water, a dark evil place, beyond the land of Ur. The sisters, Greta and Hagar were witches, better known as the Twins. Their castle sat along the Isle of Drake. They hatched a plan to abduct Juliette so the two kingdoms would not unite with a *marriage* that would come against them as one force.

The next paragraph stated that King William and King Fredrick both sent five of their best soldiers to go find her. When they did not return, William secretly sent two spies to locate the soldiers and to find his daughter. On their return, they informed William what had happened.

Two days into their travel, the spies discovered the soldiers within the Forbidden Land, owned by the Twins. All ten, plus their horses had been turned into stone. Some were sitting by fires, some walking, while others were resting in tents.

The only thing that stood out was a hawk that had perched itself on the rigging line of the main tent. It too had been turned into stone. Not being able to carry any of the men back, the spies decided taking the hawk for proof.

They wrapped the hawk inside a wolf pelt and continued onward toward Black Water to try and rescue the Countess themselves.

When they reached the village of Orbed, they met a peasant girl by the name of Shana, who worked for the Twins. She told 'em that she was heart-sickened to see Juliette locked up and feared she'd soon be killed. She told the spies everything she knew.

Shana… hmmm, she sounds like the peasant girl I saw waving to me within my dreams.

Suddenly, the storage door opened. It was James.

"I couldn't sleep. Thought I'd come down and sit a spell," he said.

"I couldn't sleep either, James. Glad you're here. Come in and shut the door."

"What did you find?"

"This," he replied, lifting the book. "Have a seat."

James settled next to him on the floor.

"I found it under the deer covered lid. It's a book of the Royal Kings of Ur and their families."

"Wow."

"Wow is right. I've been reading about King William Tyrus' family. Have you ever heard of him?"

"I've heard the name but cannot recall when."

"Biblical you think?"

"It does sound biblical. However, looking at the dress she is wearing. If he and his family were from those times, they wore wool clothing."

"Maybe Gabe was right. Someone changed her dress," questioned Ted.

"They could have."

"Alright, read to here and catch up - then read the rest aloud."

"As you wish, sir," he replied, taking the book.

Ted watched James read to himself and then come to the part of the two spies and what Shana had told them.

During Shana's visits with Juliette inside the dungeon, Juliette confided in her of what had happened.

The day before the wedding she, Juliette was traveling from the Southern Kingdom back to her father's castle when the Twins' soldiers ambushed them and overtook her carriage.

Before her escorts confronted the soldiers, a strong gusty wind came down the road. Out of the twirling dust, the evil witches, Greta and Hagar appeared.

Juliette's escorts fell to the ground in fear.

"Down with you, my sweet little Countess," ordered Greta.

Frightened, Juliette did as she asked.

This was Juliette's first encounter with them. Awful things they were with their hideous green faces, crooked noses, and wicked hands; their long fingernails sticking out like daggers. The witches' soldiers looked menacing as well; sitting upon their horses wearing black armor with shields and swords.

To Juliette's surprise, they released her four escorts so they could go back and inform her father, King Willam that she had been abducted. Their only order or more so, threat, was, "Tell William to not send a soul, for they will be torn to pieces by the hounds of hell."

After her escorts rode off, Hagar turned on her heels. "Take this beauty back to the castle."

With that, the two raised their capes, spun in a circle and vanished into thin air.

During her journey to the castle, Juliette stated to Shana that the trip was long and grueling; through the Valley of the Damned, several villages, the Dead Forest, and then onward to the castle itself – a dark, gloomy, place; bitterly cold. It reminded her of a large vulture with its disgusting bald head and cruel sharp beak sitting high on a bluff overlooking the Isle of Drake. The water was as dark as coal; thus they named the castle, Black Water.

Upon opening the gates, she was greeted by a pack of evil looking hounds, three-foot- high at the shoulders with menacing eyes; their canines dripping with saliva. Their snarling taunts made her run inside the castle as the guards shoved and pushed her along.

Shana stated to them that it was the first time she saw Juliette as she was being escorted down into the dungeon, a place that smelled worse than death. She felt sorry for the Countess and slipped down to see her on several occasions.

Then, one morning, the Twins came. They gave Juliette some food and something to drink. That was the last time Shana said that she saw Juliette. She was forbidden to ever enter the dungeon again.

Shana then informed the two spies that she was secretly seeing the castle's hound keeper, Bulmen. Shana knew if she told him to keep the hounds penned-up for the night, the two could slip in unaware and rescue Juliette. The keeper did as she asked.

"Stop!" said Ted.

James set the book in his lap.

"I can't believe this. Shana *is* the peasant girl I saw in my dreams. She was the one waving to me, then I saw a secret tunnel, which I suspect leads to the dungeon," he said blindly staring at the floor. "My dreams have been the same for a week now, James."

James sat there looking at Ted drifting.

He waited to hear what else he had to say.

Ted glanced up at him. "I remember it clearly, James. After entering the tunnel, I heard her calling out to me… Barrington, Barrington, please I beg, come save me, save me. I was running and running - calling back,

I'm coming, I coming… then I'd wake up."

"That is truly astonishing, sir. I'm perplexed by it all."

"I'd say. I'm as puzzled as you are.

Please, keep reading."

"I will. Now where was I…. right here."

When the two spies found Juliette down in the dungeon, they were horrified. She was not herself. They knew the witches had placed a spell on her. After carrying her out of the dungeon, and getting as far as they could, they decided to bring her back to Lyon Head under the cloak of darkness so she would not to be seen.

When King William and his wife, Victoria saw their daughter, they were mortified. King William then secretly ordered the two spies be executed so they would never tell a soul. From that day forward, Juliette was kept hidden up in the tower from the outside world.

Throughout the kingdom and villages, all that was known about Juliette was - she had been abducted by the Twins and was possibly dead.

"Oh my God!" gasped Ted. "What, sir."

"I just figured it out."

"Figured out what, sir?"

"That is no doll sitting there." "No?"

"This is Juliette, Countess of Lyon Head. I'd bet my soul those evil witches turned her into a doll," he said, hastily getting to his feet.

James watched him walk over to her.

"You see, James. That's why her hair is human and she has no stitching," he continued with his back to him.

"You think?"

"Yes, and here is something else that's puzzling," he replied, facing him.

"What?"

"What happened to Ryan Wilson? People just don't disappear; especially when they're dead."

"I don't know what happened to him, sir. It's hard to believe he wasn't there when the police went down to the truck."

Ted turned back staring at the doll. In that moment, it was like striking a match to flint; the whole thing coming to light. "You're the only one who can save her," he whispered Ryan's words. "Oh my God, I just remembered."

"What?"

"Ryan said something else before he died."

"What was that?"

"Just find the ke.." he replied, thinking back. His face went slack. It finally dawned on him. "I know what he was trying to say now." "What?"

"Just find the key," he sighed. "I can't believe it. I can't believe it."

"You can't believe what?"

"I know where the key goes." "You do?"

"Yes, here - help me place the trunk upright."

Once settled, Ted had James look inside.

"What do you see?"

"I see the bottom of the trunk, sir." "Look harder."

"Wait… I think I see what you're talking about."

"What do you see, James?"

"The bottom of the trunk looks like a door."

"It's a door alright, and those two holes on the side are for the key."

James slowly stepped away; staring at the back of Ted's head. "You're a very smart man, Mr. Barrington," he said in a deep straight tone.

Ted caught the change in his voice.

"Excuse me," he replied, facing him.

"I've waited a very *long* time for someone to finally discover the hidden compartment and the secret of the trunk."

"You've waited…." questioned Ted, trying to grasp his words.

"Yes, sir; you're the first one to do it," he replied, walking over to the doll. "You are correct. You're assumption is right. That is Juliette Tyrus, Countess of Lyon Head; and… as your son pointed out, someone *did* in fact purchase her a new dress thinking she was just a doll."

"Is this some kind of a joke?" spat Ted, unsure of the man standing in front of him. The one he had hired to run his New York hotel and then come live with him and run his three estates.

James bypassed that comment and continued. "I had an inkling that it would be you who'd finally solve the secret to the trunk. I waited for the right moment to present myself to you, and the opportunity came so simple when you needed a concierge for your hotel in New York."

"Who are you?" gritted Ted; knowing now that James had never graduated from Yale. It was all a lie. Before he could question him on that, James continued.

"That is of no importance. What is, however," he replied, unbuttoning his suitcoat, loosening his tie and then removing a chain from around his neck.

Ted's anger disappeared while focusing on what the chain was carrying; a pure gold skeleton key.

"It wasn't your wealth or, that you're a very intelligent man that the trunk ended up with you. You see, sir… you come from a very distinguished family line yourself, Mr. Barrington."

With his mind in neutral, Ted said nothing.

"I'm sorry that it took such a tragic accident in order for you to take the trunk, but as you can see, it worked."

Numb, Ted was still unable to speak.

"Ryan Wilson did not die. He just wanted you to believe he did."

"Where did he go?"

James again bypassed that question. "It was so pleasing to see you falling helplessly in love with Juliette and that you promised to take care of her and keep her safe. You have that chance right now, Mr. Barrington."

"I have that chance right now?" he scoffed; hearing that ridiculous statement.

"Yes, you have a chance to undo the spell and change her back."

"Really… how? She is sitting right here." "Take the key and open that door."

Ted turned toward the trunk. "What happens when I do?" he asked, turning back to James.

James was gone. The key on the chain lay at the feet of Juliette.

"Where are you?" he said, searching the room. "I need to know what to do after I open the door."

The room remained silent.

This has to be a joke, if not, it's pure madness, he thought, walking over to her. He knelt down, picked up the chain then looked into her eyes; more so her parted lips, as if she was speaking. In that still moment, he knew what she was saying. He heard it within his dreams a thousand times - *Barrington, Barrington… please, I beg, come save me.*

Her helpless words struck deep inside his heart springing forth anger. "I will," he said, standing. "I will go and break the spell the witches have placed over you and return and make you my wife."

At the trunk, he took one last look back at her sitting there then placed the key inside the two holes.

4

As Ted opened the door, he gazed into a swirling blue haze. Through the mist, further out he could see mountain peaks far off in the distance; sweeping white clouds and flocks of birds flying by. As he reached out to feel the wet mist, in an instant, a brilliant flash of light engulfed him. The energy reverberated throughout his body; then he was gone.

Before he could comprehend what had happened, he found himself standing on a rocky platform at the edge of a cliff. In front of him was a massive forest of giant redwoods, stretching skyward. Below the canopy, were smaller yellow flowered trees that hung over what appeared to be a path; an entranceway into the forest. The large leaves were dark green, the limbs ash color.

Overwhelmed, scared, not knowing what to do – that faint little voice in the back of his head whispered – *You've lost your mind, Ted. What have you done?* As those thoughts weighed heavily on his heart, he looked about for James. Where did he go if not here? He called out to him. Nothing but silence came back on the gentle breeze.

He slowly turned in a circle staring at the rough terrain all around him. Below, out past the cliff was a valley. Scattered on the ground were large boulders and rocks amongst the greenery. High overhead on the other side were impressive mountains; their peaks adorned in white sweeping clouds.

"Who is he, who is he," a voice came from within the forest.

Startled, Ted quickly spun around.

"We don't know, we don't know," another voice whispered.

"Is someone there?" he called out.

Wild hoots and cackling came back.

Ted hesitantly stepped down from the bluff.

His movement scared the miniature spider monkeys with white rings around their eyes. They raced out of the underbrush and ran into the forest.

Ted stood back holding his chest; their quick reaction frightened him. With his heart pounding, he proceeded to the path and walked underneath the flowered trees.

Within the branches and leaves, large, palm-size, butterflies, gold in color with blue spots on their wings were dancing to and fro amongst the flowers. He stood there amazed never seeing such beautiful creatures before. *Is this the land of Ur; Juliette's home?*

While pondering that, he walked down to the end of the path. There, he stopped observing the sheer depth of the forest. It looked old; ancient as time itself. The ground was covered in leaves; the undergrowth made up of tropical foliage and dead debris covered in moss. Over the top of the small hill up ahead was a misty blue haze drifting outward through the trees.

Apprehensive to even move, he slowly walked up the slope to see what was on the other side. When he reached the top, he held his breath taking in a single white tree in a mist filled clearing. It too looked ancient with its thick roots entwined around the base.

Just above the base, imprinted in the trunk was a face. It was well defined like smooth driftwood, washed ashore. The image had a beard and bushy eyebrows made-up of single strains of wood woven together. The nose was flat except for the hollow nostrils that stuck out. Eyes closed, it appeared to be sleeping.

Above the branches within the blue haze were small, mystical Manta Ray like creatures swooping though the mist then outward into the forest; as if playing. *I must be hallucinating… sea creatures flying through the air like birds on the wing. What kind of place is this?*

As he stood there awe-struck, admiring the scene before him, a deep voice spoke, "Who are you?"

It startled Ted. He quickly jumped back, tripping over his feet and falling over. When he glanced up, he was stunned; the face carved in the tree was looking at him.

"Did you… did you say something?" "Yes, who are you?"

Nervous and unsure of what to say, Ted slowly got to his feet. A part of him wanted to run; the other part was too frightened to even move. With a shaky tone in his voice he said, "My name is Ted Barrington. I haven't a clue to where I am. I just stepped through the door and now," he paused, "I'm utterly lost," he continued, looking about. "You see, I thought James, my butler would be here to assist me and…" he continued rambling on and on.

Within the foliage tiny barks and cackles were heard. Small creatures were peeking out from within the foliage; the monkeys, rabbits, chipmunks, raccoons and squirrels. A beautiful Doe and fawn stepped out to take a look.

"Humm," replied the tree. "One cannot be lost while standing at the beginning."

Ted faced the tree. "Did you say the beginning?"

"Yes, I am called the Beginning, for everything in the Realm starts here."

"The Realm," he repeated. "Am I in the land of Ur? The place I read about in the book."

"The book?" he questioned, thinking back to the Shadow carrying a book while walking alongside Shoeshon, the mighty bull elephant. He let it go; wanting to know more about this man.

"Yes, it's a book of the Royal Kings from Ur. It has all the kings and their families within; starting with the first king - King Hess and his family."

"Where did you come about such a book?" he asked, already knowing.

How do I tell him my story and have it appear that I haven't lost my mind? What do I have to lose at this point – it's already gone. "You see, I was given an old trunk. I discovered the book hidden in the lid. Inside the trunk was…" he said and then paused, "was Juliette Tyrus, Countess of Lyon Head."

The Beginning raised his wooden eyebrows staring at Ted. "Did you just say, Juliette Tyrus, Countess of Lyon Head?"

"Yes."

The Beginning drifted back, remembering when the Shadow and Shoeshon came to him with Juliette draped over Shoeshon's tusks. The Shadow informed him of her demise and that he was going to remove her from the Realm to keep her safe until they could break the spell. That is when *he* saw the *book* within the Shadow's hand. He granted the Shadow his wish and now… his thoughts drifted. *This man is stating he has her.* "If you have Juliette, why are you here?"

"I'm here to remove the spell the evil Twins placed upon her."

"The witches of Black Water?"

Cackles and hoots came forth from the animals; hearing him speaking of those wretched things.

"Yes."

"For one who appears to be lost you seem to know much."

"I only know of what I read in the book. I wish I had brought it with me, for the rest," he said then stopped.

"It may have been wise to have brought it with you. Not that it would help taking on the Twins. Their witchcraft is powerful. But what interests me even more is your name."

"Ted Barrington?"

"Yes, I heard word from a wise ol' owl sometime back that Juliette was not in love with Richard, son of King Fredrick of the Southern Kingdom."

"The book never mentioned that," replied Ted. "I only know that the witches abducted her to stop the wedding between the pair."

"They did in fact abduct her to stop the wedding but, little did anyone know. Juliette was actually in love with a man by the name of Sheppard Barrington, Lord of Corset."

"Sheppard Barrington!" replied Ted, thinking back to James telling him that he came from a distinguished line himself; his own family tree.

"Yes. I suppose she met him during one of her many travels outside the Northern Kingdom. It was she, her father used to appease the towns and villages to keep the people on his side, and it worked in some villages; for they loved Juliette. Who could not help but to love her; her beauty is beyond the stars."

"Her beauty is beyond even that," sighed Ted.

"Humm…. I utterly agree," replied the Beginning. "It was the ancient one who brought her here to escape the Realm until such a time as this."

"The ancient one?"

"Yes, Shoeshon, the mighty bull elephant carried her back to the beginning. She was draped over his tusks in a feeble state. He walked her down the pathway you just came from. There at the edge, he let her body slide into the portal which would take her to another place and time."

Ted nodded trying to take it all in. *Who was on the other side to receive her? Was it Ryan Wilson?* He hadn't a clue. "I stand here now, because," he replied; not sure of how to say it. "It was my butler, James who gave me the key to open the door and enter the Realm," he continued, hoping the Beginning knew James.

The Beginning stared at him. He knew whom Ted was speaking of and continued, "In the Laws of the Realm, if one takes a wife and they die, it is up to the brothers to see that she is well taken care of. If one is not married, they must marry her."

"But Juliette and Sheppard were not married? So why was I given this?" questioned Ted, holding the golden key around his neck out for him to see.

Heavenly sighs spilled forth from the animals.

Even the Beginning went wide eyed seeing it himself. *The magic within that key, coupled with love could change everything in the Realm.* "You're right, but they loved one another enough to have married. It was her father who was passing her off to appease King Fredrick."

"If I may ask." "Yes, go on."

"With all of my ancestors before me, why was I chosen?"

"That answer lies down the path," replied the Beginning, rolling his eyes sideways.

Ted Glanced in that direction. It was heading deeper into the forest.

"Where does it lead… to the Northern Kingdom?"

The wise ol' tree hesitated to speak. "It will lead you to your destiny if your heart so desires to fulfil your quest."

Ted's knees went weak hearing that. "I do, with all my heart desire to save her," his voice sounding shaky.

"If you make it back, I'll know you succeeded in your mission. Go now. Just follow the path."

"Wait, before I go, what is out there?" "Out there?"

"Yes, anything I need to worry about?"

"Humm, there are many things out there that could end your quest. Evil roams the Realm seeking new victims."

"And they are?"

"The wanderers, drifters, men without souls; then there are the predators, such as hyenas, wolves, wild hounds, and beware of the poisonous creatures; like scorpions and snakes."

That alone made Ted want to turn and head back to where he had just come. But what held his stand was the look in the Beginning's eye.

"How far is it to the Northern Kingdom?" "That depends on which way you go.

Just follow the path and it will lead you there. If you leave the path for any reason, you may end up worse than Juliette."

"Is there anyone who can assist me on my journey?"

The Beginning stared at him for a moment. "There are some who may, but beware, some may come as sheep, but are wolves. I wish you good luck."

Ted took in a deep breath and thanked him. With a tremble in his stride he set off down the path.

Once he departed, The Beginning called out to his trusted friend, "Major."

A beautiful grey falcon flew down and perched on a branch near his face.

"Find the Guardian. Have him watch over Ted as he makes his way to the Northern Kingdom. We must give the *Promise* safe passage until he reaches the gates. He holds the key to the Redwood Forest; with it - he has the power to understand the language of the animals - with that, I'll give him the power to command the animals as I have; for I am the Redwood Forest."

Overwhelmed with that revelation, Major stood erect. "We'll guard him with our very lives, Grandfather."

"See to it."

From the branch, Major set off on the wing to find Dewclaw, the giant grizzly bear; the Guardian of the Redwood Forest.

"Jasper," called Grandfather.

A beautiful black ferret with deep blue eyes scampered out and sat in front of him.

"Come up here."

Jasper climbed his trunk so Grandfather could whisper in his ear.

With his secret mission laid out to him, the ferret, took off though the woods.

The Beginning, known to the animals of the Redwood Forest as Grandfather, closed his eyes while thinking of the man Ted called James. A smile slowly appeared upon his wooden face as he went soundly back to sleep.

5

As Ted proceeded down the path, he was beside himself; feeling as if he were living in a dream, reality long gone. He was sure James would have been there but, he and Ryan Wilson vanished from his life like stars in the night to deal with this all on his own.

Fifty yards from the Beginning, he stepped out of those thoughts, studying the rugged terrain around him. Even though the Beginning said this path would lead him to the Northern Kingdom, he still felt lost; out of his elements.

Never before had he ventured into a forest alone, especially one so primitive and without supplies. With his mind now fixed on his situation, he gazed up at the blue haze filtering through the red woods, the large vines encasing the trunks as if trying to strangle them.

Below, along the ground, the tropical foliage and moss covered debris felt moist. He stopped to wipe his brow listening to the wild bird calls, hoots and howls; sounds he had never heard before. Gazing deeper into the interior, the forest frightened him. *I wouldn't even dare venture in there.*

That thought made him think of the animals the Beginning told him to watch out for; hyenas, wolfs, wild hounds and the poisonous creatures. What scared him the most was the hyenas and wolves. *Alone, without protection,* his mind reeled, scanning the ground.

Up ahead he spotted a fallen tree; next to it were large rocks and limbs. He picked up a limb, busted the branches and held it within his hand. He wished he had a knife to make a sharp point. Just having something to protect himself, not that it would, made him feel more at ease.

By mid-afternoon, he felt tired from walking. He looked for a place to rest; somewhere higher than he was. Just down the path, he saw a large rocky out crop and dead fall leaning against it. He walked over, climbed up and rested his back against the trunk with his feet hanging over the edge.

Hours later he awoke. The forest had all but disappeared; nothing but darkness. Gaining his senses he sat there listening to the sounds in the night. Haunting sounds that crept up his spine. Even the buzzing insects flying by seemed large.

As he sat there, off in the distance, he heard many things coming. They ran by then circled him. He knew they had gained his scent. *Am I high enough,* he thought not wanting to move. They continued to circle. Some leaped up trying to grab him. *Wolves,* his thoughts screamed.

Terrified, he pulled himself tighter to the trunk and beat them back, or at lease tried to with the limb. Then suddenly, the attack stopped. They were still there. He could hear them sniffing the wind. Behind him, he heard another creature coming; this one much bigger.

The wolves scattered in every direction. Hearing them run sent alarm bells off in his head. He knew he was now in serious trouble. *This beast could reach up and grab me.* He stood to get higher up; then he froze. The thing was right below. He could hear it breathing, could hear the large pads circling.

He sat their listening then everything went dead still; except the insects. He knew it had not left. It was down there somewhere.

In the wee hours, Ted finally fell asleep. When he opened his eyes, he could not remember drifting off. Out front and in every direction, the fog lay heavy in the air. He could even taste the moisture on his lips. Slowly standing, stretching his aching muscles he stood there listening. Nothing… not a sound except the birds and monkeys off in the distance.

His knees gave way thinking of climbing down. *What if it's still here somewhere?* He went to sit, thinking he'd stay the morning but, he was famished. He had not eaten in a while.

With limb in hand, he slowly made his way off the boulders staying close to the deadfall leaning against the rocks. On level ground, he stood there listening; as if trying to hear a pin drop. The silence was frightening as he took several steps outward to check behind his position. Fear instantly grabbed him seeing a large grizzly bear sleeping. As he stepped back to climb up, a twig snapped. The bear opened its eyes.

You're a dead man, his thoughts raced.

Just then, the bear stood, shaking its massive head. Its dark eyes bore into him, freezing Ted. He knew if he tried to turn and climb up, the bear would be on top of him in seconds; ripping him to pieces. *To be eaten alive;* gripped his heart. It made his whole body tremble. Without another thought, he fell to the ground in the fetal position; something he heard to do when facing a bear.

Ted heard the bear walk up grunting. It came so close he could feel its warm breath upon his face. With his eyes closed, he said a prayer; knowing his quest was over before it even started.

As he waited to be attacked, his son, Gabe flashed before him. His smile, his laughter; the good times they had. With his mind numb, trembling, and thinking through his life, the bear walked away and sat down.

Ted slowly opened one eye. He could hear it right behind him. He did not want to move – just breathing was hard enough.

As he waited, he heard a large bird fly up and land overhead. The bird called out. The bear grunted. With his mind on edge, he glanced up to see a large grey falcon sitting there. Then, above the falcon flying through the trees came a dozen white birds with golden head plumes and gold laced within their wings. They circled and landed in the trees around him.

What is going on? Why hasn't the bear attacked?

"Lord Barrington," he heard a man say.

"Who's there," he replied, keeping his head down.

"Stand up," the man said. "Dewclaw will not hurt you."

Dewclaw? The bear must be his pet.

Before he could answer, the bear walked up and nudged him. Ted's whole body trembled with fear. The bear nudged him again. This time he turned and looked at it. The bear stepped back.

Ted slowly sat up, looked about for the man but no one was there.

"You see," said Major above him.

Ted glanced up at the majestic grey falcon with razor sharp eyes. "Did you say that?"

"Yes. Stand up."

I'm in the world of make believe, he thought, slowly getting to his feet.

"Dewclaw is the guardian of the Redwood Forest. He will guide you until the valley. There, you'll continue to the Northern Kingdom where your destiny awaits," continued Major.

"My destiny," repeated Ted.

"Yes, your destiny. Go now, follow Dewclaw."

Ted looked at the bear.

"You can talk to him. He's not much for words, however."

"I see," replied Ted, thinking of the wolves Dewclaw chased off and then *he* staying the night with him. He nervously reached out his hand.

Dewclaw walked up and sniffed it.

"I'll be."

Dewclaw turned and started walking.

"Go," said Major. "Thank you."

Major took flight, so did the white birds.

The farther he walked behind Dewclaw. He wanted to ask the bear some questions. What did he have to lose?

"Who told you to come and protect me?"

Dewclaw lifted his head, ears back; while walking.

"You do understand what I am saying?"

Dewclaw stopped. Ted halted.

The bear turned and looked at him. "It was Grandfather."

"Grandfather?"

"Yes, the Beginning; he is the forest. He rules all that is within it. He's been here for thousands of years."

"He told you to protect me... why?"

"You are on a quest, a mission that we all want you to achieve."

"Saving Juliette Tyrus?"

"Yes, she is the most beloved human to all the animals. We call her the Countess of Ur."

Ted stared at him for a moment.

"There is much you do not know." "You're right."

"In time, you will," replied Dewclaw, turning back toward the path.

Ted looked at the limb in his hand. *I don't need this,* he thought, tossing it.

"I will take you as far as the valley where the Redwood Forest ends. Be careful the rest of the way," said Dewclaw over his shoulder.

Ted nodded.

An hour later, Ted saw the forest opening up. Further out, he could see a valley coming into view. There were mountains on either side. At the edge of the forest, Dewclaw stopped.

Ted walked up alongside him. "Thank you, Dewclaw for escorting me."

"Look for Major. I'm sure he'll be watching you from above."

Ted glanced skyward then out over the lush green valley. "I will, thank you," he replied, running his hand along Dewclaw's back.

Dewclaw stood there a moment watching Ted heading into the open plain. *The Promise has much to learn before taking on the evil Twins,* he thought, turning and walking back into the forest. *We'll be there; we will be there when needed.*

6

Ted walked out of the forest unsure of himself. He wanted to look back at Dewclaw but decided against it. How far he had to go to the village was beyond him. He just hoped he'd make it there soon; food was on his mind.

As the valley curved, near the base of the mountains, he spotted smoke rising up within a grove of pine trees. *Campfire,* he thought, thinking of food.

At the thick grove, there was a trail. He wondered if the person or people were friendly. His stomach won over, he proceeded onward. At the end, he stepped out into a small clearing. To his surprise, there was a hut. Out front, was a pile of wood, several buckets next to a busted hitching post. The grass covered roof looked as dry as a desert; the small windows covered with tattered cloth. The place appeared abandoned.

"Hello… is anyone there?" he shouted, eyeing the small corral; the fence half over, the gate missing.

He heard the door slowly creak open. He glanced back to see no one.

"Hello," he again said, walking up and peering inside. A savory aroma filled his senses; something was cooking on the stove. Inside, the interior looked rustic, abandoned as well. There was a table, two chairs, and a log- framed bed. In the back, next to the fireplace was a rocking chair. Someone was sitting in it.

"Hello."

The person said nothing.

As he walked over, he saw an old figure with long white hair and beard. Only his eyes, nose and cheeks could be seen. He looked brittle, worn to the bone; his clothing not much better.

"Good morning?"

The man slowly opened his eyes. They were blue, sharp and clear.

"I'm sorry to intrude but, I saw the smoke from your chimney." "It gets cold at night."

"I'm sure it does," replied Ted, glancing over at the pot simmering on the wood stove. "That smells good, do you mind?"

"No, help yourself."

As Ted fixed a bowl, the old man said, "You've been on a long journey, Lord Barrington. Come, sit a spell."

Awestruck by his words, Ted just gazed at him. "Lord Barrington," he questioned the title. "How do you know me?" he asked, taking a seat.

"I know all things pertaining to the Realm."

"Who are you?"

"My name is Patch."

For the first time in his life, Ted found himself without words. The only thing he thought he could add was how he came into the Realm. "I was given this," he said, lifting the gold key from out of his shirt Patch eyed the key. "In order to obtain that, you must have discovered the book of the Royal Kings of Ur."

"Yes."

"And the story of Juliette Tyrus?" "Yes."

"You solved the secret of the trunk?"

He knows everything, he thought, dumbfounded. "Yes."

Patch nodded. "Not many know of Juliette's whereabouts."

"Does that mean some people believed she is dead?"

"They do, but you and I know that she is no longer in the Realm."

"Does her mother, Queen Victoria think she is still in the tower?"

"She does. What assisted us in keeping this secret is she locked the tower and has resolved to never going up there again."

Ted nodded.

"You know," said Patch. "In order for you to break the spell, you must kill the witches of Black Water. Are you willing to do that?"

Unsure of himself, Ted hesitated to answer.

"While you're pondering that, there is something you need to know."

"I need to know everything."

"And you will. Stay a few days. It will give us plenty of time to talk and," he paused, "in the meantime; I have some things that need mending."

Ted thought of the busted fence and the gate. "I will."

"Before we start, I also want to inform you."

"Go on."

"There are those in the Realm who have the power of knowing."

"Knowing?"

"Yes, knowing that you are here." "How; are they like you?"

"No, they belong to the darkness." "What is this *knowing*?"

"I'll put it this way. How does a spider *know* it has something on its web?" "It feels the vibration."

"Correct."

"I'm confused."

"Everything is connected together like webbing. Those with power may not feel the vibration a spider would feel, but they have a knowing."

Ted again nodded.

"As soon as you entered the Realm, some knew you were here."

"Are you speaking of the Twins?" "Yes."

Ted sighed shaking his head.

"Lift your chin, Lord Barrington. They do not know why you're here, which is to your advantage."

"Alright."

"One more thing you must also know."

Ted could not only see it coming, he heard it in Patch's voice.

"There is a great evil behind the Twins; a power the Realm has not seen yet, but I know it's there."

"You feel the vibration?"

Patched smiled; catching the line.

"Yes, as like a spider. Now finish your meal and then we'll see to fixing my fence."

"OK."

In the time Ted stayed with Patch, he learned many things about the land of Ur. On the last day before departing they sat once again.

"Before you go, there is a map in that chest along with some clothing. Take the clothing and map. Study it thoroughly. If questioned where you come from, or are asked directions, you'll know the names of the villages, rivers and such."

The chest was old and brittle as Patch. He took the map and changed out of his clothing. Afterward, Patch told him to take the sword over the fireplace.

"I never used one," he replied, gazing at it. "That is truly a remarkable piece," he continued, stepping up and studying the thing.

The blade was as shiny as silver. There was a dragon carved into the blade shooting fire. The handle was metal with a gold stripe running through it. The handle itself was bound with black rope; the tip gold. "May I?" he asked, taking it down. He ran his finger along the edge.

"It's as sharp as the day it was forged," said Patch.

"How old is it?"

"It has been here through the ages; forged by the flames of a dragon. Those that know swords will know it is Ty-ka-kian steel."

"Tykakian steel; forged with dragon fire," repeated Ted, mystified. "Don't tell me there are dragons here."

"They have been gone for a thousand years."

"A thousand years," he questioned, looking down at the sword. *Wow,* he thought.

"Become one with the sword and it will serve you well."

Ted stared at him, wanting to know more. "Become one?"

"Yes, as if it was an extension of your hand."

"OK," he replied, not quite sure what he meant.

"There is a man named Gabriel, he'll teach you how to use it. He lives in Goshen, which is the first village you'll come to."

"What will a sword do against the Twins?"

"An average sword is useless against them. This one however, might give you an advantage to escape if need be. Turn the blade sideways toward the glowing embers."

Ted stepped back, turned the blade flat toward the fire. The glowing hot coals reflected off the sword onto the wood mantelpiece. It started to burn as like a magnifying glass would burn paper if held in sunlight. "Unbelievable."

"It will pierce and cut through anything," added Patch; with a twinkle in in his eye.

Patch's expression spoke volumes. Ted stood back and placed the sword out in front of him, then slowly moved it through the air back and forth.

"As you will see, it will also protect you from those that may want to harm you."

"Harm me?"

"In the Realm there are many who seek the weak. Some will come as sheep, but they are wolves."

"I'll keep that in mind. Tell me, though. I never asked but… where is the Realm located." "It's known across the twelve seas as the Kingdom in the Clouds. You'll know what I mean once you see it."

"Across the twelve seas?" repeated Ted, thinking where on Earth that would be located. Nothing came to mind. He had to ask.

"You speak of time, Lord Barrington.

Understand this." "Yes."

"The twelve seas came about in the time of Capricorn."

Ted cocked his head.

Patch smiled. "Time in the Realm is not like your time in the Great Beyond, Lord Barrington. Years to us are like centuries to you. Juliette was abducted eight spans ago, in the time of Orion."

"You call it the Great Beyond."

"Yes, and there is only one man who can come and go through the portal of time. I'll say no more and hope that gives you some understanding."

"OK, tell me this then." "Go on."

"What about the Southern Kingdom I read about?"

"The Southern Kingdom was born out of fire. When King Tyrus was a young king, he was very vociferous and taxed his people to the breaking point. His dear friend, Frederick Lennard tried to convince him that he'd lose the kingdom if he did not stop. William paid no mind. Frederick then left and went to the southern villages, where he convinced them to separate. They did and made Frederick king."

"I see."

"They fought for many years, that is… until William's youngest daughter, Juliette came of age and Frederick's son, Richard fell madly in love with her. But she was never in love with him; she was in love with your cousin, Sheppard."

"The Beginning told me that."

Patch smiled. "As you may now know, their love affair would not have set well with her father, King William. They would secretly meet at night in a stretch of forest both sides called neutral territory. Anyone could travel through it."

"Then along came Richard."

"Yes," he sullenly replied. "I remember the day as if it were yesterday. She rode into the village of Corset with her escorts not expecting Richard to ride in with his men. She was ordered out of her carriage. Not knowing the young Countess, Richard was in for a fight. She stepped down and said, Richard, son of King Lennard, you are a barbarian. The people here don't want what you're selling, so be off with you. Richard took in the young maiden and liked what he saw."

"So she is fiery woman?"

"Yes. Juliette could have cared less if Richard had her and her men seized. Instead of apprehending her, he let her go. On his return to his father, he told him that there was a way of bringing both kingdoms together."

"And the rest is history," added Ted.

"I'm afraid so. But now that she is… incapacitated, the wedding was called off with Richard. And," he went on to say, "now that Sheppard is dead, she belongs to you, Ted."

"I understand the Laws of the Realm, but where I come from she does not belong to me. She can choose whomever she wants. And besides, I'm from the future."

"A future she'll get to know and love."

Ted laughed.

He waited for his laughter to subside. "Before you go, keep it in mind, the Twins have eyes and ears throughout the Realm. There is one in particular who sits on King William's council. His name is Lord Nelson. He is a spy for the Twins."

"Really?"

"Yes."

"What does he look like?"

"He has long brown hair he wears in a ponytail. He also has a distinctive scar over his left eyebrow."

"OK."

"With this information, you'll gain access to King William's inner circle. The ones he trusts and confides in. He will not be happy hearing it coming from a stranger but, he'll know it's the truth when you mention my name."

Ted weighed that up. He had no clue how to present himself before the king. He asked Patch about it.

"It all depends on how he receives you. If he wants an audience alone with you then it would be easy to inform him. If he sees you with his council, you'll have to decide when to tell him, because Lord Nelson will be there."

Ted nodded.

"Now again, trust no one, even if they come under the cloak of friendship, or those who may want to assist you on your journey."

"I will."

"Good. Just follow the trail heading north. It will lead you through the valley back into a small forest then on to Goshen. Gabriel owns the Tavern and Inn. Give him one of these," he said, handing Ted a pouch of gold coins. "He'll know it came from me; the rest is yours. Also tell him you'll need a good horse. You know how to ride?"

"Sort of."

"If its head is down, the horse is in charge. Kick it in the side and pull up on the reins. When the head is up – ears back, you're in charge."

Ted thanked him and stood up. "How long have you lived here?"

"All my life. Now stay safe and watch your back."

"I will," he replied, heading for the door. He stopped and looked back. "Oh, I wanted to ask, what are the white birds with golden plumes and gold laced in their wings?"

"They are Grassland Pipers; they are a very unique bird; as smart as eagles."

"Thank you," he said, opening the door and leaving.

After Ted had left, Patch got up from his chair. He looked at the partially opened door thinking; *through the spans of time, we finally have a Barrington worthy of this mission.*

He waited awhile before walking out. All alone on the small porch, he called for his horse. It came out of the deep grove of pine trees behind the hut and trotted up to him. He patted its flank and got up into the saddle.

7

As Ted proceeded to Goshen, field rats scampered along the water's edge, making their way to the hidden tunnel. Inside, they scurried until they reached the dungeon; where filthy men sat awaiting their fate. Not a sound could be heard except for water dripping; pooling in holes in the hard cobbled floor.

Here at Black Water, the dark castle sitting high on a bluff overlooking the isle of Drake; if you are captured, you'll not see the light of day, nor will you return to your loved ones. Anger the Twins and your doom is sealed. They give those imprisoned three choices. They could be fed to the water beasts that live in the isle, go by fire, or be boiled alive.

Greta, the older of the two, sat on her bed running her fingers through her long matted hair. Her sister, Hagar was looking out the window when her stomach went into knots. She buckled over.

"What be with you sweet sister? Eating those rats again," she lightheartedly giggled.

"Nay, I haven't had a field rat in weeks. I sense an unforeseen power."

"What be it; spill it before we go to bed," snarled Greta.

"Can't you feel it too?"

"Nay, I only get that way when I sense the Shadow near. What is it, sweet sister?

"Someone has entered the Realm.

Someone we do not know." "Male?"

"Yah."

"Does he have power?"

"Yah, but my bones tell me he's not aware of it yet."

"How can he have entered the Realm? You mean, he came from across the twelve seas?" suspiciously asked Greta.

"I'm not sure, but I'm sure of one thing, though."

"What is that?"

"He is here for no good purpose."

Angered by that comment, Greta fumed. She quickly got up and hurried to the door. The guards stood erect.

"Summon Egmon to the tower at once!" "Yes, Madam Greta."

"The Tower?" questioned Hagar.

"If you had brains, you'd be dangerous.

Our crystal ball will show us this man."

Without another word, the two dashed out like flames from a wick.

It was a dingy room overlooking the dark water below. Hagar lit the candles while Greta quickly proceeded to the crystal ball, sitting adjacent to the war table; where miniature horses and warriors sat waiting to be moved across the map of the Realm.

Hearing subtle footsteps, they turned seeing Egmon, the protector of the water beasts. He was a ghastly disfigured dwarf with one bluish-white eye. He was hard to look at with half his face lower than the other.

Years ago, as a young boy, the two found him in the backwaters of Mead. There, they saw him standing at the water's edge tossing deer parts into the river. Surprisingly to their fright, two large creatures with razor sharp teeth appear from the depths. In utter disbelief, they watched Egmon allow the forty- foot behemoths to swim right up to him; where he'd reached out and pat their snouts.

After speaking to the boy and learning that his family disowned him due to his disfigurement, he was living in a cave within a small inlet. It was there that he came upon the beasts when they were still small.

Greta, a heartless witch, held no pity for the child. She only wanted the creatures to protect the castle. So they took Egmon in. He was more than pleased to come live with them as their loyal and trusted servant.

"My Ladies," said Egmon. "Why up so late?"

"We have a visitor in the Realm," replied Greta.

"A visitor, said Egmon with a gleam in his bluish-white eye. "Will I be feeding 'em to my pets?"

"Not just yet," she replied. "We need to know *why* he is here first before taking any actions."

With that, Greta softly placed her hands upon the crystal ball. "Show me the man who has entered the Realm," she ordered, rubbing the circular object.

The ball turned a light blue and then clouds appeared. As if flying overhead, the Redwood Forest came into view. The vision soared downward skirting the landscape. Up ahead, a man was walking down a trail. The vision circled him.

"Well, well, what do we have here?" cackled Greta.

"It's a man alright, a handsome one at that," sang Hagar.

"Handsome?" spat Greta. "He looks to be heading to Goshen."

"That he is," agreed Egmon.

"Hmmm," said Greta, walking over to the balcony. She stared out into the pitch-black of night while tapping her long pointed fingernail on her chin.

"What be on your mind?" asked Hagar.

"Handsome," murmured Greta. "I have an idea," she continued, facing them.

"Egmon, I want you to go to Port Griffin and find me a maiden. She must be a virgin, you hear me."

"How will I know?"

"Good question," she replied, thinking. "Find me a young thing, no more than twenty."

"Your wish is my command." "Take several men with you." "What shall we do with her?"

"Why Egmon… show the pretty thing our cozy little dungeon," she mused with a cruel smile.

Egmon bowed then left their presence. "What are you thinking?" asked Hagar. "You said he was handsome."

"He is."

"Well then, tell me sweet sister, what handsome man would turn down a beautiful young woman?"

Seeing the sinister twinkle within her sister's eyes, Hagar smiled rubbing her hands. The fair maiden wasn't going to Goshen – her sister was. She quickly dropped that thought and frowned.

"What's with the displeasure?"

"We used to be beautiful. Now look at us."

Her disgruntled comment caught Greta off-guard. "Do you want to upset *Zesbrew?*" "No, never."

"Then be wise with that tongue or he just might hear you."

Hagar sat down still in dismay. *I wish my father had never discovered the wretched thing on that sailing ship; the Bestow. He would have continued his life as a nobleman in Black Water; instead, he became the king; a stupid one at that.*

Her thoughts continued drifting. It all started by her parents whispering at night. They heard it every evening when the lights went out. It became too much to bear. They cornered their father while he saw them off to bed. She'd never forget his words; "Now what I'm about to tell you can never leave this house and," he said, looking back at their door, "don't ever tell your mother I told you."

With raised brows, they shook their heads promising to never say a word.

"After that terrible storm, my friends and I discover a ship washed ashore in Dragon Bay."

He called it the Ship of Fools. Little did Hagar know then – it was her father and his friends that were the fools for rowing out there to see what had happened.

To her father's ghastly surprise, he along with his friends found the entire crew dead. The scene before them looked like a bloody mutiny had occurred; men fighting men. Skeletal remains had swords stuck in them. Some were beheaded, while others were hung.

In the Captain's stateroom was a grizzly find. The Captain was sitting, a sword through in his chest. A skeletal body lay near his feet; an arrow stuck in the poor man's skull.

Upon examining the captain's journal, it was discovered that the ship's name was the *Bestow*, belonging to a far off kingdom in the 7th sea called Carsinia.

With no answer in the journal to why the crew went stark raving mad, they continued their search. When they struck below in the bowel of the ship, there before them lay a chest filled with gold, silver, rubies, and gems.

They also discovered a four-foot high wooden carving of the most hideous creature they ever laid eyes on. It was tied to a stanchion which they suspected was taken along with the treasure.

Hagar cringed within her thoughts. She knew why *now* the mutiny had occurred. Months after they had gone onboard, her father believed it was the treasure each man wanted for himself. That was not the case. It was the evil four–foot carving.

"Are you listening to me!" scolded Greta.

Hagar quickly snapped back to the present staring at her sister.

"Yah, I'm listening," she huffed, walking over to the caldron. She gazed down at her reflection in the still water. There was nothing she liked about herself. Not her green skin, her crooked nose, and or, her pointed chin. Years past, her eyes were a beautiful sky blue. Today, they were as dark as coal.

The only part she did like was her hourglass figure. With all the grieving lumps however, she knew no man would ever want to touch her again. *Power*, she thought. *I'd give it all away just to be beautiful again.*

Greta strolled over, placed her arm around Hagar and looked down at her own reflection. "Hold your head high, sweet sister. We are the witches of Black Water. We rule the Forbidden Land and all who live within it. We can have whatever we want."

Hagar pouted.

"Enough of this sadness; it will bring terrible things to us," she spewed, heading for the door.

Hagar knew what she meant, *Zesbrew*, the evil wooden carving… better known as the Entity that now resides below in the catacomb of the castle.

Hours later, Egmon returned and summoned the witches to the dungeon. Before hitting the last step, they heard a soft female voice asking why she was there. The guard in return told her she'd know soon enough; and *soon enough* was now coming down the dark, damp corridor.

"Will you look at that," beamed Greta, staring at the beautiful young maiden before her.

"Why am I here? I've done you no wrong."

"Open the gate," ordered Greta.

As she entered the girl stepped back frightened.

"You're right," said Greta. "You have done us no wrong. I just need something from you," she continued, walking up to her.

The girl relaxed a moment, giving Greta time to place her hand on the poor girl's shoulder. "How old are you, my dear?"

"Twenty two." "Your name?" "Clara Brown."

"Have you ever been with a man?"

"Why no," she gasped, "my father would," she said and then immediately stopped talking, seeing Greta's eyes light up. "What do you want from me?"

Greta leaned into her.

Clara flinched having Greta's revolting face so close to her.

"I only need your beauty, that's all," she hissed, grabbing Clara by the throat.

Clara went to scream.

Greta quickly pulled Clara toward her then placed her mouth over hers.

"Let me goo…." she muffled, trying desperately to fight her off.

As Greta deeply inhaled the breath out of the poor girl's lungs, her eyes bore into Clara. She could taste Clara's savory beauty filling her veins.

Clara's facial skin slowly turned dead- white. Her eyes shrank within their sockets. She stood there, legs trembling until she shriveled up like a dried prune. All that was left of ol' Clara was her sickly white skin stretched over her skeletal remains; inside clothing that looked too big for her frame.

With that, Greta let the dead girl go. Her bones dropped to the floor in a heap. As they did, Clara's skull disconnected and rolled across the floor toward the wall.

With a gleeful smile, Greta beamed,

"What do ya think?"

"You look enchanting," said the guard; stunned.

"You do," agreed Egmon.

"Greta," gasped Hagar. "Why did we not have Egmon get two young beauties?"

"Because, sweet sister, I'm going to Goshen alone."

8

By the time Ted entered the village of Goshen the sun was setting. On the outskirt, he spotted a man sitting near the horse stable, whittling a stick.

"Can you point me in the direction of the tavern?"

"Just up on the right; you can't miss it." "Thank you."

Ted worked his way through the bustling crowd of buyers and sellers with their carts of fruit and vegetables; live chickens, others selling woven baskets and assortment of trinkets.

After walking past a man standing on a horse-drawn wagon lighting street lamps, he spotted the tavern. The sign overhead was a Bed and Wine Glass; the words Gabriel's Tavern & Inn written over the top.

It was a small rustic pub reminding him of the pubs in Ireland with its wooden interior and big stone fireplace. Two waitresses were serving the men at the tables, while a group was gathered along the bar.

Those at the bar glanced at him as he walked up to the end and stood there. The Bartender was a stocky man with full black beard and bushy eyebrows. He poured a wine, pushed it across to someone then went down to Ted.

"What can I get you?" he asked, wiping his hands on his apron. "A glass of wine." "Food?"

Ted raised his brow. He hadn't eaten since morning.

"Tonight we're serving lamb and gravy?" "That'll be fine."

"Have a seat at one of the tables. The waitress will serve you. I'll bring you your wine."

Ted took a seat in the corner. When the man came over, he asked, "Are you Gabriel?" "Yes. What can I do for you?"

He pulled out the gold coin from Patch and handed it to him.

Gabriel flipped it several times then stared at the stranger. "Where are you staying?"

"Right now… nowhere."

"I've got a room upstairs. Last one on the right."

"Thank you."

While eating his meal, outback of the tavern the wind picked up; swirling through the grassy woodlands. Amongst the shadow of the trees, a beautiful woman suddenly appeared carrying a suit case. She checked herself then proceeded around to the front.

The door opened. The men at the bar turned to see who had walked in. Clara took off her hood in the doorway, allowing her blonde flowing hair to drape over her shoulders. She presented a quaint little smile to the men gawking at her while allowing her eyes to roam over the patrons. The one she saw in her crystal ball was sitting alone eating his meal.

Gladdened that he was there, she strolled up to the bar.

Gabriel walked down to her.

"May I have a glass of wine, please?"

"Sure. Would you like something to eat?" "Yes, I'm starving," she lavishly sighed.

"Lamb with gravy?" "That'll do just fine."

"I haven't seen you in Goshen before.

Staying long?"

"Not sure. You have a room?"

"You're in luck. I have one left." "I'll take it."

He slid the Inn registry across to her.

"Upstairs; room five on the right."

She thanked him, grabbed her wine glass, and proceeded over to a table adjacent to Ted.

Ted smiled with a nod. She smiled back.

"Your dinner, ma'am," said the waitress. "Thank you."

While eating her meal, she was a bit dismayed that the man had said nothing, as if she weren't there. She thought she'd strike up a conversation.

"You look familiar. Where are you from?" Ted wasn't expecting that question; especially from a young woman like her. "I come from a distance shore; a place called Crisco."

"I've never heard of it."

"I suppose you wouldn't have. It took me months to sail here."

"You come by way of ship."

"Yes."

"Across the twelve seas, I assume?" "Correct."

"I've never sailed. Don't like the water.

Your name?"

"Ted Landen," he lied.

"I'm Clara Brown. Are you staying here long?"

"No. I'm heading north."

"Really?" she gushed. "I'm heading to the Northern Kingdom to visit my parents. Maybe we could travel together?"

Patch's advice or more so warning came front and center; *careful of those you meet. They may appear harmless, but really are wolves.* To him however, Clara seemed more naïve then a threat; asking a stranger to accompany her north. He tried to brush her off; gently. "I'll be staying a few days before moving on," he said, hoping she'd tell him she'd be leaving in the morning."

"I'm in no rush. Seeing I'm traveling alone, I wouldn't mind some company."

With her quaint little smile and those telling eyes, he figured he'd take her up on her offer and ensure she made it there. "OK," he agreed.

"Great. Just let me know. In the meantime, I'll do some shopping."

After his meal, Ted bid her a goodnight and departed.

Gabriel followed him up the stairs.

It was a small room with a window. Ted walked over and looked down at the road.

"I saw you talking to that lady?"

"She said her name was Clara Brown," replied Ted.

"I've never seen her before."

"She sounded nice. She wants to travel with me to the Northern Kingdom; not that I told her I was going there – just heading north."

"Before you do, make sure she is alone."

The expression on his face was another warning sign. "I will."

"So you met Patch."

"Yes, I spent a few days with him."

In the Realm there are only a few who know Patch. It made Gabriel pause for a moment; *who is this man standing before me?*

"How do you know him?" asked Ted.

"I think it's best we do not ask too many questions. I am now your humble servant; what can I do for you?"

His words surprised Ted. *An old man living along the mountains, in a rundown hut… what made Patch so special that Gabriel was now his humble servant?* "Patch said you would give me a horse and teach me how to use this," he replied, showing him the sword."

Gabriel looked at it then met Ted's eyes. "You must keep that sword hidden; at least the blade. Those that know swords will know that is Tykakian steel; forged from dragon flames and has a legendary history behind it."

Ted nodded, gazing down at the sword.

"Have you ever handled one?" "No."

Ted brought the sword up and placed the blade sideways. The steel began to glow.

"In all my days," gasped Gabriel.

"Can you teach me how to use it?" "Do you have several months?" "No."

"That is a difficult thing to teach in a short time, especially one that holds such power. You must be careful with it. I suspect it will slice through anything; rock, wood, armor and well… you get the idea."

Ted nodded. "At least teach me enough so I don't look foolish."

"You sleep tonight. Tomorrow, I'll take you out to our cabin. Give me at least three days, if that's alright?"

"That'll be fine."

"I've got a friend who can help run the tavern with my wife while I'm away."

"Great."

"Sleep well. See you in the morning." "Thank you."

With that, Gabriel departed.

The following morning, the ride out to Gabriel's place by wagon was along a river surrounded by forest. When they entered a meadow of high grass, rolling hills and large embedded boulders - the river curved north. The road leading to his place continued westward.

Gabriel's cabin sat amongst a few trees covered in shade. There was a small corral, barn and chickens walking about.

"This be home for me and the wife."

"Nice place. Any children?"

"Sadly no. My wife is barren."

Ted let it go. What else could he say?

"I'll teach you the art of the sword around back. The ground there is hard and level."

"OK."

That same morning, Clara sat by her upstairs window watching the two men climbing into a wagon below. *It appears I'll need a horse.*

At the stable, she captivated the stockman with her swaying hips and telling smile. He was more than pleased to assist her in picking out a horse; a tall brown chestnut with white spots. As she trotted away, she thought of her own horse, Dracon. He was a black-velvet stallion with streaks of white through its mane.

She called him Dracon, because that was his name. Well, it was the name of her lover, who decided to leave her once she became a witch. She would have none of it, nor would she tolerate another woman having him either… so, she cast a spell on Dracon; changing him into a horse, the one she now rides at Black Water.

Clara rode the Chestnut out of the village, through the forest until she came to the meadow. Seeing the cabin in the foreground and the wagon out front troubled her. She wasn't expecting this; the two ending up here.

Her torment subsided when Gabriel's plump little wife, Rose came to mind. *She may have the answers I need,* she thought, riding back.

At the tavern, Clara caught up with Rose changing out her bedding.

"Did you enjoy your ride this morning?" she asked.

Not knowing how she knew she had a horse, Clara said *yes*, and then asked a question herself, "I was wondering."

"Go on."

"I spoke with Ted last night. He said he was from Crisco. Have you heard of it?" "No."

"He said he came by way of ship; across the twelve seas in a far off land."

"Really?" she replied, wondering where this conversation was leading.

"I asked him if I could accompany him on his journey north. Myself, I'm riding to visit with my parents in the Northern Kingdom. You think it was wise for me to ask him?"

Rose casually sat on the bed. "I've never met the man until last night; same with Gabriel."

"I see," she replied a bit surprised. "Yes."

"I thought they were friends when I saw them riding out together this morning?" questioned Clara.

"All I know is – he was sent to Gabriel."

"By whom?"

"Gabriel wouldn't say and I don't ask questions. It helps in a marriage to just trust."

Clara raised her brow to that comment. *If Rose only knew who she was talking to; it would probably be the death of her.*

"Someday when you get married, you'll see."

Clara stood up and walked over to the window.

"Why the fuss?"

She turned and sighed. "I just wanted to make sure I can trust this man if I traveled with him, that's all," she lied.

"Well, if it settles your heart my dear," she replied, getting up, "my husband only knows good men. If he was sent to see Gabriel I'm sure you can trust him. Now – I have a million things to do," she continued, heading for the door.

"Wait."

"Yes?"

"Where did they go this morning?"

"Gabriel took him to our cabin to teach him how to duel with a sword of all things."

"You'd think he'd already know."

"Not really. Some men are scared of 'em.

Now, enjoy your day."

After the door closed, Clara turned and stared out the window. "I need to know who sent this man to Gabriel," she murmured, rubbing her chin. Feeling the soft flesh made her lift her hand to her face. *I don't have much time left playing Clara Brown. Soon I'll return to my fabulous self.*

With that twirling inside her head, all she could hope for was staying young and beautiful until she and Ted were on their way. *One night alone on that dark winding road, he'll tell me everything. No man can resist my love potion.*

9

Morning of the fourth day, Ted and Clara were ready to leave. As Gabriel assisted Ted with provisions and water for their trip, he glanced over at Clara fixing her saddle. *So young and beautiful; such easy prey – or was she?* He took nothing for granted. In the Realm there were many spies. The North, the South, and the witches of Black Water had them.

When his wife Rose came out, he dropped those thoughts. "You two have a safe trip," he said to the pair.

"We will," replied Clara. "I have a strong man watching over me," she continued, mounting her horse. "Are you ready, Ted?"

"I am," he replied, shaking Gabriel's hand. They stared at one another. Ted's gratitude of Gabriel assisting him, and Gabriel's knowledge of who Ted was, lay within their eyes. No words needed to be spoken. He then thanked Rose and got on his horse. With a sturdy kick, the horse turned and headed down the road.

When the two were out of earshot, Gabriel whispered, "I don't trust that girl."

"Oh now," fused Rose. "She's a bit naïve; most young women are."

"Would you allow our daughter, if we had one, to travel alone to the Northern Kingdom?"

Her answer was quick; *no.*

Ted knew from the map Patch gave him that they had approximately twenty miles before Shendor. He mentioned it to Clara.

"I'm in no rush; unless you are."

"No. I figured we could do at least10 miles per day or more."

"That's fine with me. Is there anywhere in particular you are going?"

"For now, I'm heading to Shendor. Tell me, do your parents know where you are?"

"Yes," she laughed, "my father works for the king's finance minister. My mother has a leather shop adjacent to the market square," she lied.

"Really… that must be nice."

"It is. I love the castle and all its splendor."

"I've never been there."

"You've never seen it, why… one day you should go. You'll see what I mean."

"I find it hard to believe that your parents allow you to travel alone like this."

"I can take care of myself. Well, sort of. I've been traveling this route since I was a child with my parents. I know all the dark places."

"Dark places?"

"Yes. Are you married?"

That caught him off guard. "I was." "What happened?"

"She was in a carrr…." he started to say then quickly recovered, "a carriage accident."

Hearing the trouble in his voice, she glanced over at him. "I see you're still fond of her."

"Yes," he replied. *I almost blew it.* "Tell me about the dark places? I've never heard that phrase."

"You know the forest caves near Mount Leer. You never know what could be lurking inside."

Not knowing, Ted just nodded.

"I've encountered wolves and hyenas before."

"Best we stay clear of them."

"We must, they're terrifying creatures that roam the Realm in packs," she said, thinking of her sweet pet hyena, Rye. She glanced down at the handle of his sword. "How well are you with that?"

"Just learning."

"Just learning… at your age?" "I never had a need of one."

A man who crossed the twelve seas and now traveling alone in a far off land thought he had no need of one… and now he does, she thought, drifting on that.

Why… he's been lying to me the whole time. I hate people lying to me. It's worse than leeches crawling up my neck. He really thinks I'm stupid. Well Clara Brown was certainly stupid but, this fabulous witch is as cunning as a fox, she mused glancing in his direction. "If trouble be near, can you defend us with that sword?"

"I most certainly can," he boasted, not really knowing if he could.

"I sure hope so," she subtly replied.

Her comment made him turn and look at her. From her boot in the stirrup up to her shoulders she was a wee little thing; no more than five-feet four.

Seeing him checking her out; she paid no mind; hoping he liked her busty appearance. Most men did.

"Sometime before the sun sets we'll need to find a place to rest for the night."

"There are a few spots up ahead," she said.

As nightfall approached, Ted and Clara had made good time. They stopped once for lunch and continued until the sun was setting. "We'll make camp in there," he said, pointing off the road at an old dead trunk, "with the thick canopy overhead it will keep us out of the weather."

Clara glanced over. It was an ideal spot to work her magic. Besides, she had no intentions of staying until they crossed the river up ahead. Tonight, she would know everything about Ted Landen.

After their meal and a warm fire going, she asked if he wanted a drink of wine. "It's from the Canter-Berry vineyards in Navarro."

"I wouldn't mind. It may help me sleep tonight."

She got up; teasingly swaying her hips. After getting her flask she waltzed over and settled in next to him.

It was the first time she was so close to Ted. Her eyes were sky blue, her lips lush and tender.

"Have you ever drunk the wine from those vineyards?"

"No."

"You're in for a treat, try it."

Ted took the flask and drank. It was as smooth as silk going down. "Well?"

When he handed it back, he felt strangely attracted to her; as if he had drank a dose of passion instead of wine.

"Well?" she again asked, seeing his eyes taking her in.

"I… I.. it's so sweet, so…" he lustfully murmured.

"Ted." she whispered, moving closer.

"Yes," he replied, heavenly gazing at her. "Take another sip," she teasingly suggested, putting the flask to his lips. She smiled as he lavishly drank as if it were the nectar from the Gods. It was in some ways – it was her sweet love potion; no man could resist.

When he stopped, his attentive words were all she wanted to hear. "You are the most exquisite creature I've ever seen."

"Such flattering words, Ted. I suppose you'd like to kiss me?"

"Yes, so very much so."

She moved her nose inches from his. "Before I allow you to, tell me, where are you really from?"

"Crisco."

"Truly you speak? It's just that…" she sighed with a slight pause. "How could you not have been to the Northern Kingdom? It sits along the coast within the 12th sea, the Sea of Presidium? Isn't that where your ship had docked?"

"Well, I… I didn't…" Buzz ….

"Shoo," spat Clara to the bee flying around her face. The bee flew off.

"Please tell me the truth, why are you here? If you tell me, I'll let you kiss me for a thousand years."

"A thousouunds yurrs," slurred Ted, now feeling faint like.

Buzz…. buzz…. buzz….

"Shoo you wretched things," she spat, swatting the air. Before she could get Ted to confess, a horde of bees appeared out of nowhere. The more she fought them off; the angrier they became, attacking without mercy.

"Ouch, ouch," she screamed, getting to her feet. They were in her hair, on her face and all over her arms and hands.

"Get off of me, get off of me," she frantically shouted, stumbling backwards and falling over a log. As she desperately tried defending herself from the brutal stings, she glanced over at Ted not being stung at all; just lying there in a drunken state.

"He's the Shadow," she cursed, standing up. She raised her hands, spun in a circle and vanished.

After she had left, the bees hovered over Ted for a moment then flew off into the forest.

In the courtyard, back at Black Water, the wind picked up. A miniature dust devil appeared then Greta stepped out of the swirling dust. "Curses," she hissed, storming toward the castle's entrance.

"Madam, your face," spoke a guard.

"My face… my whole body has been stung. Ensure the walls are protected, watch out for bees!"

"Bees, Madam Greta?"

"Yes. Summon Egmon for me. I want him and a few guards to fetch several buckets of river mud and bring them up to my room, fast!"

"As you wish, Madam Greta."

At the big double doors a guard stepped forward and opened them. She hurried past and ran through the dark corridor lit-up with torches. Above the flames were stone vultures perched on pillars looking down at her. After entering the Gable, the large hall where her and her sister's thrones sat, she took a side passageway and ran up a flight of stairs. Pushing open her bedroom door, she grabbed the bell on a table and rang it.

Hagar turned from the oval mirror where their seamstress was fitting her with a new black gown. "Greta!" she gasped. "What happened?"

"Bees, that's what happened. I believe the man in the crystal ball is the Shadow."

"The Shadow; how could that be? He was coming from the Redwood Forest?" she belted. "Leave us," she ordered their seamstress.

"I could just slap myself. He said he came by way of ship across the twelve seas," grunted Greta.

A side door opened. In ran their chambermaids.

"Hurry, get me undressed. I have Egmon coming with buckets of mud."

"Yes, Madam," they replied, alarmed by her appearance.

"Your face!" gasped Hagar, walking over to her.

"My face! Why… I feel as if I've been stung a thousand times. Mix me up an ointment that'll sooth my body after the mud dries and sucks out these stingers."

Hagar strolled over to her cabinet. "Let me see now," she chimed, looking along the shelf. "I think a bit of chopped up lizard tongue, a dash of crushed fish eyes, some green chives, hmmm," she sang, reading the labels. "Here is what I'm after; and a pinch of dried monkey brain. I'll mix the entire brew in a vat of warm whale blubber. That should do the trick."

There was a knock on the door. A chambermaid opened it. It was Egmon along with two guards with buckets of mud.

"Set them down and I'll take 'em over," he said to the guards.

"As you wish," they replied, not wanting to look.

Egmon carried the buckets over to the tub. It was the first time he had seen Greta naked. She was an awful sight to behold. Afterward, he quickly hurried out to a balcony where he could get some fresh air. Looking up at the stars above, he whispered, "I may not be a pretty sight myself, but her," he paused, shaking his head, "I'd kiss a bullfrog before ever kissing that."

While Greta soothed her swollen body, she told Hagar everything.

"So, he said he was from Crisco at first and then he was just about to tell you the truth when the bees came?"

"Yah, I almost had him spilling his guts," she spat. "I wish he were here right now – I'd be spilling 'em with a sword."

"If that is true then he is not the Shadow. The Shadow would have been too smart to be caught off guard like that."

"You're right, sweet sister. At the time, my mind was in fits seeing him just sitting there; not being stung at all."

"What kind of bees were they?" "Those nasty Zenith Bees."

"Oh… they're a nasty lot. They would have even attacked the horses, I'd suspect."

"Yah, sweet sister" agreed Greta, thinking back. "He said his name was Ted Landen."

"Ted Landen," repeated Hagar.

"Well, to my surprise, he also told me that he had never seen the Northern Kingdom. How could that be if he came by way of ship? Like I said, I could just slap myself; hearing him telling me that and not making a point of him lying to me."

"You have something there," replied Hagar, smearing more mud on Greta's face. "I would have slapped myself too. You think he works for King William?" she asked, studying her sister's eyes.

They stared at one another for a moment. "He may be. Or, we're missing something."

"What is it?"

"Why would the bees attack me and not him?"

Hagar thought of that. "Are you thinking maybe they came to protect him?"

"What else could it be? If so, that frightens me, sweet sister," she said, gazing up at the ceiling.

"Frightens you? We've never been frightened of anyone, except the Shadow, who has the power to change."

Greta's gaze shifted from the ceiling down at her. "The more I think, the more troubling it becomes. We've never had to face angry bees before neither."

"You're right, and if they are protecting him…"

"You said he had power he wasn't aware of having?" asked Greta, raising a brow.

"I did," replied Hagar. "He might now, though. Where do you think he really comes from?"

"I don't know, sweet sister." "Wait a minute," said Hagar. "What?"

"You said he told you he was heading north."

"Yah."

"I betcha he is heading north to see King William."

"Now you're thinking, sweet sister. He could have been summoned by the Shadow on behalf of King William. But why?" she asked not having an answer.

Seeing Greta in a twisted state, she waited to hear what was on her mind.

"Why would this man be summoned? They got the Countess of Lyon Head back - so he can't be here for us. Maybe it has something do to with King Frederick. You know those two don't like one another?" she said, grabbing more mud and smearing it around her neck. She flung what was left in her hand.

"I'm not sure of that, Greta. They may have the Countess back, but they'll never be able to break the spell. Little ol' Juliette will remain a doll for a thousand years," she cackled.

"Hold your laughter, sweet sister. My gut tells me we'll be seeing this man again." "You think?"

"Yah, you can count on it."

10

At Daybreak, Ted felt something nudging him. He awoke in a haze; his horse by his side. Sitting up, he noticed Clara was gone; her Chestnut horse tethered to a limb.

When his eyes locked onto the flask, it all came back. He could still taste the sweet wine. *If you tell me the truth, I'll let you kiss me for a thousand years; a thousand years,* echoed inside his head. *Clara wasn't the naïve young lady I suspected she was. She had to be one of the witches, but how?*

Drifting on that, he looked down seeing dead bees. He picked one up. *Strange,* he thought, looking at the bluish green insect with a yellow stripe on its back. *The thing is as big as my thumb.*

As he sat there mystified, the ground began to shake. Something huge was coming. Quickly to his feet, he turned seeing an enormous elephant with a huge trunk and long tusks. Its wrinkly grey skin was covered in a light moss. He looked ancient; as old as the forest itself.

The mammoth beast shook its massive head. Its deep grumbling caused Ted to step back. As it approached; twenty feet… ten feet… Ted's heart quickened. He fell to his knees; scared.

The long trunk came forward sniffing him. Out of fear, he spoke with his head down. "I am Lord Barrington," he said, stating his title; hoping it would protect him.

The next thing he heard was the flapping of wings. A bird landed in the trees overhead.

"Major," said the elephant in a deep tone.

"Good morning, Shoeshon. Lord Barrington is on a quest to save the Countess of Lyon Head. Grandfather has granted him safe passage."

"I see," he replied, eyeing the man before him.

"Stand, Lord Barrington," said Major.

Ted looked up at the majestic falcon sitting on a branch.

When he gazed upon Shoeshon he was overwhelmed. Shoeshon was the biggest elephant he had ever seen, and those eyes, those dark brown eyes bore right into his soul.

"That in your hand is a Zenith Bee. They are known for their vicious sting. They have the capacity of killing," said Shoeshon.

Ted glanced down at the insect.

"Gabriel dispatched his carrier pigeon to me thinking you may be in trouble. I quickly took flight and requested the bees to save you. I am glad I did; for Clara Brown was actually Greta; the evilest of the two witches," said Major.

"How… how did she do that?"

"I heard word on the wind that she killed a woman to become her. It's not the first time." "Wicked things they are," added Shoeshon.

"I'll keep that in mind."

"Do that. You never know who is who in the Realm," replied Major.

"So," said Shoeshon. "You met the Beginning, the one we call Grandfather?"

"Yes."

Shoeshon leaned toward him. "You may not know this, Lord Barrington, Grandfather is the forest. He rules all things. The plants we eat, the fruit from the trees and the shrubs. And… as you know now," he said, lifting his trunk upward toward Major, "he can call upon the animals and the insects to do his bidding. Major is like the hand of the king to Grandfather."

Ted glanced up at him.

Major tilted his head conceding Shoeshon's words.

"Only a few know that Grandfather even exists," continued Shoeshon.

"I see," he said. "Do the Twins?"

"No," said Major. "That would be the end of us. Right now however, what is important is getting you to the gates of the Northern Kingdom. Will you escort him to Shendor?" asked Major.

"I was heading that way." "Good."

"I'm off then," he replied, lifting from the branch.

"Are you ready to leave?"

"Yes," answered Ted. He quickly gathered his things. After untying the Chestnut, he got in the saddle and nudged the horses to move out.

"How long have you been here?"

"I was born into the herd many years back."

"I'm sure it was."

"Do I look that old?" lightheartedly grunted Shoeshon.

Ted laughed and continued onward aside him.

"We'll be crossing a river soon."

"Would that be the Crystal River I see on my map?"

"Yes. The forest will change on the other side."

"Change?"

"It will become very dense with many hills and caves."

"Greta mentioned them. She called 'em the dark places."

"There are only two animals you need to fear out here. One is Silver eye and her pack of hyenas, and, Split-tooth the Alpha male and his pack of wolves. They roam the dead forest in the Forbidden Land more often than here."

"I met the wolves already. They smell like nothing I've smelt before. Foul things they were."

"They are at that. I can smell both creatures, miles away. Most of the forest animals can."

"Silver Eye?" questioned Ted.

"Her eye is really not silver. It just looks that way. She lost it in a fight with Thor, the mighty bull elk. From then on, we in the forest nicknamed her that."

"Split-tooth?" he asked.

"One of his canines hangs out of the bottom of his lip."

Ted nodded. He'd never forget either description.

At the river's edge, Ted halted watching the slow moving current. The river stones sparkled from the cascading sunlight between the limbs stretching over. The larger boulders half submerged were covered in a light green moss.

Looking over the river, the forest was very dense with lots of hanging vines from limbs. Without a word, he followed Shoeshon across to a path.

Ted could not see a thing behind the huge elephant. It wasn't until they entered a clearing he could come abreast of him.

"Is it like this the whole way?" he questioned, taking in the rugged terrain with grayish volcanic rock jetting up from the earth. "Yes, but this path goes all the way to Shendor. All the animals use it."

About a quarter of a mile out from Shendor, Shoeshon stopped. "This is as far as I go. Just around those trees up ahead you'll come to a small valley. Shendor is not far from there."

"Thank you for escorting me."

"Call upon me anytime, Lord Barrington."

"I will, if need be."

"Be vigilant; evil is lurking all around."

Ted nodded.

Shoeshon turned and slowly made his way back into the forest.

As he did, Major swooped down and landed on a branch.

The elephant stopped.

Major whispered the secret to him.

Shoeshon glanced back to where he had left Ted.

When his eyes came forward he said,

"Lord Barrington is the *Promise*."

"That he is. We must protect him with our very lives if he is going to save the Countess."

To Shoeshon, Juliette Tyrus, Countess of Lyon Head was the queen of the Redwood Forest; the most precious woman in all the Realm.

Her love for the animals was apparent. She never needed to call. They would come from far and wide when she traveled there. Sometimes, she'd step down from her carriage and greet the animals; her escorts were always amazed seeing them gathering around her.

11

Ted walked out of the forest into a meadow of rolling green hills; filled with an array of white and blue flowers. Around a bend, he came upon a farm. A woman was out front working in her garden. She was wearing a gray wool dress and white bonnet tied under her chin. On the side of the cabin were colorful hummingbirds drinking from a feeder.

"Hello," he greeted, dismounting his mare.

She turned, wiping her hands on her apron. "Good morning," she replied, eyeing him up. He was staring at something. She glanced that way.

"I've never seen such wonderful hummingbirds."

"They're called Royal Hummingbirds. I've seen them in the forest on a few occasions and have been trying to lure them out to come to my feeder. I was hoping they'd love sweet strawberry juice."

"It appears they do."

To her and his surprise, the birds flew over to Ted. They circled him; hovering motionlessly in front of his face.

"Good morning my friends," he humorously greeted, lifting his hand. One landed it on it.

"I'll be," she gushed. "They seem to like you," she continued, walking up to the small picket fence.

Ted was amazed himself.

One chirped. He understood what it said.

"She said they love strawberry juice."

"She what?" the woman laughed, thinking he was kidding.

"The light-blue one is Bree, and these are her friends, Mylee, and Nera."

"Now, sir, you really are making fun of me, aren't you."

"No," he replied, extending his hand. The hummingbirds looked at her.

"What is your name?"

"Donna Gillum," she answered, keeping her focus on the birds.

"Say good morning, Donna."

The birds began chirping.

"Who are you?"

"I'm Ted Landen," he lied, not trusting anyone again.

"I wish my husband was home to witness this."

With her husband not home, Ted thought it wise to ask for some water for his horses and be on his way.

"Bring them around back. The well is next to the barn."

"Thank you."

As he turned for the gate, the hummingbirds flew back to the feeder.

Upon entering, Donna asked, "I suppose you can talk to the cows, sheep and pigs as well?"

"No, I can't – maybe it's because they've been domesticated."

"You cannot talk to your horses?"

"I do. They seem to hear me but say nothing back."

She laughed.

After taking care of his horses and filling his flask, Donna stood by the gate watching him leave. *My husband will laugh when I tell him this.*

When her husband, Ben returned home that night – he did not laugh. He had heard word from his cousin Lord Nelson that someone by the name of Ted Landen had come; someone the Twins suspected was working for King William and or, the Shadow. *So… the man comes visiting my wife on his way to the Northern Kingdom,* he thought. *He also can speak to the hummingbirds. I wonder if he can speak to those bees,* his thoughts drifted. *That is certainly news the Twins would want to know. They'll pay handsomely for it.*

"You don't find it strange?" she asked.

"Yes, I think he was pulling your leg," he replied, keeping his thoughts to himself. "I must go and see my cousin."

"At this hour of the night?" "Yes."

"Why all of a sudden do you need to see him?"

"Business, my dear."

"Business… phooey… you always say it's business when you spend days with him."

"Well," said Ben, grabbing his coat. "I might surprise you with a new dress. You'd like that, wouldn't you?"

"New dress; I'd rather have my husband sitting down with me for supper."

"I'll be back in three days. I'll eat with you then," he replied, walking out the door.

While Ben rode off to the Northern Kingdom to give his cousin Lord Nelson the news, Ted trotted into the town of Shendor.

It was a large village with mud-brick buildings. The dirt street was wide and busy with horses, carriages and kids running about. In the middle was an Inn. He dismounted.

Across from him, outside the trading post, two men were leaning against the wall, watching Ted securing the horses and then entering the Inn.

"That's him," whispered Lutz.

"It sure is. That's Greta's Chestnut," added Gavin. "What do you want to do?"

"We must find a way of giving the Twins' potion to him. Once he's out, it will be a long ride back to Black Water."

Lutz nodded, glad to see Ted Landen wasn't traveling with them bees. He heard word of Greta being stung. It was the last thing he wanted to deal with.

"Afternoon, you have any rooms available," asked Ted at the Inn

"Yes," replied the clerk. "How long will you be staying?"

"Just tonight; I'll be heading off in the morning."

The clerk grabbed a key. "Sign the registry book."

Ted signed his name.

"Room 4, upstairs on the left."

"Thanks."

The room was like a million other rooms; a bed, dresser, nightstands and a window. He placed his belongings on the bed then walked over looking down at the road.

There was a knock on his door.

"Come in."

A lady entered carrying a bowl, towels and soap. "Good day. These are for you to wash up," she said, placing the items on the dresser. She went to leave.

"Wait."

"Yes."

"Where is the best place in town to eat?" "Cooper's, it's just down the road on the right."

"Thank you."

After securing his horses in the stable, Ted walked into Cooper's for a meal. Two men came in right after him. He turned seeing them strolling past and taking-up residence at the bar. He noticed the long knife in a shoulder harness on the tall one and then his eyes drew down on both their swords. *They look like trouble,* he thought, heading for a table.

Dinner was a nice slice of beef, corn and biscuits. It went down well. He drank the last of his port and stood up. After paying the man at the counter, he walked out into the still of the night. *I'll check the horses before going to bed,* he thought, heading over to the stable.

After opening the big doors, he noticed the stable-hand was gone. His horses were in the last two stalls at the end. Before reaching them, he heard a scampering noise.

A black ferret rushed in from behind.

"Hurry, you must get out of here." "Who are you?"

"My name is Jasper – waste no time, trouble is coming."

Ted hurried over and opened one of the rear doors.

"Going somewhere?" he heard a man say.

He slowly faced him. *It's the two from Cooper's.* "What can I do for you?"

The short fat one drew his sword. "You can drink this and then we're all going for a ride."

Ted stared at the man then eyed the taller one drawing his long knife. "I've drunk enough wine tonight, thanks."

"This isn't any wine," replied the fat filthy man.

"That's right, and seeing you have no bees to protect you now, you best do as we say," said the taller man.

It's the Twins' henchmen. With his mind racing, thinking of what to do, he glanced up in the rafters. Sitting along the beam were six large Grassland Pipers. *I'll be a son-of-a- bitch,* he thought, dropping his gaze upon the men. *If I order them to attack, will they?* He had nothing to lose. He took two steps back; quickly drawing his sword. "I am Lord Barrington and I'll drink nothing you have," he grunted, pointing the sword at them. "ATTACK," he shouted.

The Pipers lifted off the beam and flew down toward the men. In a flash, the bird's plumes went from gold to blood red.

The two men yelled out, wildly swinging at them. They hit the floor overwhelmed by the birds attacking; pecking at their faces, arms and legs.

"Tell your witches, I command the animals," said Ted; watching the mayhem.

Neither could reply as they desperately fought the winged menace going for their soft flesh.

One drove its beak into Lutz's lips; ripping a section off. Another plucked out one of his eyes and ate it.

"My eye, my eye," screamed Lutz, rolling over in pain.

Gavin got to his knees, his head and face badly bleeding. "You rotten birds," he cursed. "Let's get out of here," he moaned, getting up. The Pipers clung to him as he raced out the doors.

Seeing Gavin leaving, Lutz stumbled to his feet. He covered his bloody face; his right eye gone, his upper lip ripped off and half his lower ear missing. He staggered out the doors still fighting the birds pecking at his head.

After the two had left, Ted stood there a second looking to see where the ferret was hiding. He spotted him sitting on a wooden rail just overhead. "How did you know?"

"I'm a spy. I was sent by Grandfather."

"Grandfather," repeated Ted. Before he continued, the front door opened. Ted quickly turned thinking the two men were back.

Instead, it was a man wearing a long black hooded coat. One side was tucked behind his sword.

"Are you alright?"

"Yes, who are you?"

The man said nothing, turned and departed.

Ted looked up at the ferret.

"I've seen him before. He works for King William," said Jasper.

Ted glanced back at the door. *Maybe he's a spy; was probably following those two? I'm sure he saw the Grassland Pipers. He just might mention that to the king.* Ted dropped those thoughts and faced the ferret. He had questions.

"Tell me," he said, "how did you get here? The Beginning is several days' ride."

"Juno, the great eagle brought me here.

He's out back."

"Juno?" he repeated, walking over and opening the rear doors. There on a high branch he saw the majestic bird.

The eagle looked down at him then flew off toward the mountains.

After going back in, he reached out his hand. "I guess you and I are a team," he said.

"That we are, Lord Barrington," replied Jasper, climbing onto his hand then gathered himself on Ted's shoulder.

Back in his room, sleep evaded Ted. The more he tossed and turned, the more his thoughts circled inside his head. He thought of home, his son, his business; those that worked for him. He thought of this quest, his decision to take it, and now, going home sounded better.

He rolled over opening his eyes. Jasper was sitting by the window looking out. *What will you tell them? That you want to go home; you're all done with this mission to save the Countess? What would Grandfather say?*

*What would the rest say? They're all depending on me. They have come to my aid, have rescued me and now…*his thoughts drifted.

"You can't sleep?" asked Jasper.

Ted sighed.

"You have much to do, Lord Barrington.

Best you sleep."

His words sat there tapping his heart. *You see,* he thought. *They're all counting on me, and besides that, how do I return?* That thought made him think of the Beginning; whom he now knew was Grandfather.

He remembered what Grandfather had said; if you make it back here, I'll know you have completed your task. *Then what? How do I get back to my world?*

"Lord Barrington."

"Yes, Jasper," he replied, glancing over at him.

His look said it all; go to sleep.

"I will," he said, rolling over and closing his eyes.

Ted awoke more vigorous than the previous night. The one thing that dispelled all his ill thoughts was Juliette. His love for her was more than overwhelming; she was like a torch to his soul. Immersed within her loving arms was his ultimate goal; and he'd see it through to the end, having her forever.

He slipped out of bed seeing Jasper asleep by the window. After washing up he nudged the ferret awake and they left the Inn.

Outside, dawn was breaking. People were up; walking through the hazy morning sunlight. With both horses ready, he placed Jasper on his shoulder and quietly rode out of town.

After passing the last house, he rode into the forest toward the Northern Kingdom; a place he was eager to see.

12

With Lutz in grave pain, his eye gone, lip torn apart and missing a piece of his ear and Gavin not feeling well himself, he could not take hearing the moaning any longer. As soon as they reached the safety of the forest, he halted and got down from his horse.

"What are you doing?"

"Dismount and come over here," grunted Gavin.

Lutz slipped off his horse and staggered over.

"Lie down," said Gavin, unwrapping Lutz's head. He shrieked seeing the mangled socket and his lip hanging off. There was nothing he could do but wash out the empty socket and cover it up.

Lutz's scream was intense; every nerve in his body shook.

"Now drink this; it will ease the pain."

Lutz poured the wine over his lip. He screamed from the burning sensation.

"Drink, you bloody fool," said Gavin.

Lutz carefully placed the bottle to his lips and guzzled the wine. Three bottles later, he remained drunk, dizzy with port all the way back to Black Water.

As the two trotted up to the castle, a guard shouted down to open the gate.

Once inside, soldiers asked what had happened. None was willing to inform the Twins. They left that to Egmon.

Egmon marched them straight to the tower, overlooking the Isle of Drake.

When the Twins entered, they were outraged.

"Where is Ted Landen," shouted Greta.

"You mean, Lord Barrington," replied Lutz.

Greta's eyes bore into him. "What did you say," she spat, storming over to him.

"His name is Ted Barrington, Lord Barrington. That's what he said right before he had the Grassland Pipers attack us."

Greta spun on her heels looking at her sister. Greta's expression said it all. The truth is finally known. Ted Barrington is Sheppard Barrington's cousin.

"Grassland Pipers," hissed Greta, training her attention back on Lutz.

"Yes, hundreds of them," he exaggerated. "I lost an eye, part of my lip and a piece of my ear," he groaned, patting his bandaged face.

"Pipers; you poor thing," she sighed. "Let me see," she continued, lifting the bloody cover. She stood back disgusted.

Lutz could see her expression again change; her cold, dark eyes were like daggers.

"You still have one good eye, so why didn't you stay and capture him!?"

"Madam Greta," he moaned.

"Can you still see?" she barked, standing back with her hands on her hips.

"Why, yes."

"Well then, show me how far you can see," she said, walking toward the balcony rail. Hagar stood there confused with her sister's antics. She glanced over at Egmon. He shrugged not knowing what Greta was up to.

Lutz strolled over.

"Get up there," ordered Greta. "Get up there?"

"Yes, I want to know how far you can see."

Lutz reluctantly climbed up. It was a fifty foot drop to the dark water below.

"Look out there."

Lutz gazed past the Isle toward the remains of the volcanic island on the other side.

"Well," snapped Greta.

"I can see past the top of the volcano." "Anything else?"

"Yes, I see the silvery moon."

"Good, because that's the last thing you'll ever see," she snapped, pushing him off the rail.

Lutz screamed all the way until he hit the water and went under.

"What have you done," shouted Hagar. "Come, sweet sister."

Hagar and Egmon ran over.

Gavin seeing their backs to him silently crept for the door to escape.

Greta hearing him, called out to her pet. The foul creature got up and headed for Gavin. He quickly turned placing his back against the door. Rye held her stance snarling at him; ready to pounce.

"Leaving so fast?" cackled Greta keeping her eyes forward on Lutz.

"No I… I'll be waiting right here," he replied, staring at Rye.

"Over there," shouted Egmon, pointing at two large heads appearing above the water.

Greta's eyes fixed on the beasts. She smiled seeing Lutz frantically swimming toward the breakers below the castle.

The behemoth monsters glided over toward him.

"Will it be one bite or two," she smirked.

Hagar was not amused, but could not look away.

"One bite and he'll be gone," replied Egmon.

As the creatures with their long tails swam toward their prey, one turned its long head sideways and grabbed Lutz tossing him into the air. His terrifying scream could be heard across the Drake. The other took hold, and tossed him again.

"Oh, they are having fun," giggled Greta.

Lutz bleeding badly could hardly swim.

The large crocodile drifted up to him and grabbed his legs. The other came up and took the rest. With one powerful jerk, Lutz was ripped in half; both getting a snack.

While the beasts enjoyed their meal, Greta slowly turned and glared at Gavin.

"Madam, Greta," he pleaded.

"Don't Madam Greta me," she hissed. Lutz was gone in one bite, how long do you think you'll last with my sweet pet, Rye?"

Gavin slowly lowered his eyes on the hyena; her jowls dripping with saliva. It was the last thing he wanted having that foul smelling thing tearing him apart.

With a wave of her hand the door opened. "Seize him," shouted Greta to the guards.

They rushed in and took hold of Gavin.

"What are you going to do to him," asked Hagar, worried.

"I'm not going to do anything," she mused, lifting her pointed chin. "He will decide for himself. You have two choices."

Gavin waited to hear.

"We'll set you free at the front gate of the courtyard and see if you can escape from Rye or, follow Lutz to the deep water below; which will it be?"

Gavin looked out over the balcony into the dead of night while thinking; *a quick death or, slowly being torn apart.* It was a death he could not bear. Without a word, he pulled away from the guards and ran toward the rail. With one giant leap, he went over the rail.

Greta turned seeing the last of him. "That was easy," she mused, rubbing her hands.

Hagar glanced at Egmon. He simply smiled.

"Egmon," said Greta.

His smiled disappeared. "Yes, Madam Greta."

"I want you to take five good men and go capture Lord Barrington before he makes it to the Northern Kingdom."

"But, Madam," he replied. "That's a two day ride. He'll be there in a day."

Greta's eyes became like angry black marbles. "Rye or the rail?" she hissed.

Egmon wasn't sure if she was kidding. He never gave her a chance to continue. He ran out of the tower screaming.

Greta laughed hearing his boots echoing down the circular staircase.

"You wouldn't have?" scolded Hagar.

"Nay, sweet sister. I love Egmon. I just wanted to scare him a bit, that's all," she giggled.

"You," spat Hagar. "Leave us," she ordered the guards.

They bowed and walked out.

When the door shut, Hagar spun on her heels folding her arms.

"Why are you upset?" "They were good men."

"Good men," she grumbled. "Good men would have Lord Barrington kneeling before us."

"What if Egmon doesn't capture him?"

That did not set well with Greta. She certainly wouldn't toss him over the rail nor have Rye rip him apart. She sullenly strolled over to the balcony.

Hagar stood there waiting.

"If they do not capture him, we'll have to place the castle and surrounding villages on high alert," she said, facing her sister. "War is coming. I can feel it."

Egmon with five good men in armor, rode hard all night; through the villages of Orbed and Tribow. They stopped in Bissell to rest their horses and speak to Mani; an old warrior.

While drinking port at the tavern, Mani and his men sat and listened to Egmon. Not a sound was heard as he spoke. When he finished, Mani stood up.

All eyes gazed at the ox of a man wearing a wolf pelt coat with white rabbit skins draped over his shoulder. "How do you defend against a man who somehow has the animals protecting him?"

Heads turned this way and that not knowing or having an answer.

Mani continued, "We all know that no man or army can fight the Shadow and win. Now this one has come. I say go back to the Twins and tell 'em to prepare for war, if that is his reason for being here; seeking revenge for the foolish thing they did by abducting the Countess of Lyon Head."

Egmon stood up in his small black cape. "I and my men must try and capture him before he makes it to the Northern Kingdom."

"You said he was in Shendor," one man questioned.

"Yes."

"You'll never make it sitting here," another spoke up.

"Are any of you willing to come? I'll speak highly of you to the Twins if you do. Their coffers are filled with gold, silver, rubies and gems."

"You cannot guarantee that anyone volunteering would be paid," said Mani.

"No, I can't guarantee that but, know this… Greta will be very pleased if Lord Barrington is kneeling before her. I'm sure in her delight she'd be more than happy to pay each man a handsome reward."

"I'll go," said Fons.

"Me too," added Drew. Rex and Lory stood up. Egmon looked at Mani.

"We'll all go," he said, heading for the door.

Egmon smiled, nodding to his men. They got up and followed him out.

The eleven men – five soldiers including Egmon from Black Water and the five from Bissell rode out of the village. They made good time through the Dead Forest and onward through the Valley of the Damned. Upon reaching the natural rock bridge separating the two sides, they halted.

"We'll cross on foot and rest on the other side," said Egmon.

"You have one hour to rest, gentlemen," said Mani, "then we ride again."

13

"Rider approaching," yelled a guard on the Northern Kingdom wall.

The Captain rushed over.

"One man, with a pack horse, Sir." "I see him."

As Ted trotted out into the clearing with Jasper, he halted; stunned by what he saw. He had traveled the world. Seen the castles of Europe, the architecture in France along with touring the Roman Colosseum, but what stood before him now – was spectacular. The Northern Kingdom began in the plains and went up a sloping mountain side.

At the top was Lyon Head Castle; the structural peeks adorned in white mist. The front of the kingdom was a forty-foot, white- washed wall, made of sandstone blocks; stretching clear across the open field. The entrance was protected by a draw bridge expanding over a moat. To the left, beside the mountain, he could see blue water; *the Sea of Presidium*, he thought, thinking of the map.

In his mesmerizing trance he never realized what was coming behind him; hundreds of Grassland Pipers swooping above the tree-line and settling within the branches. Along with the Pipers were a swarm of Zenith Bees darting through the forest, landing on the outer tree trunks.

Just then, Jasper heard the pounding of hooves. He stood up on Ted's shoulder and growled.

Ted turned seeing a group of rough looking men riding hard toward him. Terrified, he frantically pulled up on the horse's reins. The horse reared sending him flying back. Jasper leaped from his shoulder, rolling several feet in a ball through the grass.

From the balcony of the king's chamber, the first hand to the king, Lord Hartman took in the scene. "Your Majesty, come see this."

King William hurried out to the balcony.

Ted quickly settled his horse. As soon as he mounted with Jasper, the gang surrounded him. He sat there as an ugly looking dwarf rode up and placed his horse in the center.

"Well, well, if it isn't Lord Barrington." "What can I do for you gentlemen?"

"Gentlemen," repeated Egmon, looking about his men.

Laughter erupted.

"You have a date with the Twins," said Egmon. "We're here to escort you to Black Water."

"Really," replied Ted, spotting over the little man's head dozens of Grassland Pipers perched within the tree line. He leaned back in his saddle as if not to have a care in the world.

Egmon did not like Lord Barrington's posture or his unamused attitude. "A man all alone without his little friends to protect him, I say is a fool," he said, pushing back his cape and leaning forward.

Jasper leaped off Ted's shoulder, ran up the horses' head and growled; baring his teeth.

"Look at this feisty varmint," laughed Egmon. "I guess you do have *one* little friend to protect you today."

Again the men laughed.

Egmon stopped laughing seeing Ted's smug expression. "You're coming with us. If you cause any trouble, Mani here will shoot you with an arrow. Not bad though. We aren't taking a dead man back. The witches want you alive."

Ted said nothing.

That pissed Egmon off even more. "Your sword," he grunted, holding out his hand. "Slowly now; real easy like."

Ted nodded, reaching down to pull it out then quickly brought his fingers to his lips and whistled.

The horses reared from the sudden ear- piercing sound. Before Egmon and his men could settle their horses down, from out of the forest trees, the Pipers swooped into the air. They flew low, just above the ground; the bees right after.

Drew spotted them. "We have trouble coming!" he shouted.

Egmon and Mani glanced in that direction. Their eyes grew wide watching the gold laced within their wings and the plumes on their heads turn blood red.

The men all panicked. Their horses scattered in every direction desperately trying to escape the birds' vicious attack.

By the hundreds, the bees caught up, entering the fray; repeatedly stinging the men. Several fell off their horses. All they could do was run for their lives. The Pipers circled swooping downward catching their talons in their hair - bees stinging their faces, arms and hands. They fell in balls covered in bees; their moans and screams deafening, then all went silent.

Seeing this, Egmon shouted to his remaining guards to retreat.

Mani gathered his horse, bees all over him; Pipers attacking. "Retreat, retreat," he shouted, mounting and riding off.

The men dispersed with bees and birds all around them. Once they made it back to the trail, the Pipers flew high in the air watching the men racing off on their horses. They then circled back to the open plain where Ted was standing.

Ted looked at the big birds overhead, continued checking the dead men lying on the ground and then spotted a wounded bird. He walked over and picked it up.

"Lord Barrington."

"Yes, my feathered friend."

"When you see Grandfather, tell him…"

Ted watched its eyes close, its head roll to the side. With a deep sigh, he gently laid it down. "I'll tell Grandfather how brave you were."

"Your Majesty," said Lord Hartman stunned.

"I saw it. I want to speak with this man.

Gather my council."

"Yes your Grace."

As Ted trotted toward the drawbridge, the multitude of Grassland Pipers stayed with him overhead. The bees stayed in the open grassland in a giant swarm. Once he made it to the draw bridge, they took flight back to the forest.

The guards on the wall along with their captain looked up at the sight.

"What do you make of this?" asked a guard.

"I haven't a clue," replied the captain, shifting his focus on the man, riding up to the bridge, "but we'll know soon enough. Get word to the king."

"Yes, Captain."

Ted halted at the drawbridge.

"State your business," asked Captain Torres from above.

"I need to speak with King William." "Why?"

Ted glanced at the guards next to Torres. "I think it would be better if I spoke to you alone."

Torres stared at the man for a moment. He knew the king would want to see him. "Alright, let him pass. I'll meet you in the courtyard. I want several men to go out and retrieve the dead."

Two guards stepped forward from the entrance holding spears.

Ted dismounted and escorted his horses across the bridge.

After entering the gate, each step he took, he felt himself truly back in time; back to the Roman days. The cobble stone street, whitewashed walls, the hanging flower baskets. The people dressed in wool clothing; soldiers wearing silver breast plates, short tunics, and leather sandals.

In the center of the courtyard was a huge statue of a lion in full armor. In the corners were beautiful stone statues of royal guards, fifteen feet tall, holding standards and spears; their flags fluttering in the breeze. Just then, Captain Torres appeared from a flight of steps.

"Your name?"

"I am Lord Barrington," he said, looking over Torres' shoulder at a woman wearing a blue hooded coat. As she walked by, she glanced his way; her eyes seemingly taking him in.

"Are you related to Sheppard Barrington, Lord of Corset?"

"Yes."

"I've never seen you before." "I come from a far off land."

Torres nodded. "What's with the Pipers?" "They seem to like me," he replied with a glint in his eye. He shifted on the woman. She turned and headed up the street. After rounding a corner through an alleyway, she changed into a dark-skinned man of India descent.

Just then, soldiers on horseback came trotting into the courtyard.

Torres stepped aside.

The one wearing a dazzling uniform with lavish plumes streaming from his silver helmet dismounted.

"This is Lord Barrington. He is requesting to see King William," said Torres.

"That he will," replied Cornel, Captain of His Majesties Royal Guard. "The only Barringtons I know are from Corset."

"Sheppard Barrington is my cousin. I, myself, come from a far off land."

His words intrigued Cornel. *He must be here due to his cousin being killed.* "Who were the men after you?" he asked, side stepping his thoughts.

"I'd suspect the Twins' henchmen, Sir."

Coming from a far off land, how would he know about the Twins… his thoughts drifted, *why would they be after him?*

"Captain," said Torres, pointing up at the birds, perched on the walls, roofs and chimneys.

"He can also explain that to the king.

Mount up and follow me."

As the group proceeded down the cobbled stone street, Ted looked for the woman wearing the blue hooded coat. When they entered the market square where people were buying and trading their goods, he spotted the coat, but wearing it was a dark skinned man. Riding by, the man looked up at him.

"How long have you been traveling?" asked Cornel.

Ted glanced his way; thinking. "For many months," he replied, keeping his story straight; being from a far off land.

"Your business here or, do I need to ask, due to your cousin now dead."

"That is one reason. The other is to break the Twins' spell over Juliette."

Cornel looked at him seemingly thinking if Lord Barrington had a clue to where she was being hidden. He had to ask – somewhat. "What do you know of her?"

"I know everything, if that's what you're asking," he replied, staring into his eyes.

"Everything?"

"Yes, and I'm well aware not many know where she is right now."

Cornel nodded wondering who had told him. "Your cousin was in love her."

Ted glanced down the cobble stone street then looked at him. "Yes, I got news via a letter," he lied. "How do you know that, Captain?" he asked in return.

"She confided in me."

Ted sat back in his saddle.

"You can trust me, Lord Barrington. No one knows about their love affair but me."

"I guess one of such standings needs to have people watching their backs."

"There are no truer words spoken; however, I don't think I'll ever forgive myself for allowing her to be abducted."

"Together, we may change that, Captain."

That comment not only surprised him, it filled his heart with hope. A slight hope, for how could they kill the Twins. No one had an answer. *Maybe Lord Barrington does.* He was anxious to know. "I'm sorry Sheppard took it upon himself to try and save her," he said, changing the subject.

"So am I."

"King William does not know why he tried to do that."

"So you kept your word; even from him?" "Yes, and from her mother as well."

As they proceeded to the castle, inside the walls, Lord Hartman called for the king's council to assemble.

Lord Nelson opened his door when a guard knocked. "Forgive me for interrupting, my Lord; the king seeks your presence with the rest of his council."

"Why?"

"We have a visitor." "Visitor?"

"Yes, my Lord. A Lord Barrington has arrived seeking the king's presence."

Hearing the name, Nelson seemingly glanced back at his cousin Ben Gillum; Donna's husband standing behind him. "Give me a moment. I'll be right down."

The guard nodded and departed.

Nelson shut the door. "Did you hear that?"

"Yes, he told my wife he was Ted Landen," said Ben

"Well, we now know that his name isn't really Ted Landen… it's Ted Barrington; I'd suspect he's Sheppard Barrington's cousin."

"That he is," replied Ben, "which leads me to suspect his reasoning for coming here."

Nelson stared at him while thinking; *yes, he knew why Ted was here.* Through the Twins' spies, they had learned that Juliette was secretly seeing Sheppard. He wondered if Richard and she had married, would the two have continued their love affair. It did not matter now. The fool man tried to save her himself and was taken by the hyenas. His body was discovered, well some of it that is; scattered about the forest floor.

"You think the Shadow requested him to come?" questioned Ben.

"Who else could have?" he said, washing his face.

"I'm surprised however; if it were the Shadow who requested Ted to come, why didn't the Shadow tell King William that Juliette was seeing Sheppard?" asked Ben.

Nelson grabbed a towel while pondering that. He knew the Countess was close with Captain Cornel also. "Maybe he and Cornel swore an oath to her not to tell anyone; even her father and mother."

"It doesn't matter, Lord Nelson. This news will set well with the Twins."

"It will. I want you to ride to Black Water and inform the pair straight away."

"I'll ride out tonight and hopefully return with pockets full of gold, rubies and gems."

Nelson could already feel the items within his hands. "Tell 'em I'll get word back as soon as I hear what this *Ted* has to say to the king."

Ben nodded and headed for the door.

After he left, Nelson proceeded to the council chamber.

Ted and Cornel dismounted at the steps of the castle; an elaborate structure with grayish marbled steps and white-washed pillars. Men in white robes were standing at the entrance of the castle above them.

After following Cornel up the steps, they proceeded through the archway with sculptured statues on either side. As he came to another chamber men and woman wearing elegant clothing were standing there whispering to one another as they walked through.

Cornel turned down a passageway and walked up to a door. "Wait here," he said.

Ted looked at the guards standing there.

Neither spoke a word.

Five minutes later the door opened.

"The king will see you now."

Not knowing what to expect, Ted deeply inhaled and entered.

Cornel escorted him up to a long table with men in fine clothing sitting there.

The king stood up.

"Your Majesty, this is Lord Barrington."

"Your Grace," greeted Ted, bowing. When he lifted his head, he gazed at the king in his bright blue outfit with a white ruffled lapel and cufflinks. His appearance was sharp; so were his facial features, especially his dark peering eyes.

"Lord Barrington," greeted William, taking in the ferret on his shoulder. "Does your friend have a name?"

"His name is Jasper," he replied, glancing at the men sitting there; one in particular, Lord Nelson. Before he continued, he knew he'd have to expose this traitor. "Your, Majesty," he said. "Forgive me if I seem a bit nervous."

William waited. "Please, speak up."

"What I have to say may be best if I told you alone."

"Alone!" grunted Lord Hartman.

"The king never sits alone with a stranger for the first time," soundly added Lord Bright, William's Financial Advisor.

Ted looked from one to the other. He then eyed the king; who held an expression that stated; say what you have to say in front of my council.

"OK," said Ted. "On my way here, I got word from a reliable source that you have a spy within your council."

The room instantly erupted. Men stood up shouting, so did Nelson.

"Sit down!" ordered William.

The men grumbled taking their seats.

"Lord Barrington requested to speak with me alone. You all objected and now don't like what he said," spoke William.

"But your Majesty," argued Lord Bright.

William held up his hand. He looked at Ted. You received word from whom, may I ask?"

Ted hoped when he said the name, the king would know he was speaking the truth. "Patch… his name is Patch."

"Patch," he repeated, cocking his head. "Yes, your Grace."

"This is outrageous," one man shouted. "Who is Patch? another man questioned.

William slowly turned his head and replied, "He's an old friend." As he looked back at Ted, he thought, *why didn't the Shadow tell me himself that I had a spy on my council?* He dropped that thought and asked, "Do you know who it is?"

"Yes."

"Guards!" shouted William.

The men around the table got nervous not knowing who it was.

The guards rushed in; swords drawn.

Lord Nelson's heart quickened; while internally praying he hadn't been exposed.

"Who is it," demanded William.

Ted whispered in Jasper's ear. Jasper went down the table and sat in front of Lord Nelson.

The men were astounded by this.

William glared at Lord Nelson; one of his most trusted servants.

"Your Majesty, do you truly believe that I, your humble servant would be a spy!" he blasted. "And this," he continued, pointing at the ferret. "This stunt is outrageous!"

Groans and anger spilled forth from the group. The men could not believe it themselves.

Furious, William pounded the table. "Have my physician place Lord Nelson on the wheel."

The guards stepped forward, seizing him.

"Your, Majesty. You're making a terrible mistake," pleaded Nelson, being dragged out.

"Tell the physician I want a *full* confession, I want to know everything – this day."

"Yes, your, Majesty," they replied, knowing a *full* confession was the worse torture one could bear.

Nelson knew it too. He had witnessed it himself. "Your, Majesty, please… I beg of you. There is no need for this. I am your most humble servant," he cried out.

After the door shut, Nelson could be heard begging for his life all the way down the corridor.

Angered, William sat down. He waved his hand for Ted to sit.

"Nelson a spy," said Lord Bright. "It's beyond my thinking."

"It is at that," Lord Hartman agreed.

William eyed the two then focused on Ted. "Before you tell us your reason for being here, please explain to me the Grassland Pipers and Zenith Bees. How did you get them to attack the Twins' men?"

Wanting to hear themselves, the group pushed back their thoughts about Nelson. They were intrigued with this man having a smart ferret called Jasper and the birds and bees protecting him.

"I come from a far off land," said Ted, not wanting to explain with all those sitting there.

"How can you come from a far off land being Sheppard Barrington's cousin? Were you not born in Corset?" asked Lord Hartman.

"One can travel," replied Ted.

The response was quick; laughter. William lifted his brow to Hartman. Hartman sighed feeling foolish.

"I have come to your kingdom to try and save your daughter, Juliette."

"How dare you," grunted Lord Bright. "Juliette is dead."

"Silence," shouted William. He then focused on Ted. *My daughter is in the tower. Not many on my council know that, but this man does.* He knew right then that the Shadow was involved with having Ted come here. *But why… Was it that he was able to control the animals? I saw it first hand and Ted by-passed my question.*

"With all due respect," said Ted, looking about the men at the table. "I would like to speak with you alone, your Grace."

"Now, after informing us that we have a spy, you want to speak with the king alone," said Lord Reese, William's Administration Minister; in charge of the castle's affairs. "If you have more to tell the king, you can say it right now."

Ted glanced at him then shifted his eyes on William.

"Out, everyone out," ordered William.

Grunts of displeasure resounded from the group making their exit.

William waited until they had left before continuing. "Now," he said, getting up and pouring two glasses of wine. He handed one to Ted and sat down. "Before we speak of my daughter, what about the Pipers and bees?"

"As you may know," he replied and paused, "your daughter loved the animals. She frequently visited the Redwood Forest."

"I am well aware of her journeys there."

"Did you know they would come right up to her?"

"No," he replied, stunned hearing that.

"The Realm is full of mystery, magic and such."

William sat back. He knew that as well; *the shadow, the witches and now this revelation of his daughter with the animals.* "With you living in a far off land, how would you know all this?"

The king's question sat there between them. He figured he'd start at when he entered the Realm. Everything before that, his world, how he happened upon the trunk, and the book would have been impossible to explain.

When Ted finished, William sat back. "As a young man, when my father was king, I traveled to the beginning of Realm."

"The beginning?" repeated Ted, thinking of Grandfather.

"I guess you can call it the beginning. All I saw was the cliff line and a valley way below."

"What about the tree?"

"The white tree?" questioned William, thinking back.

"Yes."

"I did not know what to make of it; especially the carved face in the trunk. It looked very old. I suspect it had been there for a very long time, even before the Northern Kingdom ever existed, I think."

He never spoke to Grandfather, thought Ted. He let it go. "That's where I entered." "From where, the valley below?"

"Yes," he lied.

"I see."

"After reaching the ridgeline and entering the forest, I came upon the white tree. To my shocking surprise the face spoke to me. It said, "Who are you?"

King William sat back stunned hearing that. He could not imagine such a thing as a tree speaking. As he stared at Ted, something washed over him. The man sitting across the table was different. He felt it as soon as Ted entered the chamber. He had to know, and sharply asked, "Where are you from, really?"

Ted knew from the tone in his voice and those peering eyes staring at him that he'd better tell him the truth. Hearing Nelson begging for his life down the corridor was something he wanted no part of; to be put on the wheel and interrogated himself, whatever the *wheel* was. "I'm from another time," he replied, knowing that answer would produce more questions from the king.

William sat there for a moment just looking at him. In his mind however, he was connecting the dots. *It had to be the Shadow who brought him here. Then again,* he drifted. *Does Ted even know the Shadow's true identity?* William figured Ted didn't know and with that, he wasn't about to expose the Shadow to Ted. Not just yet, at least. So he simply changed the subject. "How much do you know of my daughter's plight?"

"I know everything, your Majesty. After the Twins placed that spell on her, your wife, Victoria ordered her hidden away in the tower. Before I go on, though, what is the situation between you and King Frederick?"

"We settled our differences." "You have?"

"It was quite simple actually. After calling off the wedding between Richard and Juliette, my brother, Prince Andrew married Frederick's cousin Noreen. We all knew they were secretly seeing one another and let the two carry on.

"My wife, Victoria wasn't happy with it but, that is what Frederick and I decided. Now," he said, "what else were you going to say?"

"This may upset you, your Grace," he replied. "Juliette was in fact in love with my cousin, Sheppard. They were having an affair. That is why I wanted to speak with you alone, well… and to tell you about Lord Nelson."

Astounded by that revelation, William stood up. He walked over and poured himself another wine. He lifted the bottle to Ted.

Ted shook his head. "They were madly in love with one another, your Majesty," he continued.

"So," William replied, coming back to the table. "I've always wondered why Sheppard tried to rescue her. Now I know why he did."

"Love is a funny thing, your Majesty. It has no rhyme or reason, it doesn't think, but only feels."

After Ted said that, the room went silent for a moment.

"I never heard it quite like that before, but you're right. And I guess that is why you are here because Sheppard and Juliette were lovers and should have married. With his death, the Laws of the Realm would have granted you the right to marry her."

"Yes, I am aware of that."

"I'll tell you what, Lord Barrington," he said, sitting down. "If you kill the Twins and break the spell over my daughter, she will be yours to marry."

That is all Ted wanted to hear.

"Some on my council do not know where Juliette is."

"I suspected that from the outburst," he said, keeping Juliette's whereabouts to himself.

"Are you hungry?"

"Yes, your Majesty."

"I'll have the chambermaids prepare you a room, then fix you a bath. While you're settling in, my cook will bring you a meal."

"Thank you, your Majesty."

William rang a bell. Four chambermaids came in. With William's instructions, Ted followed them out.

14

As Ted was settling in his room, Lord Nelson was dragged into the physician's chamber. He was immediately stripped of his royal gown and then placed on the upright wheel; a circular contraption with wooden cross members. His hands, feet and head were bound to the wooden cross beams; tightly securing him to the wheel.

Romulus, better known as the physician, was a tall thin man with bushy eyebrows, dark needle eyes and an odd looking nose. He seemed pleased doing his service for the king. William wanted a *full* confession. Seeing Nelson was a trusted servant, one who sat on the king's council, Romulus wanted more.

He walked over to his table and opened his cloth haversack, allowing Nelson to see his fine instruments laid out before him. It was something Romulus did to all those that were sent to him; so they'd see what kind of pain they may endure for days if they remained silent.

He picked up a few sharp instruments and began studying them. That alone was enough to loosen Nelson's tongue.

"I'll tell you everything."

"Oh… I know you will," replied Romulus, walking over with a razor sharp cutter.

"OK… Alright," he started pleading. "Yes, I worked for the Twins. I just ordered my cousin Ben Gillum to ride to Black Water to inform them of Lord Barrington's arrival. That's what you wanted to hear, right?" he immediately confessed, hoping there would be no torture.

"Well, that was quick. It's not too often I get someone to confess so fast," he said then paused, "however, what I'm after is more of a serious matter."

Nelson swallowed.

"How long have you been a spy for the witches of Black Water?"

"Two years."

"Two years," he repeated, turning away then quickly facing him. "So," he said, pausing for a moment. "You were doing their bidding around the time Juliette was traveling to and from the Southern Kingdom?"

"Yes," replied Nelson, nervously looking at the cutter. He knew what they were used for. He sat on several of Romulus' interrogations. The blood, the screams were too much to bear in some of his sessions.

"Did you tell them where she was going and what route she took?"

Nelson hesitated knowing his answer would anger him. You see, Romulus was a mad-man that lived for nothing but one thing – dishing out pain. Romulus thrived on it.

With not wanting to answer his question, he watched as Romulus walked over to the side of the wheel, pried open his tight fist and cut off his pinky finger.

Nelson's terrifying scream bounced off the walls.

"Did that hurt?"

As his whole body shook, gasping moans were all that came out.

"I'll ask you again. Did you inform the witches of the times and route she traveled?" "Yes, yes…. Please… no more!"

That drove into Romulus like a knife. He went to the other side and cut off his other pinky.

Nelson's eyes rolled back; his bounded feet and arms violently shook; stretching the leather straps.

"How did you tell them? I never saw you leave the kingdom."

I can't do this. What will happen to Donna?

His pause was enough to upset Romulus even more. He bent down and cut off his baby toes. Agonizing moans escaped Nelson's lips; saliva rolled down his chin.

"I'm waiting."

"I told Ben Gillum. He's my cousin,"
Nelson finally cried out.

"Ben Gillum, you say?" he repeated, coming nose to nose with Nelson.

"Yes."

With a remorseful expression, Romulus poured out his undying devotion for the countess. "I loved Juliette; the entire kingdom did. She was the most enchanting creature I had ever seen, and yet she never had an up- right chin toward anyone. She loved the children, the poor and gave of her time to them."

Romulus's loving words were softly spoken but, his steely eyes were stone-cold anger; straight from the pit of hell.

"I wish now I had never told him to go and inform the Twins," replied Nelson; saddened by his actions.

"I suppose the price was too great to give up," Romulus shot back. "What did they pay you for your service," he continued, raising a brow.

"The wealth of a king."

Romulus was right. He did it for greed; the Twins did pay him a handsome price for his two years of service. Sickened by that, he turned, walked over to his table and picked up a razor sharp scalpel. When he turned and faced Nelson his eyes bore into him. "The wealth of a king you say."

Nelson said nothing. He knew if he did, it was over. Romulus would go stark raving mad. With his silence, he did anyways.

Without warning, he slashed Nelson's chest, his rib cages, and then slipped the blade down his thighs. The cuts weren't deep but the pain was excruciating. Nelson was losing it. His mind was shutting down.

Romulus saw his eyes roll back and he wasn't done. He drove the scalpel underneath each of Nelson's fingernails; removing them one at a time.

All that was heard from Nelson's lips was gibberish, gasps and moans.

Romulus tossed the scalpel and pulled up Nelson's head. His face was as white as a sheet. "If you think you are going to get out of this by passing out; you're highly mistaken," he spat, letting go of his head. As he went to leave, Nelson spoke up.

"Please, I beg of you. Kill me quick and get it over with."

Romulus stopped and faced the traitor. He knew if he tortured him to death and then told William that it was *he*, Nelson who set up Juliette to be abducted, William would probably remove his head as well. That wasn't going to happen. But… before he went and told the king, he walked back over, picked up the scalpel and slowly sliced off Nelson's ears. With that, he stormed out to inform the King his findings.

An hour later, Romulus returned with four soldiers.

Nelson opened his eyes seeing blurry figures entering the chamber.

With anger in his stride, Romulus picked up a knife and walked up to Nelson. He cut the straps binding him to the wheel.

Nelson fell into a heap on the ground.

"What are you doing?"

"I have spoken to the king. He wants you burned at the stake immediately, which means, regrettably," he replied with a sigh, "you'll get your wish of dying a quicker death. Take him away."

The soldiers seized Nelson and manhandled him out of the room.

He cried the whole way into the outer courtyard where traitors were beheaded, or burned at the stake.

A crowd of his Majesties' Royal Court stood there watching Nelson being tied to the pole, blood still oozing from the sides of his head.

"You traitor," one shouted.

"You'll pay with your life for what you have done," another yelled.

"We trusted you, so did the king," they went on and on.

Nelson looked up at the balcony.

King William was standing at the rail staring down at him. "You… of all my loyal servants, Lord Nelson. The Queen has ordered you not to be tortured to death. You'll be burned at the stake for your treacherous affair with the witches. The Queen now lies on her bed crying knowing it was you who did this to our beloved daughter."

Nelson wanted to say he was sorry; however, he was even weak at saying that.

As the wood was lit, the heat getting hotter - all Nelson could think about were Ben and Donna. *What will happen to them?*

The flames got bigger, the heat unbearable. Nelson screamed as his clothes caught fire. He was engulfed within the flames violently fighting to get free. Then it was over. His head went down.

The Royal Court turned and walked out. King William stood there watching Nelson cook; the black smoke rising up. He shook his head and departed the scene himself.

15

That same evening, Egmon and the men made it back to Bissell. Mani was still furious when he rode into town and dismounted at the stable.

"What happened to you," asked the stable hand.

"We were attacked; lost a man because of this idiot," replied Mani, watching the dwarf walking in. "Look at him," he continued, "he sustained nothing," he spat with a slight nod of his head.

"I lost a man too, Mani. I was smart, though, I used my cape to hide from those nasty bees and birds."

"Bees and birds," questioned the stable hand. "You all look awful," he said, looking at their swollen faces and bloody gashes on their heads.

Mani faced Drew, Fons and Rex. His expression said it all, time for revenge. The four quickly drew their swords and introduced the points to Egmon and the witches' guards.

"Drop your weapons," ordered Mani.

"What are you doing?" he replied; scared. "You're going to pay for this," shouted Mani. "Tie 'em up!"

The stable hand panicked and ran out.

As Egmon watched him flee, he knew he was in serious trouble.

"Tie his feet also and hang him over the rafter. Any of you move, we'll slice you to pieces," grunted Mani.

Once they dropped their swords, Mani walked over to the hot coals in the barrel and placed his sword inside. "I think it's time you felt a little heat yourself, Egmon."

"Heat… I think you're taking this a bit too far, Mani," replied Egmon, eyeing the barrel.

"I am! Just look at my face, look at their faces," he shouted, pointing. Egmon looked at them; even his guards' sustained wounds.

"I want the gold, Egmon!"

"You'll get the gold, trust me," he replied, facing him.

"How?"

"I'll tell Greta what you did."

"She'd just laugh," he spewed, pulling his sword out of the fire.

"Mani, now listen here," said Egmon; worried. He'd been through enough with people kicking him around for being an ugly dwarf. This however, was even worse.

"Shut up," grumbled Mani, walking up to him hanging upside down.

While Mani was tormenting Egmon, Ben reached the outskirts of Bissell on his way to Black Water to inform the Twins of Lord Barrington's arrival. As he entered the village – it seemed empty. Not a soul in sight. He rode to the end of the street. Horses were out front of the stable; light coming from inside. He dismounted and walked up to the door.

"Mani, please, no more," begged Egmon.

Ben peered inside. His eyes grew wide seeing Egmon hanging from the rafters and Mani teasing him with his sword. *I've got to get to Black Water, fast.*

Like the wind he rode onward to the castle. At the entrance, a guard on the wall shouted, "State your business?"

"It's me, Ben Gillum, Lord Nelson's cousin. I need to see the Twins immediately. Mani has Egmon and the Twins' guards tied up inside the stable in Bissell."

"Open the gate."

Ten minutes later the entire castle was in an uproar.

"Gather our horses," ordered Greta, walking down the steps to the open courtyard. As her gaze took in Ben, she stormed over to him. "Who did you say has Egmon tied up in the stable in Bissell?"

"Mani and his men, Madam Greta…. Also, Lord Nelson sent me to tell you that the man you are after is not Ted Landen. His real name is Ted Barrington, Sheppard Barrington's cousin. He is now with King William."

Every word out of his mouth was like poison down her throat. "First off, we already know all about Lord Barrington."

"You do?" he said; surprised.

"We do have spies, Ben," she lashed out. "Two of them now lay in the bellies of the water beast. Would you like to be next?"

"No, please, I am your loyal servant," he gushed, kneeling before her.

Her eyes took in the pitiful sight. It pleased her seeing him on his knees begging. It warmed her evil heart. "Get off your knees my loyal servant and take us to Mani," she said, turning and facing Bulmen. "Release the hounds."

"Release the hounds," questioned Hagar. "We could be there in a split second, Greta."

"No, we ride; I want the hounds with us." "As you wish."

Bulmen entered the dark corridor unlocking each pen setting the dogs free. They came out snarling ready to pounce on anything.

The soldiers stepped back in fear.

When the hounds saw Greta, they cowered, whimpering toward her.

"Come, my pets," soothed Greta, patting a few. She mounted her horse and took off out the gate.

When they came to the stable in Bissell, the Twins dismounted. Greta pointed to the right – six hounds went that way. She pointed to the left – the rest went that way; surrounding the place.

With a wave of their hand, the two transformed into swirling black smoke drifting through the cracks in the stable doors.

Drew and Fons saw the smoke and began yelling.

Mani quickly turned seeing the smoke; then the Twins appeared.

Greta's eyes fell upon Egmon hanging there. She shifted her angry telling gaze upon Mani holding a glowing hot sword.

Just then, Rex bolted out the front doors. The hounds pounced on him ripping him to pieces. The sound was wicked, the screams even worse.

"Anyone else wanting to leave?" hissed Hagar; eyeing Drew, Fons and Mani.

Mani quickly fell to his knees. "Madam Greta, we were only having a bit of fun; isn't that right, Egmon?"

Greta glanced up at Egmon. If his face wasn't awful enough to look at, it was even worse with several swollen lumps from bee stings. She felt sorry for him with his small black cape. It brightened her heart when their seamstress made it for him.

"Off your knees," she spat.

Mani stood up on wobbly legs. Greta lifted her hand toward him.

He felt a powerful grip around his neck then he was floating upward into the air.

"Now, this is what I call fun. Don't you agree, sweet sister?"

Hagar turned toward the other two. She twisted her hand and they began floating upward as well.

"I can't breathe," cried Mani.

"That is the whole point, Mani. You're not supposed to."

"Madam, Greta," said Egmon, twirling around as if he wanted down.

She waved her hand; the rope untied itself and lowered him to the ground.

She then let Mani drop to the floor. He laid there choking.

"Now tell me; what is this all about?"

"I asked Mani and his men to come with me to capture Lord Barrington."

She walked over to him. "Well, where is he?"

Egmon mournfully lowered his head and told her everything.

"Grassland Pipers and bees this time," she cackled, staring at her sister.

"He has a gift," said Hagar.

"He must," added Egmon. "The animals do his bidding."

"How," shouted Greta.

Mani wanted to speak but refrained. He knew his life was in grave danger.

"I told Mani that you'd pay him a handsome price for bringing him back," said Egmon.

"You did," she oozed; wide-eyed.

"Yes," replied Egmon, still staring at the ground.

Oh, the disgusting thing he was. How could she not love the little man frowning with sadness? Her soft heart then instantly turned stone-cold. "I'll pay them alright. I've got 11 hounds that haven't been fed tonight. Well, not all of them. Some got to eat."

"We don't want your gold," whimpered Mani.

"Gold! You were expecting gold; you little worm?"

"That's what Egmon said."

Greta glared at Mani sitting there. She could have killed him outright for passing it off on Egmon. "Guards," she shouted.

They stepped forward.

"March these men back to Black Water."

That was an eight mile hike, Mani thought, but he wasn't going to tell her that.

She caught his eye. "You now work for Egmon as his trusted servants."

"For how long?" asked Drew.

"Why, my dear man, for the rest of your lives. Now, get up!"

Fons, and Drew got to their feet.

"Their horses?" questioned Hagar.

"Bring them too. I want you sweet sister to place hounds in front and hounds in the rear just in case one thinks he can escape."

"What about our wives?" asked Fons.

Greta strolled over to him. "Your wives, why," she harped, thinking. "I guess they'll have to marry other men; for you'll be forbidden to ever leave Black Water again."

Fons began to cry.

"Tears of a fool," she hissed, heading for the back doors. "Come, Egmon, tell me what you're going to do now that you have loyal servants of your own."

Egmon thought of that. After what Mani had done, he'd make sure Mani knew his place from now on. "First off, they'll make my bath, set out my clothing and…" he went on and on as he and Greta walked out the doors.

16

When Greta, Hagar, and Egmon escorted Mani and his friends back, Shana, the peasant girl in Ted's dreams, stepped out from the stable. She wasn't surprised seeing the three men shackled like dogs. *Such fools,* she thought, *treating Egmon that way.*

"Take them to the dungeon. Give 'em thirty days to think about their new lives as Egmon's loyal servants," ordered Greta.

Shana quickly reentered the stable, stowed away the buckets and shovels while listening to Greta continuing her rant. The screeching sound of her voice made her cringe. *With all this going on, it's now or never,* she thought.

She quietly exited the back door and headed up a flight of steps. After hurrying to her bedroom, she shut the door and sighed.

For days now she had thought of leaving Black Water for good. If she were caught, she knew she'd be alongside Mani, Fons and Drew in that filthy dungeon.

She sat on the bed; panic-stricken. *If I am caught, will they boil me alive, feed me to the water beasts or,* her thoughts twisted, *would they turn me into stone like Pristina.*

Not many knew where poor Pristina, a chambermaid had gone. Shana knew. Pristina was caught red-handed sneaking around in the catacomb below the castle.

Shana got up and walked over to her window. She stared out into the dead of night drifting on the vision of the young girl frozen in place just inside the entrance of the tomb of Greta and Hagar's ancestors.

On the nights Shana had slipped through the hidden passageways, searching the castle herself, she discovered the catacomb. To her luck, she came to a steep stairwell leading down.

She almost lost her breath seeing the rats scurrying up from the darkness below. As she descended, she was surprised seeing light from torches at the bottom. When she took the last remaining steps and made it to the cold damp floor, she halted. There before her, was the gate entrance, Pristina locked inside. She looked as if she were fleeing from something; her head slightly turned, eyes filled with fear.

With her mind still adrift, Shana turned from the window and sat once again. She thought of the times she was foolish enough to hide in Greta and Hagar's chamber closet. There was a trap door in the floor. It led to another secret passageway allowing them to escape if trouble was near. On one of those nights while listening – she was shocked hearing a male voice. It sounded like a wretched snake hissing. Whoever it was, they called him *Zesbrew*.

That was the last thought she had as she got up and quickly packed her belongings. Slowly opening her door; she peered out into the corridor. The coast was clear. She quietly walked down to a flight of steps. At the bottom, she hesitated; listening for any guards; nothing but silence. She crept through the corridor to a room which had a hidden wall. Behind it was another flight of stairs leading down. When she hit the bottom, there was nothing there; just a carved out section of rocks that looked as if the builders were going to expand the castle but never finished.

She remembered discovering the place long ago and would come down to just escape the evil above. While there, she watched rats coming in through the rocky enclave. She wondered if they were coming in from the outside world.

Two weeks of digging in the dead of night, she exposed an opening to a tunnel. The smell was awful; it sat like tar up your nose. Dropping to the floor she covered her face trying to see in the dark. To her surprise, she saw what appeared to be light streaming in through brickwork at the end.

When she went down to investigate, she could smell the fresh air. The light was actually the moon bathing the outside world just behind the wall. It took her one month to finally dig out the bricks and crawl out. To her surprise, she was standing at the side of the castle, near the back, adjacent to the Isle of Drake. She could hear the water rolling along the breakers.

Not realizing then, at the end of the tunnel in the opposite direction was the dungeon. When she finally stumbled upon it; searching the length of the tunnel, she again saw light streaming through brickwork. With her knife she slowly opened the mud between several bricks and peered inside. She was shocked to know this secret – another way into the dungeon.

Tonight, when she dropped to the cold damp floor, she never looked in that direction. She hurried to the bricks leading to the outside world – her escape. After she crawled through, she replaced the bricks and stood tight against the wall shaking; gulping fresh air like a fish out of water.

To her left the Drake; to her right the front of the castle. Straight out; the forest, with a thirty yard clearing she had to run without being seen.

She stepped away from the wall and looked toward the front. All she could see was the light from torches bathing the ground; not a guard in sight.

She took in a deep breath and dashed across the clearing to the forest edge. Hiding behind a tree, she stood there a second listening to the water rolling along the breakers. Knowing what was lurking out there made her shiver. She remembered seeing the mammoth water beast swimming along the shoreline the other day. They were terrifying creatures with razor sharp teeth.

Without another thought she headed deeper into the woods; keeping out of sight of the guards on the wall. Two hundred yards in, she headed north; to her village of Orbed where she could steal a horse.

As she walked, it became cold and very dark; hard to see a thing. If that wasn't enough to keep her senses on high-alert, the terrain was unbearable to navigate. An hour into her journey, she heard something coming; more than one. It was the awful smell that caused her to panic; *hyenas.*

One ran past her, then another one. She quickly picked up a large broken limb; turning this way and that. *Run,* her thoughts screamed. From tree to tree she ran, keeping her back against the trunks. Their awful taunts and snarling turned her stomach into knots. As she went to run to the next tree, her foot got caught on a protruding tree root.

She tripped and instantly felt herself free falling down a ravine; sliding and twisting over rocks and debris. Near the bottom, her body was tossed into the air. She landed hard, hitting her head on a dead tree trunk; sending her into complete darkness.

The hyenas stood there glaring at her, but none dared to slide down after her; it was a fifty foot embankment. Silver Eye took off, the rest followed. She raced along the edge of the sloping terrain where they could enter the ravine.

Before Silver Eye could, a hand reached down and felt Shana's pulse. The girl was alive. The person grabbed her and dragged her through the ravine and out the other side.

When Shana came to, her vision was a blur. She could see sunlight; but strangely it wasn't coming from the forest canopy. It was coming through a small circular window. *Where am I?* she thought, reaching up to feel the lump on her head. To her shock, she felt a cloth bandage.

Opening her eyes, she realized that she was not in the forest. She was in a hut. Netting with vegetables hung from wood rafters. She could hear chickens outside.

"You're awake," said an ol' woman.

Shana looked over seeing her sitting there in a rocking chair. She was a small slender thing with white long hair and wrinkly face. "What happened? Where am I?"

"You are in the forest with me now. Last night the hyenas came and almost took you."

Shana thought back. Her memory too was a blur. "Who are you?"

"My name is Tess," she replied, getting up and checking the girl's wound. "You're very lucky."

"I' am at that. My name is Shana," she replied, watching the woman lifting the cloth and checking her wound.

"You have a nice cut, but it will mend well. Why were you in the forest in the dead of night?"

"I," she said, "I'm escaping from Black Water."

"Black Water! What were you doing there?"

"I was a chambermaid for the Twins; not of my choosing, though."

"I see," said Tess, sitting down.

"No one has a choice in the matter. You do as you're told or your fate is sealed."

"I know. I met those evil witches long ago."

"You did?"

"Yes, it was after my parents had died of the plague. I too, took ill myself. Lost sight in one eye and became feeble minded."

Shana gazed at her one greyish eye. It looked like glass. "You don't sound feeble minded."

"I was for a time; then I just kept up the act so people would leave me alone."

"I see," replied Shana, slowly sitting up and looking about. It was a very small hut with a bed, table and chair. There were things hanging from everywhere. She glanced out the open door. There were small cages with chickens inside. Out past them she could see the forest.

"Tell me," said Tess. "How long have you worked for the Twins?"

"Longer than I wanted to."

"Have you ever heard the name *Zesbrew*?"

"Yes!" she replied stunned; staring at the woman relaxing in her chair. "How would you know this man called *Zesbrew*?"

Tess slightly smiled; *she thinks he's a man.* "First, tell me what you know of him."

"Alright, while I was there, I'd slip out at night and search the castle. I got to know it well. One night while listening to Greta and Hagar inside their chamber closet, I heard a man's voice. It sounded awful. Like a snake hissing. Then I heard them call him *Zesbrew*."

"I'll be," gasped Tess. "That thing is alive."

"What thing?"

Sit back and listen."

Shana nodded.

"After I lost my parents and was acting feeble minded, I was sitting on the rocks off Dragon's Bay looking at a ship that had washed ashore. It was probably fifty yards out; its hull stuck in the thick sandbar.

"While sitting there, I saw the Twins' father, Esaul; he was a nobleman at that time, and his friends heading to the beach to go out to the ship. When they walked by me, I started mumbling to myself. Knowing my condition, they paid no mind."

"You're talking about the ship called the Bestow."

"That's right, and I also saw what they brought back too."

"Really?"

"Yes, it was a treasure chest and a four- foot high wooden carving of the most hideous thing I have ever seen."

Hideous thing! "Go on," she pushed.

"It looked like a crotchety old man with a long-stretched face and long nose with flaring nostrils. He had sunken eyes, bushy eyebrows over them. His arms were small, but his hands and fingers were long. His body," she said, shaking her head. "He had a small pot belly, thin legs, knobby knees, and long feet and toes. The wooden man, if you could call him that, could not have been too heavy; Esaul was carrying him behind his friends who were carrying the chest."

"Was this wooden carving, *Zesbrew*?" "Shh... just listen."

Shana sighed.

"After they brought that thing and treasure back to Black Water, everything changed. The four men that went aboard with Esaul soon disappeared along with their wives. Esaul then convinced the soldiers to kill the king, the queen and all of his council. Afterward, he became king, an evil one at that.

"I never knew that."

"What year were you born?" "In the year of Pisces."

"That was twenty years ago. This all happened in the year of Virgo."

Shana nodded. "That was a very long time ago."

"It was."

"So what made Esaul kill the king and queen and take over? I mean, he was at that time a very wealthy man with that treasure."

"It wasn't the treasure that made him kill the king, it was *Zesbrew*."

"I'm losing my mind with all this," said Shana, trying to connect the dots.

"Don't lose it just yet. I have more to tell you."

Shana waved for her to continue.

"It wasn't long after when Esaul was king that he and his wife had two daughters; twins." "Greta and Hagar," murmured Shana.

Tess nodded. "They grew up spoiled, and in time, had an encounter with *Zesbrew* themselves."

"I'm seeing a picture," said Shana.

"It gets worse. After that encounter, they killed their parents and took over as the Witches of Black Water. They capture all the land and villages up to the rock bridge. That is as far as they went.

"As a young king, King William set it in stone that they'd go no further. They held that until, King William's friend, Fredrick Lennard enticed the southern villages to go in with him and set up a new kingdom."

"I'll be," whispered Shana, drifting in space.

"And as you know now, what set the flames for war between the Northern Kingdom and Black Water were Greta and Hagar abducting Juliette."

"You believe a war is coming?" "Yes."

"Is that why this Lord Barrington has come?"

"This Lord Barrington will be the one who starts it."

Shana sat there a moment. She knew now that she must get to the Northern Kingdom and inform King William. She stated that to Tess.

"Before you go, you need to hear all that I have to say."

"I think you've said enough."

"No, there is more you need to know before you go."

Shana sat back. "*Zesbrew* is a Relic." "What is that?"

"A relic is like a spirit, something that has been and always will be."

"Oh... my..." gasped Shana.

"I know this, because… one day while I was out, the Twins came to me. I played stupid. Hagar feeling sorry for me asked Greta if *Zesbrew* could help me. "Nay, sweet sister," she said, "we must keep the relic hidden."

"I'll be a fried goose," said Shana. "We must keep the relic hidden," she repeated Greta's words. "I know where they keep Zesbrew hidden."

"Where?"

"He resides in the catacomb underneath the castle," she replied, getting up. "I must be going."

"Not just yet." "No."

"There is more."

Shana plopped her fanny down. "I may be as old as you before I hear the rest of your story," she sighed.

Tess smiled. "Now, my dear, if you do not hear the rest, you won't have the complete picture as you confess to have."

"Alright, I'm listening."

"I once overheard some sailors talking about a place called Shem which lies along the shoreline within the Sea of Benn Aron, the 4th sea of the twelve.

"The ruler was Ruskin. He was a very wealthy king; his treasure worth a thousand kingdoms they said."

"Was that the treasure the crew of the Bestow took?"

"Yes; the sailors in port stated that the crew also took a wooden carving that was inside King Ruskin's secret chamber. I can't imagine the horror Esaul and his friends discovered when they went onboard that ship that night. The entire crew was dead."

Shana sat back in a minefield of thought. "This may sound strange, but do you think *Zesbrew* was placed inside King Ruskin's secret chamber to guard the treasure?"

"It's possible or," she said then paused, "it's also possible that *Zesbrew* could be the keeper of the treasure, wherever *it* goes -*he* goes. Can you remember what *Zesbrew* and the Twins were talking about that night?"

Shana stared out the window thinking. She turned and looked at Tess. "Even though his voice was harsh, like a snake hissing, he spoke as if he were courting them."

"Courting them?"

"He spoke with a flattering tongue, that's what I mean. I remember him saying, *my gorgeous creatures, so warm and tender. Your beauty is beyond the stars;* their beauty beyond the stars," she repeated. "Can you imagine that? They are the ugliest things I have ever seen."

Tess sat back. While in thought she gazed at Shana. "You just unleashed the secret of *Zesbrew*."

"I did?"

"Yes. It's his flattering tongue that places people under his spell. If you ever encounter him, do not look into his eyes or listen to his words."

"I most certainly won't."

"Now, before you go," said Tess, getting up from her rocking chair. She grabbed a cup and walked over to her. "When you get to the Northern Kingdom you tell King William that for them to defeat the Twins they must kill *Zesbrew*."

"How… how do you kill a spirit?"

"They must find a way. Drink this," she replied, handing her the cup.

Shana looked inside. "Is it water?" "Drink!"

Shana drank some.

"All of it."

Shana emptied the cup and handed it back to her. The lights instantly went out inside her head. When she awoke, she was lying in the forest. The hut was gone; so were Tess and her chickens.

What just happened? she thought; dazed and confused. She touched her forehead. The bandage was gone.

Was I dreaming? Did I really speak with Tess?

She sat up and instantly froze seeing that she was lying on the ground just on the outskirts of her village. "What in the dickens," she fussed, looking about. *I'll wait until tonight to steal a horse and then go immediately to see King William. There is so much he needs to know.*

17

While Shana was looking for a place to lay low until evening, Ben Gillum, Lord Nelson's cousin was riding hard toward the Northern Kingdom. He wanted to tell Nelson that the Twins already knew of Lord Barrington's true identity. The Twins paid Ben a handsome reward for conveying the news they had obtained. This payment was to appease the pair in their continued efforts; Lord Nelson was in fact one of their most trusted spies who sat on King William's council. That was more valuable than gold and silver.

"Captain, Torres," shouted a guard.

Torres walked over. He saw Ben coming out of the forest. "Get word to the king fast!"

The guard ran down the steps to the courtyard and mounted a horse.

When Ben rode up to the drawbridge, Torres needed to buy some time. "You're back," he shouted down.

Ben halted on the bridge. "Yes, Captain. It's hard finding excuses to get out of the house."

"I'm sure it is," *you lousy traitor.* "How is your lovely wife?" he asked with a warm smile.

"She's fine. Have you seen Lord Nelson?" "Yes, he was talking to the king when I was up there."

"Thank you," replied Ben, trotting past the entrance guards.

They looked at one another with devilish grins.

Ben rode through the hustle and bustle of the city, and dismounted at the castle steps. A stable hand rushed out and gathered his horse.

"What a beautiful day," he said, glancing up at the clear blue sky.

Captain Cornel walked out pleased to see Ben. He knew the king would be pleased as well. "What brings you here today?"

"I need to speak with Lord Nelson."

Cornel placed his arm around Ben and escorted him inside. "Lord Nelson said you went home?"

"Yes, having a farm you can't be away too long."

"I'm sure you can't. I think Lord Nelson was with the king in the courtroom."

"The courtroom?" he questioned, wondering why the king would be there. The courtroom was never used unless a trial was taking place.

"For some reason he wanted to be alone today," he lied.

"I see," replied Ben, eyeing the Captain, "hiding from his wife I suppose," he whispered.

"I won't get into that with you, Ben."

"I understand; I have fights with my wife too."

"I wouldn't know. I haven't a wife," he replied, waving at Ben to open the courtroom door.

Ben nodded and entered.

When the door shut, Cornel called several of his men over. "Guard the door. Do not let him out."

"Yes, Captain."

Ben was surprised seeing only the king lazily sitting back with one leg over the armrest of his chair.

"Ben," he said, excited seeing him.

"Your Majesty," he replied, bowing. "I was told Lord Nelson was here with you."

"He was… then he left in a hurry; said he had a lot of things to do."

"I see."

"He looked like a chicken with its wings on fire, actually."

With that said, he wanted to excuse himself to find Nelson and tell him what had happened at Black Water, and to split the payment for their undying service to the Twins. However; you never excuse yourself from the king. He excuses you.

"So where have you been keeping yourself?"

"I was home with the wife. Tending a farm is a lot of work."

"I'm sure it is. How is your wife?" "She's fine, your Grace."

William slowly removed his leg and sat up. "I've been sitting here thinking, Ben."

"Yes, your Grace."

"Since we're in the courtroom, tell me, what would be the charge for lying to the king?"

That question caught Ben by surprise. "Being a farmer, I'm not familiar with the laws your, Grace. However; I do believe it would be a very serious offense."

"Well, I have someone here that could help us."

Judge Regus walked out from behind a curtain.

Ben went tense. *I don't like this.*

The door to the jury room opened. In walked a jury of men.

"What is this?" asked Ben, feeling suddenly ill.

"I asked you where you have been." "Yes, and I told you, your, Majesty." "You lied to me Ben. Why?"

"Your Majesty, why would I lie."

"You again just lied," he replied, training his attention on Regus. "What is the charge for lying to the king?"

"Death, your Majesty."

Ben fell to his knees. "Please, why are you doing this to me. I'm your faithful servant; trustworthy in all affairs."

"That's another lie, Ben. How many times can I kill you?"

Ben looked at the judge and then glanced at the jury. Not one smile.

"Oh please, let the poor man off the hook and tell him," said William.

Judge Regus stood erect, placing his hands on the podium. "We discovered that Lord Nelson was a spy for the Twins. He gave a full confession to the king's physician then was put to death by fire."

The king's words flashed before him kneeling there; *Nelson looked like a chicken with its wings on fire.* The color in Ben's face washed out.

"I'll ask you one more time. Where did you go," ordered William.

"I went to Black Water."

"Well, I'm glad you said that, because," he said then slightly paused, "my physician enjoyed his time with Lord Nelson. There wasn't much left of him to torch. The one thing he did mention during his interrogation was - he sent you to Black Water to inform the Twins of Lord Barrington's arrival."

Ben's heart sank. He knew his life would soon be over. How he was going to die was now his biggest worry. "Yes, your Grace."

"Lord Nelson also confessed that it was *you* he sent to inform the Twins of Juliette's comings and goings," said William in a sharp unmoving tone.

Ben felt ashamed to say it. He looked at the floor. "Yes I did," he replied, placing his hands together as if praying. "Please, your Grace - have mercy on me."

The doors to the courtroom suddenly opened.

William sat up.

Ben heard footsteps. They sounded light.

It's a woman; he thought. *It's the queen!*

The jury stood and bowed.

Victoria proceeded up to the front, turned and looked down at Ben on his knees. "Stand!" she shouted between her clenched teeth.

Judge Regus glanced at William.

He slowly shook his head. This was her affair, and no one, not even *he* was going to stop her from getting her revenge.

Ben gathered himself before her; keeping his head down.

"You disgust me," she spat, walking around him. "How could you do this to my beloved daughter, Juliette?"

Ben said nothing.

Captain Cornel stepped in with two guards.

William nodded for him to stand at the ready.

"You have nothing to say?"

"M'lady," replied Ben, looking up at her.

She slapped his face; the pain was instant. "Judge Regus has the jury found him guilty?" she continued, glaring at Ben.

"Yes, M'lady," he replied; knowing they did not need a jury to find him guilty; he confessed.

"What sentence has been given to this traitor?"

"I was just about to sentence him to death, M'lady."

"I see," she replied, eyeing the wretched man before her. "You can forget your sentence, Judge Regus. I'll be the one who will sentence him today," she grunted.

"Yes, M'lady," replied Regus glancing at the king.

William slowly nodded.

"So," said the queen. "You ran and told those evil witches of my daughter's whereabouts."

Ben nodded.

"Well…" she spat. "Since you like running," she continued, turning toward the judge. "Here is his sentence. I want him stripped naked, tied off to the back of a horse and have him run through every village with a sign around his neck stating – I killed Juliette."

"I did not kill her," moaned Ben.

"Oh…. yes you did," she shouted, facing him. "I want that horse at a gallop," she continued, staring at Ben. With that, she proceeded to the doors. Before departing, she spun around. "What is left of him, place on a ship and toss it into the sea. I'll not have that wretched traitor buried in Ur."

Regus slowly nodded.

Queen Victoria then hurried out; her sobbing wails echoing throughout the corridor, reverberating back to the men's ear staring angrily at Ben.

William got up and walked down to him; fire dancing within his eyes. "You can thank the heavens you're getting off easy. I would have preferred my physician to slowly strip you of your skin." he said, facing Judge Regus. "I want Captain Torres to carry out his sentence immediately," he continued, walking out to find his grieving wife.

"My Lord," moaned Ben.

William stopped.

"What about my wife?"

Without looking back he spoke. "Your wife; why… you should have been home taking care of her instead of committing treason. I sold her to the Kurtz. She is now bound on a ship to serve their king," he lied.

Ben fell to the floor sobbing.

"He's all yours, Captain Cornel," said William, departing the room.

Guards came in, hauling him to his feet. They dragged him out the front doors of the castle.

Torres rode up.

The stable hand brought him the rope.

Cornel had him stripped then he placed the sign around Ben's neck. "Go easy through the streets; let the people see him before you exit the kingdom."

"Yes Captain," said Torres, mounting his horse.

"Once you cross the bridge – the Queen has ordered your horse to be at a gallop through all the villages."

"It will be my pleasure," he replied, slapping the reins.

Ben felt the rope go tight around his wrists. He stepped out to meet his fate; a fate he knew would be worse than being burnt alive. The image of his face peeling away along with his skin while being dragged through every village was enough to make him pray to the Gods that he'd simply pass out so he did not feel a thing.

18

After Ben was taken out of the kingdom, Captain Cornel and his men rode out to Ben's farm. When Donna heard the sound of horses, she walked outside seeing soldiers dismounting near the fence.

"Donna Gillum," said Cornel. "Yes, that is I."

"You are now under the king's charge."

She placed her hands to her face; shocked.

"Where is your husband?" he asked, already knowing.

"He's with Lord Nelson, his cousin. Why? What's this all about?"

"Lord Nelson and your husband are spies. Nelson confessed and was put to death. Your husband is now being dragged through the villages."

She instantly crumbled to the floor. "My husband is a spy… this can't be true," she sobbed.

Two soldiers opened her gate and approached the steps. "Go in and pack some clothing, you're coming with us."

Donna quickly got up; tears running down her cheeks. When she returned, she saw they had one of her horses out front.

That same afternoon, three visitors flew into Lord Barrington's room.

"Lord Barrington," said Bree, hovering in front of him.

"Hello my little friends, what's the pleasure of your company today?" he questioned; surprised seeing the hummingbirds again.

"It's Donna," said Mylee. "She has been place under the king's charge.

Ted tilted his head confused.

"She's been arrested," said Nera. "For what?"

"Her husband Ben is Lord Nelson's cousin. Nelson confessed that it was Ben he sent to Black Water to tell the Twins of Juliette's comings and goings."

"Well now," he replied. "How do you know all this?"

They looked at Jasper. Ted glanced down.

"They are spies like me."

Ted slowly gazed at the birds fluttering in front of him.

"We could not tell you that Grandfather had sent us with Donna there," said Bree.

"Alright, where is she now?"

"They're escorting her into the main entrance as we speak," replied Nera.

"You three stay here with Jasper," he said, quickly exiting the room.

As Ted hurried down a flight of stairs, a guard was standing there. "Where is the king?" "After tending to the queen, he went back to the courtroom." "Where is that?"

"Down the corridor to your left, my Lord."

As he walked up to the door, the guards bowed and opened them. He walked in and stood there.

The king was on a throne, a judge was standing to the side of him behind a podium wearing a purple gown; along with a jury of men sitting there. Donna was kneeling before the king.

King William looked back. "Lord Barrington," he said, waving for him to come forward.

"Tell them I know you," pleaded Donna.

Ted looked down at her.

"Do you know her?" asked Judge Regus. "Yes, I met her on my way here."

"Have you met her husband?"

"No, he wasn't there when she allowed my horses to drink from her well. What is this all about," he asked, already knowing.

"As you're aware, Lord Barrington," said Regus. "Lord Nelson is no longer with us."

Ted nodded; he did not want to see Nelson burned at the stake. He remained in his room that day.

"His cousin, her husband," he continued, pointing down at Donna, "was sent by Lord Nelson to the Twins with information on the Countess's whereabouts. With that, they were waiting for her in the forest. Juliette was on her way back from the Southern Kingdom when they abducted her."

"I know nothing of this," cried Donna. "I believe her," said Ted.

"You believe her," repeated William.

"Yes, look at her. Does she look like a spy?"

"I'm not a spy, and if my husband is, I want nothing to do with him. My loyalty is to you King William; it always has been," she sobbed.

Ted gazed at William.

Unbeknownst to them all, out front of the castle a woman on horseback trotted out of the forest.

"Rider approaching carrying a white flag, Captain."

Torres walked over. "Sound the bell." "Yes, Captain."

Five soldiers rode out to meet the young girl.

As they circled her, she told them who she was and that she needed to speak with the king.

"Why do you want to speak with him?" asked a soldier.

"I worked for the Twins, not of my choosing. I was the one who comforted Juliette while she was inside the dungeon. If the Twins had known, they'd have boiled me alive," she added, hoping that would lend to them escorting her in front of the king.

One soldier stepped forward. "You could be lying."

Shana laughed. "I am just a peasant girl. I have no weapons. There is a lot going on at Black Water. I'm sure King William would like to know. So please, take me to him."

"Know what?"

"Ben Gillum is at Black Water. He was secretly dispatched by Lord Nelson to inform the Twins of Lord Barrington's arrival here."

The soldiers glanced at one another.

One turned and faced her. "Lord Nelson confessed. He was burned at the stake. His cousin, Ben has been here. He is being dragged through the villages at the queen's request. His wife is now kneeling before the king."

"Well then," she huffed, "then you know I'm not lying. I also have troubling news for William also."

"Follow us," said a soldier. "We'll let you speak with Captain Cornel of his Majesties' Royal Guard. He is the only one who can grant you an audience with the king."

"So be it."

Ten minutes later, Cornel quietly opened the courtroom doors and stood there. William could tell he had something important to say. He waved him up.

Cornel came forward. As he did, the court members spoke amongst themselves.

"Bring her in," said William.

The doors open. All heads turned to see who it was.

In walked Shana being escorted by Royal Guards.

Ted almost lost his breath seeing her himself. It was the peasant girl within his dreams; the one waving for him to come help.

"Forgive me, Judge Regus," said William. "I think this woman will confirm to us what we want to know."

"By all means, your Grace."

"Step forward," ordered William.

As Shana walked up, murmuring whispers went out from the jury. She looked at the lady kneeling before the king then glanced over at Lord Barrington.

"My Lord," she greeted, curtsying.

"What brings you here from Black Water?" asked William.

Donna looked up at the filthy girl standing there.

"I was going to bring you the news that Ben Gillum and Lord Nelson are spies. I heard word that Nelson was already put to death and Ben is being dragged through the villages," she replied, looking at Ted. "The Twins now know your real identity, Lord Barrington."

Before he could react, Donna placed her hands to her face and sobbed.

Shana glanced down at her.

"This is Ben's wife," said Judge Regus. "I'm sorry," whispered Shana.

"Lord Barrington," said William. "Yes, my Lord."

"Do you know this woman?"

"I saw her in a vision. She is a peasant girl who was ordered by the Twins to work at Black Water as their servant."

Shana gazed upon the man speaking. She watched his lips moving but, could not understand such words; seeing her in a vision.

"Why have you left?" Regus asked her.

"First off, if I may. I was there when they brought your daughter, Juliette to Black Water. I comforted her and tried to help her to escape. One morning, Greta and Hagar went down to the dungeon and gave her some food and something to drink. Afterward, I was forbidden to ever go down there again. I'm sorry, my Lord. I wish I could have done more."

William nodded.

Shana turned and looked at Ted still amazed at his astonishing ability.

"Anything else?"

"Yes, but," she said, looking about the room, "what I have to say, my Lord, I think should be said in private. There is much you need to know."

Regus turned and faced the king.

"Captain Cornel," said William. "Yes, your Majesty."

"I want you to personally escort Donna back to her farm. I want to know all that she needs."

"Oh… your Majesty," gushed Donna, standing up. "I will always be your most loyal and trusted servant."

William nodded. "Make a list and give it to my finance minister. I'll not have a most loyal and trusted servant," he said with a smile, "without provisions to see her through the year."

"What about me, your Majesty?" asked Shana.

"We'll find you a place to stay. Right now, I want all my ministers in the council room, including Commander Phelps," he said, getting up. "Follow me, Lord Barrington, Shana," he continued, walking out.

Captain Cornel and Donna rode back to her farm. There, he took a list of everything she needed. During that time, he found her quite attractive, warm hearted too. "I'll return in a few days to see that your provisions have arrived. If there is anything else I can do, please ask. You have the king's ear."

"Thank you, Captain. You are most welcome any time," she said with a warm tender smile.

Cornel nodded, got on his horse and looked down at her. "I'm sorry about your husband."

She sighed hearing that. "He was hardly here. I've always suspected when he told me that he had business with his cousin, Lord Nelson, and would be gone for days, he was in the city fooling around with the harlots at the pub. Now I know he was actually a spy for those evil witches. Today I'm in mourning – tomorrow I'll be done with him."

Cornel raised a brow. *What a foolish man.* "See you in a few days," he said, riding off.

19

The council filed into the room; some not happy having this peasant girl standing before them, especially in her filthy condition.

"Please," said William, waving his hand toward the two empty chairs for Ted and Shana to sit.

The king's advisors looked at Shana; she gazed back at them feeling their stares.

"Let me start by asking," said William.

"I'm sorry, your Majesty for my appearance," she interrupted, gazing down at herself. "I am dirty, tired and needing a bath."

"I'd say," smugly remarked Lord Hartman.

His comment struck her. She knew they were all thinking the same thing; she wasn't however, going to be dismissed due to do her appearance. She had information they needed to hear. "Your Majesty."

Seeing her distain, he waved his hand for her to continue.

"After Egmon and Mani's men were brought back, the same men that tried to capture Lord Barrington, I knew it was time to leave. I spent the night in the forest. Was entertained by hyenas, and while running for my life. I tripped and fell down a ravine.

"The last thing I remember was being tossed into the air and then," she said, pausing for a moment, "I woke up inside a hut. If that ol' woman hadn't rescued me, I'm afraid I'd not be here right now. The hyenas would have taken care of that."

William casually glanced at his men sitting there. They seemed to have lost their tongues hearing her demise.

"I see," said William. "Tell me, how long have you worked for the Twins?"

"Several years; I hated every minute of it."

"Why do you come to us now," asked Commander Phelps.

She took in the broad shouldered man wearing an impressive uniform with a lion symbol on his breast plate. "I've always wanted to escape, but feared for my life. I saw my chance two nights ago when the castle was in an uproar. You see," she said, taking a breath, "Mani and his men where not happy being stung by those bees and brutalized by those Grassland Pipers. They were torturing Egmon and the Twins' guards inside a barn on the outskirts of Bissell.

"Ben then showed up with news of Lord Barrington's arrival. He then informed the Twins of Mani taking Egmon. That set the two on fire. Mani and his men are now in the dungeon and will become Egmon's loyal servants."

Laughter erupted. William raised his hand.

"Your Majesty," said Shana. "Go on."

"I could start at the beginning, but first, I'd like to ask if anyone here has ever heard of the ship – the Bestow?"

"I've heard of it," replied Lord Hartman.

All eyes fell upon him.

"So have I," added Commander Phelps. "After they stole King Ruskin's treasure – I suppose greed took over which caused a mutiny onboard; no one survived."

"Do you know where that treasure went?"

They all looked at one another; none had an answer.

"Maybe it was by luck that the hyenas came. If they had not, I would not have met Tess, the ol' woman in the hut. She told me the story of the Bestow and the men that went out and took the treasure from that ship."

"Don't keep the king waiting," said Lord Reese, William's Foreign Ministry Advisor.

"It was the Twins' father, Esaul and his friends. Along with the treasure chest, they brought back a four-foot high wooden carving. Tess said that a spirit resided in it – she called it a relic."

"Relic," questioned Hartman.

"Yes, that's not all. I heard that wretched thing talking."

"What?" spat Phelps.

Shana then went on to tell them everything from the beginning; how Esaul became king, his daughters becoming witches - right up to seeing Pristina frozen in place and then her hiding in the witch's closet; where she overheard Greta calling the wooden carving *Zesbrew.* She then described the horrid thing.

The men sat back flabbergasted.

"I'm beyond words. The whole story is now before us," said William. "I've heard of the kingdom of Shem within the 4th sea, but never really knew the ruler or his ways."

Silence filled the room; every man sat there trying to grasp it themselves.

"A four-foot high wooden carving, named *Zesbrew?*" murmured, Lord Reese; breaking the silence over the room.

All eyes fell on him.

"Tell us about the woman who told you all this," he then asked.

Shana sat there for a moment. Within her mind, she thought she had dreamt the whole thing, *but how could that be? I remember everything Tess had said to me.* With that twirling inside her head, she knew she'd had to keep Tess's vanishing into thin air to herself. She just went on and told 'em Tess's personal story, or what she knew at least.

When she finished, William spoke up. "I would love to sit down with her myself, that's if we knew where she went?" he said, glancing over at Lord Barrington sitting there not saying a word. "What say you about all this?" he asked.

"I'm still pondering her story, your Majesty. He then asked her a question himself. "You said that the only way to kill the Twins, or at least take their power away, would be to kill *Zesbrew?*"

"Yes."

"How do you kill a relic," asked Commander Phelps.

"I don't think you can," she replied.

"Hmm," said Ted. "If we can't kill him, we could at least destroy the wooden carving."

"Continue?" said William.

"Is there any way to trap the rats in the Catacomb?"

"Rats?" she said confused.

Smiles appeared around the table.

Ted caught the expressions. "I'm not a warrior, but I do have a mind that thinks out of the box."

"Thinks out of the box," repeated Phelps with a smile.

"Yes, like flanking your enemy without them knowing it."

Several laughed seeing Lord Barrington was wiser than they thought.

"Pray tell," said Phelps, "what's your flanking maneuver using rats?" he mused.

Before he could answer, Shana spoke up. "Forgive, me," she said. "There is a way of trapping them if we can circumvent the water used for the privies and channel it down to the catacomb below the castle. But why, may I ask, do you want to trap the rats there?"

Ted sat back, folded his arms and replied, "You trap a rat… it will eat anything to survive; even its own kind. I'd also suspect that it would even eat a wooden carving to survive as well."

"Well played, Lord Barrington, well played," said Hartman.

"OK," said Ted. "Is there something she can use to draw what the water beasts look like?"

William nodded for Reese to fetch a quill and parchment.

Shana sat there drawing. When she finished she pushed it over to him.

"That, your Majesty is a crocodile. How big?" he asked her.

"Forty-feet; their heads would just fit on this table."

The men sized that up.

"There is no way to kill 'em," spoke Phelps.

"Yes there is. They have one soft spot right between the eyes."

"Will an arrow do?" asked Willliam.

"Yes, but a crossbow would be even better. Where do they live?"

"They live in an inlet cove on the other side of the Drake. It's inside the remanence of the ancient volcano. There is a large flat rock where Egmon said they sleep."

"Any other way to get in?"

"There is a large opening at the ceiling; it's a forty-foot or more drop to the water below."

"What are you thinking, Lord Barrington," asked Phelps.

"I just want to know the entire layout.

May I see a map?"

William nodded.

Lord Reese again got up.

After placing it on the table, Shana started pointing across the map. "As you can see, the Isle of Drake cuts off the Eastern tip, here. It was created by a volcanic eruption long ago. The Eastern tip or, the portion of what remains is mostly hard lava and rocks. As you know, from the rock bridge, here - to the Isle of Drake is the area the Twins rule. The villagers hate the witches. They do their bidding out of fear."

"That is a plus," said Ted. "They could be convinced to switch sides."

"They could," she replied, "but only if they knew the Twins could be killed."

Ted stood up and walked over to the balcony.

The council waited to see what was on his mind.

He slowly turned casting his eyes over the group. "We could go by way of ship to the Eastern tip. There, we could slip in unaware to the top of the old volcano and use ropes to slide down inside the cove. The crocodiles could be killed while they slept."

"Slide down ropes?" questioned Phelps.

"We call it rappelling. I'll show you. We might even be able to shoot them from the air. The men at the top securing the ropes could hoist the person back up after he is done. Who is your best archer?"

"Captain Torres," said Phelps.

"Then he'll be the one to kill the crocs."

"May I ask," said Reese, "where are you from?" he continued with a curious mind. There was something about Lord Barrington having such knowledge and foresight in warfare without any skills in the art of war. He believed Lord Barrington was holding back his abilities. *Why he did…* sat uneven with him.

"He does not have to answer that," grunted William. "He is my special guest and will be treated as such."

All heads bowed. Each man, however, was thinking the same thing. Too smart to be just a baker's boy; a term they used when describing an uneducated man. Ted was no baker's boy, not even close.

"As I mentioned before, I come from a far off land. I've traveled most of my life. That is all I will say. So if I may," said Ted, standing, "let me dwell on this."

William nodded then called a guard. "Escort Shana to the Queen's chambers and have the queen's maids fix her a bath. They will find you a room to sleep and clean clothing to wear, M'lady."

"Thank you, my Lord," she said, following the guard out.

Ted left as well. He stopped Shana in the corridor. "I think you and I need to talk."

"Yes, Lord Barrington. I was hoping we could."

"Have a maid escort you to my room tonight when you have settled in."

Shana nodded and departed with the guard.

A knock on his door came later than he thought it would. He opened it seeing Shana with a maid.

"I'll find my way back," she said to the girl.

The maid nodded and left.

Ted shut the door. "Would you like something to drink?"

"Yes, wine if you have some."

As Ted filled two glasses and handed her one, he took in her appearance. Shana was a pretty girl, with long brown hair, nice golden eyes and well suited for the gown she was wearing; one he suspected came from the queen.

"I have many questions," she said. "I thought you would."

"How do you get the animals to do your bidding?" she asked, glancing down at Jasper. "I mean… the bees, the Pipers, and him?"

"I really don't know," he sort of lied.

"The Twins know you have power and can call on the animals and insects. I saw Greta when she came back after being stung. If she wasn't ugly enough, she looked horrid from those bee stings."

Ted let that pass and asked a question himself. "How did she change into Clara Brown?"

"That poor girl," she sighed, shaking her head. "Greta sucked the life right out of her."

"How?"

"She clasps her mouth over her victims and inhales their breath."

"That would be an awful way to die."

"I never saw her do it. I thank the Gods I never did. So," she said and then paused, "did you really see me in a vision?"

He knew that question was coming. "I have dreams. In one of them I saw you waving to me as if you wanted me to come help you."

"Is that why you're here?" "Sort of."

"You are Sheppard Barrington's cousin?" "I am; I'm a long distant cousin."

She slowly nodded; taking note of that. "Juliette told me about her affair with your cousin, Sheppard. She would have never been happy with Richard, son of King Fredrick," she replied, taking a sip of her wine. As she did, she glanced about the room, more so the bed. She cast her eyes upon him. *Sheppard was a very handsome man; Ted is even more attractive.* "Are you married?"

"I was. She died; leaving me with a son." "I see," she replied, lifting her glass while staring into his eyes.

Ted saw her lustful expression. Before he said something, she got up and started walking about the room.

He took in her gown, or more so, her figure. He felt she wanted him to look. He remembered his wife swaying her hips and cooing like a love sick hen when in a flirtatious mood. Shana was a nice hen herself.

She sat on his bed.

Ted dropped his thoughts and downed his glass. "Do you think we can kill the Twins?" he asked.

"Yes. The weaker one is Hagar. Greta is pure evil. If we can get Hagar first, we might have a chance," she replied, lying back on the bed.

Ted sat there watching her sprawl out. The next thing he heard was Shana's deep breathing. He got up and looked. She was sound asleep.

With a subtle sigh, he knew she'd been through a lot. He lifted her legs, took off her shoes and placed the blanket over her.

In the morning, Shana awoke seeing she had fallen asleep in Ted's room. She sat up. Ted was sleeping in the chair. As she tried quietly to get up, he opened his eyes.

"I'm so sorry," she said.

"Don't be. You were tired."

"I was, and the wine… well, it put me to sleep."

"I figured. After you did, I was thinking. Is there any way you could go back to Black Water?"

"No. Why would you ask?

"You spoke of a way of closing off the water to the privies."

"Yes."

"I know someone who could find a way."

Shana stared at him confused.

"Jasper," said Ted, pointing down at his furry friend.

"Him?" she gasped.

Ted looked down at Jasper. "Do you think you could find a way?"

Jasper nodded.

"Seeing it myself, I…" she gasped, taking in the ferret bobbing his head. She suddenly looked up at him. "But what if Greta and Hagar discovered I've come here to speak to the king?"

Ted gave that a thought. "How long have you been gone?"

"Four days."

"Have you ever been away that long?" "Yes, I take care of my mother."

"Is that what you told 'em your reason for leaving this time?"

"No, I left through the secret tunnel."

"That is not good," he sighed. "Let's just leave it for now."

"As you wish. I must get back to my room before they think…" she replied, walking to the door. "Thank you for the evening," she continued, leaving his room.

20

Fifteen minutes later someone knocked on Ted's door. He was surprised to see the queen standing there with her armed escorts.

"M'lady," he greeted, feeling apprehensive to *why* she was there.

"We haven't had time to talk," she replied, strolling in and shutting the door; leaving her escorts outside.

"Yes, you are right."

"I'd like to see you in my chambers tonight. William and I will be there." "Yes M'lady."

"Cornel will come and escort you." "Yes M'lady."

"Have a pleasant day," she said, walking to the door. She turned and looked at Jasper. "Does he bite?" she asked, walking over to him.

"No, he loves attention."

Victoria bent down and patted his head. "He's gorgeous. I wouldn't mind one myself," she said, walking to the door.

Ted opened it.

"Until tonight," she said, walking out.

Before shutting the door, Ted took in her escorts wearing deep blue armor, and helmets. He slowly closed the door. *That was an introduction,* he thought. *She seems very direct; not even a smile.*

The day slipped by uneasy for Ted. He hadn't a clue to what was on her mind. He waited until after dinner for Cornel to come.

Eight o'clock turned into nine and then ten o'clock rolled by with a knock on his door.

137

It was Cornel. They made their way down the corridor, slipped up a flight of stairs. He then went left then right and finally pushed open a wall; a hidden passage. Ted and he entered the queen's chambers.

Queen Victoria and William came in from an outer balcony. "Lord Barrington," greeted Victoria.

"M'lady, your Majesty."

William nodded taking a seat.

As she proceeded across her elaborate chambers, Ted took in her appearance. She was tall, very slender, with long slim arms and neck. Her brown hair now down draped over her shoulders. Her eyes were green. She had a straight nose, supple lips, and a perfect chin.

Ted glanced back to see Cornel still standing there. His assumption was right; *she* wanted to talk.

"My husband has informed me of this love affair between your cousin, Sheppard and Juliette. Is that true?"

"Yes, it is true."

She stood there seemingly gazing at him. "I wish she had confided in me. Not that I'd have any say in the matter," she said, slightly looking back; conveying to him – William was king.

"Would you have approved of their love for one another?" he asked.

"I've met Sheppard. He was by all accounts a man of integrity and Lord of Corset.

His wealth was no guess. So, yes, I would have approved."

Ted felt at ease with her words.

"Now," she continued, turning and walking away. "I hear you're a very wealthy man yourself; have traveled for most of your life."

"Yes, M'lady," he replied, knowing the king conveyed their conversation to her.

She turned and faced him. "Where are you from?"

"When not traveling, I make my home in Crisco. It's across the twelve seas," he said, shifting his eyes on William. It was apparent in William's expression that it was alright in telling her that; for she would have not understood such a thing as someone coming into the Realm from the future.

"I see," she said then laughed.

Ted smiled at her humorous reply. He found the Queen to be highly educated and very articulate. There was no - this or that – just straight to the point. Her quip *I see* was nice however; showing she had a lighter side.

Victoria then faced her husband and asked the next question. "I was told you saw my daughter in a vision?" She turned to hear his answer.

"Yes, I have seen your daughter," he replied, sidestepping the question.

"There are only a few that know where she is."

Ted nodded.

"Some on the king's council and those in this room."

With Cornel still here they must trust him like a son, thought Ted

"I have gone up and looked at her on several occasions. It's hard for me. I'm sure you can understand."

"I do."

"In truth," she said, coming up to him. "I'd rather have a portrait of her, something I could look at and remember all the good times we had and," she continued with a slight pause, "I could gaze upon her beauty instead of gazing at a doll."

Ted again glanced over at William; the king's smile disappeared with his wife's subtle remark.

"You see, Lord Barrington. To me she is already dead. That is hard for William to surmise but, that is my disposition on the matter."

"I truly understand that, M'lady," he replied, "however… to lighten your thoughts about your beautiful daughter, Juliette; to me she is not dead. I have taken on this quest to rescue her, and let it be known here and now… with every fiber of my being, I will succeed in my endeavor. You see, M'lady, love is a magical thing. From the moment I saw her, I knew deep down inside that she was the one, the one who'd complete me."

"Complete me," she whispered through her soft supple lips. It was an expression she had never heard before. It made a tear well up in her tender gaze. She felt the same way for William, without even knowing how to express it so eloquently as Lord Barrington just did. William did in fact complete her and she knew Lord Barrington would surround Juliette in that same *forever* love.

"If you do kill the Twins and break this spell, Lord Barrington, I too will grant you her hand, and I know…" she said, catching her breath, "you'll be taking her away from me."

Ted found that confusing. *How would she know where I was taking her?*

Before he could answer, she continued, "Since we are on this quest together in killing the Twins, there is someone I want you to meet."

Ted thought she was going to bring out one of their spies, someone who would give him information.

From a side entrance, a hidden door opened. Ted turned seeing the woman he saw in the blue hooded coat casually stroll in.

She said nothing as she walked up behind the queen. When she came around, she changed into the old man of India descent; the one who was sitting in the market square when he and Cornel rode by.

It caught Ted off guard.

The old man walked around him. When he came back in front, he looked like a British Noble; tall, handsome with a bit of grey splashed through his hair; supporting a well- trimmed beard.

"Tell him your name," said Victoria.

"I am Alexus Arteria," he said, removing the blue coat.

"Where are you from?" she ask.

"I'm from the past, present, and the future."

Victoria stepped up next to Ted. "I call him the ancient one – the man of many faces – he can take on the appearance of anyone. He is better known as the Shadow."

Ted looked from her to Alexus.

In an instant, Alexus waved his hand over his face and became King William.

Ted stepped back gazing at him and then looked over at William sitting in the chair.

Alexus then again waved his hand over his face and became Queen Victoria.

Ted had all but lost it seeing *two* Victoria's standing in front of him. "I'm, I'm," spilled forth from his lips.

Alexus waved his hand again and became himself.

Ted slowly shook his head.

"You see now," said Victoria. "why he is so important to us."

"I do."

"He would have never been known by the outside world if we did not have spies within the castle," she said, glancing back at William. "In truth, however," she continued, "Alexus only discovered the two spies, Lord Nelson and his cousin Ben Gillum a short time ago and had you carry the message to us. I see no harm in it now that he allowed you to give us the news upon your arrival; for Lord Nelson and his cousin had already committed their treasonous act."

He stood there listening to her rambling while staring at Alexus.

When she finished, Alexus waved his hand over his face and became Patch.

"In all my days," gasped Ted. He knew now that the man who came to the barn was him and not a spy.

"I see you are having trouble with this, Lord Barrington," said Victoria. "I can imagine why. Alexus is a gift from the Gods."

Ted nodded.

"You asked Shana to go back to Black Water with Jasper?" said Alexus.

"How did you know that?"

"I saw her on the way back from your room this morning."

Ted cringed hearing that. He did not want to look at the queen; especially now that she just gave him permission to marry her daughter. He had to say something quick. "I suppose you know I saw Shana in a vision."

"Yes."

"She came to my room last night, wanting to know how. We spoke for a while, had a glass of wine and then she fell asleep. She looked tired. I'm sure she was after what she had gone through to get here. I covered her up and allowed her to sleep in my bed. I took the couch. Not an easy way to sleep."

From the side, he saw Victoria glance at William. He slightly nodded his head. It made Ted sigh under his breath; *no harm done.*

"That was grateful of you," said Alexus. "When I met up with her, she looked perplexed.

I asked her why. She said you were thinking of sending her back to Black Water with Jasper."

Ted went to speak.

He raised his hand. "Do not be upset with Shana telling me."

"It wasn't set in stone that I wanted her to go," remarked Ted.

"I know but, it gave me an idea to go myself with Jasper. I can get in. I have been there before. This time with Jasper would be easy."

Ted agreed with a nod.

William stood and strolled over. "No more secrets."

"Yes, your Grace, they said in unison.

"Before we strike forth to Black Water and dispatch those evil things once and for all, we have much to prepare."

"Yes," replied Alexus. "If your plan works using the rats and they devour that wooden carving, I'll confront *Zesbrew* myself."

"Can you defeat him?" asked Ted.

"Now that we know the Twins' secret of how they became witches, maybe *Zesbrew* has one himself; something that would release him from this world forever."

Ted glanced at William and Victoria. Their expression was of relief hoping there was a way of getting rid of *Zesbrew.*

"It's late," she said. "Cornel, see Lord Barrington to his room."

"Yes, M'lady."

"We'll speak again soon."

"Goodnight," said Ted, following the captain out.

As they proceeded through the castle back to Ted's living quarters, Cornel set it in stone, Ted's now relationship with the king and queen. "With both of their approval of you marrying Juliette, you will become their son- in-law. That is a permanent seat on the king's council."

Ted thought of that; however, the permanent seat on the king's council – his high position in the kingdom would never take place. He was going home and making Juliette his wife. His council would be Juliette and Gabe.

When he walked into his room, said goodnight to Cornel, and closed the door, he stood there in thought.

Besides William and Victoria's approval of him marrying Juliette, something else weighed heavily on his mind. Was there truly a way of ridding *Zesbrew* from the world? *Maybe by fire, or submerged in salt water, or…* his thoughts wondered.

He thought of his childhood movies. Vampires, cowering to the Cross or having Holy Water splashed upon them; the Werewolf being killed by a silver bullet. The ideas seemed ridiculous to Ted. *Those were only silly movies,* but then again, his thoughts continued… *what if there was a way?*

21

As Victoria called it a night, back at Black Water midnight was; *the witching hour…*

Most nights, Greta and Hagar would be up in the tower scurrying around the caldron; chanting and tossing items into the pot. Tonight however, they wanted to slip down to the catacomb to speak with *Zesbrew.* They knew their failure in trying to capture Lord Barrington was going to upset him. He knew somewhat of their miss steps - but not all.

After descending the dark stairwell, they walked up to the gate looking at poor ol' Pristina; still standing there frozen in place. With the exception of those on the ship of fools, the Bestow; who were enticed by *Zesbrew's* wicked tongue to kill one another, Pristina was the only person that tried to flee his presence. Her terrifying expression said it all; death was coming.

While unlocking the gate, Greta teased her sister. "I see the rats take to you," she whispered, watching the rodents gathering at Hagar's feet.

"They come to me for food unbeknownst they'll end up in jars on my shelf."

Seeing those awful things in jars gives me boils, thought Greta, opening the gate. She grabbed a torch and proceeded down the long corridor where their ancestors slept.

Each tomb had a bust depicting who was buried there. Their parents however, had no busts; just an old shoe they had worn.

As they passed by, neither said a word; nor did they even glance that way. It was due to them killing their parents. After they did, they pulled off a shoe from each; where it now sits on their grave.

At the large structural door, fastened into the wall, they hesitated.

"You do all the talking," whispered Hagar.

"I always do all the talking," spat Greta under her breath.

With the key set in, the large hinges squeaked. Greta held the torch outward; dispersing the darkness within. The air felt damp as they entered.

What stood before them in the flame of the torch was a large chest filled with a treasure worth a thousand kingdoms. Even the chest's lid was sparking with inlaid gold, silver and gems.

"Who so mindful to visit with *Zesbrew?*" he hissed, stepping out from the darkness.

"It is us, my Lord," greeted Greta, bowing.

Hagar bowed as well.

Zesbrew came forward, turning his head this way and that taking in his lovely servants. He reached up and lifted Greta's chin.

She gazed into his deep dark eyes. "We have failed you, my Lord," she moaned.

"Failed? There is no failing," he replied, training his attention on Hagar, who by all right despised the wretched thing.

"As you know, I went myself," continued Greta. "I then sent two of our spies, who were fools. Then I sent Egmon and five guards."

Zesbrew's eyes went soft; his wooden lips turned into a frown.

"What you don't know is Lord Nelson dispatched his cousin Ben here to inform us that Lord Barrington had made it to the Northern Kingdom."

Zesbrew slowly turned with his back to them.

Greta and Hagar eyed one another; worried.

When he faced them, he placed his long wooden finger to his chin. "Is it possible to slip a ship under the cover of darkness into King William's harbor?"

The two looked at one another; thinking.

"Yes, I believe we could," said Hagar. "What captain do you trust?"

"Why… Captain Howler. He's our finest captain. He commands the Wicked; one of our fastest sailing ships," replied Greta.

"Maybe *Zesbrew* go this time."

"You, my Lord?" she questioned. "Yes, me."

"By ship?" asked Hagar.

"No, I go by carriage to the rock bridge.

I'll make my way there on foot."

The Twins were confused.

"Your eyes deceive you. Remember, with power comes wisdom. I will capture this Lord Barrington and place him on the ship."

"And have Captain Howler bring him back?"

"No. Once the cargo is safely onboard, you'll order Howler to sail across the Sea of Presidium to the Kingdom of Grim."

"But, my Lord, I want Lord Barrington kneeling before me," fussed Greta.

Zesbrew walked up and touched her cheek. "I think it is best Lord Barrington works the mines for King Bela."

"My Lord," moaned Greta; disheartened hearing that.

"Are you questioning my wisdom, sweet princess?"

"No," she replied, looking down at the floor.

Her expression melted his heart. "Please, take a trinket from my treasure."

Greta raised her head. "Yes, my Lord."

The two walked over, opened the chest and gazed inside. Their eyes instantly filled with lustful greed.

Hagar took a beautiful jade ring; Greta, a small slipper inlaid with diamonds.

"Go now my sweet servants. Tomorrow night come and get me."

"Thank you, my Lord," they replied, departing the cave-like structure.

Upon reaching the stairwell and heading up, Greta finally spoke. "We'll have Egmon take him."

"Yes, sweet sister," she agreed, admiring the ring on her finger.

After they had left, *Zesbrew* sat there thinking. *Lord Barrington will be treated well working the mines for King Bela. He works his slaves to death.*

The following night, Hagar cast a spell over Black Water. Once those in the castle were asleep, the two descended the dark stairwell. They quickly escorted *Zesbrew* through the hidden passageways to a side exit where Egmon was waiting for them in a covered wagon.

He felt the wagon rocking back and forth. Once the precious cargo was onboard, Greta walked up to him. "As fast as lightening, ride to the rock bridge."

Without a reply, Egmon slapped the reins; the horses took off, galloping into the night.

As he rode through the Dead Forest, Silver eye and her pack of hyenas watched the wagon from a bluff. Her senses told her not to attack. She silently disappeared back into the woods.

Onward he went, through the villages. Some were out. When they saw the wagon with Egmon, they hurried back to their huts scared; believing the Twins were onboard. Little did they know that it was *Zesbrew;* his dark eyes peering out from a slit in the canvas.

Once Egmon crossed the bridge, he halted near the grove of trees. Without calling or getting down he felt the wagon rocking back and forth. He sat there nervously staring out into the dark of night.

"Be here tomorrow night at this time, Egmon."

"Yes, my lord," he replied not glancing back.

He waited until *Zesbrew* slipped away before looking down at his hands. They were trembling holding the reins.

The wicked thing crept silently through the trees until he came to the clearing; the plains of the Northern Kingdom. Spying out the ground to cover before the high wall was much. There was only one way so not to be seen. He lay on the ground, stretched out his hands and transformed into a large wooden snake.

Slithering through the grass, he came upon some rocks stacked in a group near the moat. From his location he could see the guards walking out over the bridge then turn and walk back. He counted each step and the time it took when they turned and headed back to the entrance.

"Oh, Zesbrew hates water, but I must get Lord Barrington to Grim," he hissed, sliding down into the gully and swimming across. At the corner of the wall, he slithered out, went up the bank and headed down the side. When he was sure no one could see him, he transformed back into his wretched wooden self.

Glancing up the forty foot wall, one would think it was impossible. Not for *Zesbrew*. He dug his toes deep into the dirt transforming them into roots. He then lifted his hands. They began to grow; twirling upward around each other to the top of the wall. *Zesbrew's* hands then appeared; taking hold of the ledge. His feet came out of the ground and shrunk back to his hips.

Over he went onto the guard's walkway. At the corner was a lookout tower. He hid inside waiting for the sentry to return to his post. When he did, *Zesbrew* reached out and grabbed the man. His fingers changed into tentacles suffocating him.

Eyes wide with fear, the guard tried to scream.

"*Zesbrew* not hurt you. You are the bravest and wisest man in all the Northern Kingdom. You should be the king. Instead, they made you a sentinel because they hate you."

The guard stopped fighting; *Zesbrew's* soothing words placed him in a trance.

"You go and kill the sentries on the wall, then kill everyone in the castle. Once you have done your courageous deed, *Zesbrew* will make you king. Now go," he said, releasing him.

As like in a trance, the guard walked off to the second station. His sentry friend turned seeing him. "I think I'll sit a spell, if you don't mind?" he said.

"No, go ahead. My feet are killing me too."

When the sentry turned his back to him, he took out his dagger and stabbed him several times. With that, he went on to the third sentry and did the same. This time however, he tossed the poor sap over the wall. The splash was heard.

"My, my," said *Zesbrew*, "it's time to go."

He hurried to the side and hopped off the wall onto the tall statue inside the courtyard. He clung to its neck and lay silently on the statue's back.

The guards on the wall started shouting and ringing the bell.

Captain Torres came out of his office.

"What is going on?"

"Ty Davenport, Captain," a sentinel called down. "He's gone stark, raving mad."

"What?"

"He's killed a few men."

Torres flew up the steps. It was true; Ty was fighting several. Torres quickly drew his sword and waited for Ty to turn. The blade went in deep. Ty fell to his knees. Torres twisted the blade and pulled it out; causing more damage. Ty fell over dead.

Up at the castle, they heard the fortress bell. They in turn sounded their alarm, alerting the entire kingdom.

Soldiers quickly mounted and rode off toward the entrance believing they were under attack.

In the commotion, *Zesbrew* slipped down off the statue, crept out of the corner and made his way around some crates to a side street. He turned and followed it.

A woman came out to see what was happening. When she saw *Zesbrew,* she panicked. He quickly grabbed her mouth; muffling her screams. His fingers grew like daggers; one drove up her nose; two punctured her eyes. She went limp on her feet. After letting her go, he continued onward; his fingers dripping with blood.

Queen Victoria rushed out of her chambers to see Captain Cornel running toward her. "Hurry, we need to get you and your ladies to the vault."

"What is going on?"

"Not sure M'lady. We could be under attack."

"Where is William?"

"He is on his way to the Royal Hall." "Alexus and Lord Barrington?"

"They are on their way there with Shana."

By the time the Queen and her maidens reached the Hall, everyone was there. William had already pushed his throne back, exposing the stairwell leading down to the vault. The women, children and elderly were descending the steps.

"William," shouted Victoria.

He turned seeing her running up.

"Quick, go down." "Are you coming?" "No."

"William," she moaned. "Go."

She kissed him on the cheek and ordered her maidens to follow.

Ted rushed in with Shana.

"Take the steps down," ordered Cornel.

"I'm staying," replied Ted. "You go down Shana."

Just then the Hall doors opened. Ted was stunned seeing twelve men walking in. *Gladiators,* he thought, taking in their size; all bare chested, wearing nothing but tunics, leather sandals; some with bronze armbands, breastplates and brandishing swords.

"To the entrance," shouted William, drawing his sword.

When they reached the castles' doors, Torres pulled up and dismounted. "My Lord," he said, taking the steps up.

"What is going on?" asked William.

"It was Ty Davenport. He…" replied Torres, shaking his head; not believing what he was about to say.

"Speak up!"

"He went stark raving mad and started killing our guards on the wall, your Grace."

William stood back, eyeing his captain.

Alexus walked up behind the king and whispered in his ear.

William slowly tilted his head back to hear.

"I can sense the relic is here, my Lord." "*Zesbrew?*"

"Yes."

William's jaw tightened. "Commander Phelps, I want you and your men to walk this entire kingdom. Search every house, every street, every wagon and crate. Do not stop until you find this creature."

"Yes, your Majesty."

Suddenly, without warning, a distant wailing cry was heard. "Belinda, Belinda."

The next thing the king heard was horses galloping.

The soldiers dismounted and walked up to the man, cradling his wife.

"Why? Why?" he cried.

The soldiers looked down seeing blood coming from her eyes, nose and mouth.

"Get word to the king," one ordered.

"Your Majesty," whispered Alexus.

"Yes," he replied not turning around. "I have a plan."

"Go on."

"We'll use Lord Barrington and Shana as bait. You know *Zesbrew* is here for him."

William said nothing.

"Leave Lord Barrington's room unprotected. We'll wait there for *Zesbrew.*"

"Go."

Alexus walked up to Ted. "Follow me."

On their way they took Shana from the vault.

Zesbrew heard the man screaming. He knew they had found the woman. He looked up at the roofs overhead. Down from him was a wagon. He walked up, climbed onboard and then used it to hoist himself up onto a windowsill; continuing to the roof. Silently, he crept to the chimney looking toward the castle; the roofs leading there.

From one to another he jumped until he was at the last building. *No way into the front; must go around to the side.*

"You honestly think this will work?" questioned Shana.

"Yes. Now do as I say," replied Alexus. "Put cotton in your ears and do not look into his eyes. As you know Shana, he will use flattery to try and entice you into a trance, just like the guard on the wall."

Ted and Shana nodded then went searching for some cotton. None was found. "Come, Shana, let's check the Queen's chambers," said Alexus.

After they left, Ted walked out to the balcony. He knew the evil thing would come up this way.

The door opened, he turned seeing Shana walking in. "Where is Alexus?" "He went back to the king."

"Great. We're on our own," spat Ted, pulling out his sword.

"Put that away," she gasped. "Why?"

"He is of the darkness. If he gets that sword from you it will make him even more powerful."

Ted did not question her reasoning. It was the last thing he wanted. He quickly slipped it under his bed.

From behind them, *Zesbrew's* hand came up over the rail.

Shana's eyes filled with fear, staring at Ted. He heard it too.

"Don't look into his eyes," she mouthed.

From the balcony rail, *Zesbrew* pulled himself up and over; his feet touching the marble floor. Before him was his prey, with their back to him.

When Ted turned and faced him, *Zesbrew* was gazing at the girl. It was Shana; the Twins' lovely servant.

In all Ted's days of living, he had never feared anything until now. *Zesbrew* was hideous looking.

"Shana, my sweet little flower," hissed *Zesbrew,* taking his eyes off her and locking them onto Ted.

They both looked toward the floor.

"No words for *Zesbrew?*"

"My Lord," replied Shana, curtsying. "I am so glad you've come to save me," she lied.

Zesbrew walked up to her.

"The king's spies captured me and made me his whore," she spat, pointing at Ted.

"Whore," grunted *Zesbrew,* eyeing the man.

What the hell is she talking about, thought Ted.

"Who are you?" asked *Zesbrew.*

"I am the king's new animal trainer." "Why would the king give an animal trainer such a lovely gift as this?" he asked, pointing at Shana.

"I don't know," he replied, keeping his eyes glued to the floor.

"You talk to the animals?" "Yes."

"How?"

"I was struck by lightning when a child.

They believe that is how."

"You wouldn't lie to *Zesbrew?*"

"From what I know, no one can lie to you, my Lord."

Zesbrew looked from one to the other. He knew they were lying. "Shana my sweet flower, your alluring fragrant is fit for a king."

"Yes, my Lord."

"I know a king who'd love to have you." "Yes, my Lord."

"You, Lord Barrington, are wise and truthful. You belong in better conditions." "Yes, my Lord."

Zesbrew placed his hands upon both.

"You belong to *Zesbrew* now. Come with me."

"Yes, my Lord," they said as if in a trance.

They walked out to the balcony.

Zesbrew stepped aside. "Jump into the water, *Zesbrew* will take you from this place and give you a wonderful life."

Without looking at one another, Ted and Shana climbed up onto the rail and jumped.

Before *Zesbrew* leaped off, through a hidden door a chambermaid walked in. *Zesbrew* turned hearing her.

"My Lord," she said.

"Who so mindful to speak with *Zesbrew?*"

"It's I, Gloria, the Twins' favorite spy," she replied, hoping he'd treat her well.

"What words do you have for *Zesbrew?*" "I have information you need to hear."

"Go on, sweet servant."

"I overheard Lord Barrington talking to King William."

Zesbrew stepped up to intently listen.

"Lord Barrington is not from the Realm." "Not from the Realm? How can that be?" "He is from the Great Beyond, my Lord." *Zesbrew's* expression went slack. "The Great Beyond?"

"Yes, my Lord. It's in another time, well, that's how he described it to William.

How can someone enter the Realm? he thought. He eyed the woman; thinking. *There is only one who may have such power to come and go from this place; the Shadow.*

"Juliette is also not here," she added.

She was taken at night by Alexus Arteria."

Zesbrew grew angry hearing that. She glanced down at the floor in fear.

"So," he said, piecing the puzzle together. "If she is not here, then she must be in the Great Beyond, which…" he continued, turning around. "She was taken from the Realm to Lord Barrington and now he has entered seeking more than revenge for his stupid cousin. He is here to kill the Twins and break the spell."

Gloria just stood there listening to him. She knew William and his guards were on the way. "I must go now, they're coming."

Zesbrew turned and faced her. "Go, hurry, and keep us informed," he replied, walking over and jumping from the rail.

Gloria ran to the curtain, pulled it back and slipped through the hidden doorway.

Seconds later, William and his men ran in. No one was there. They rushed over to the balcony rail. Looking out, William's eyes filled with fear. "Where on earth is he taking them?"

Commander Phelps and Captain Cornel spotted Ted and Shana following the most God Awful thing they had ever seen.

"It's taking them to a ship."

"A ship, you mean a lifeboat!" yelled William.

"I would think so, your Grace," said Cornel.

"Go and report to Captain Burlap. I want my navy to set sail at once. I'll not let that evil thing take them away."

"Yes, my Lord," the two replied in unison.

<h1 style="text-align:center">22</h1>

Just outside the harbor, in a secluded area, Captain Howler's boat crew stood patiently waiting at the shoreline. It was hard to see with the fog rolling in.

"That's them," whispered a boat crew, pointing down the beach.

"Remember, do not look into *Zesbrew's* eyes while he's speaking," warned the other.

"Come, my servants," said *Zesbrew*, to his captive prey.

"My Lord," greeted the crew, seeing Ted and Shana as if in a trance.

"Take Lord Barrington to King Bela of Grim. This flower I give to Captain Howler for his troubles."

"Yes, my Lord," they said, assisting the pair into the boat.

Before making his escape, *Zesbrew* waited until the lifeboat had breached the incoming waves and was rowing hard toward the ship. He then walked up over a bluff of high grass and continued down the shoreline until he reached the forest; where Egmon was waiting for him.

"The boat is returning, Captain," said a deckhand.

"Quick, lower the ropes."

As the boat approached, Howler saw the young woman. "Why is she coming?"

"She is a gift for your troubles, Captain."

"Hurry, let's get them onboard," he whispered, eyeing the enemy ships at anchor in the harbor.

Once the two were on deck, Howler ordered Ted to the Brig and Shana to his stateroom.

They walked liked zombies to where they were being escorted.

"Maintain silence about the deck," ordered Howler. "Mr. Pickens," he then said, "see to the anchor."

"Aye, Captain."

"Mr. Allen, ready the sails. Come about to starboard and takes us out to sea."

"Aye, Captain."

When the Wicked made her turn and headed for deeper waters, Ted was escorted below. As he descended the ladder, the pungent odor became stronger; foul smelling men, filthy quarters, laced together with animal excretion from goats, pigs, chickens and possibly rats. Like the wretched stench of death, the foulness sat in his nostrils like tar. It made his eyes water.

I have to get out of here, he thought. It was a feeble thought; for he knew it would take King William's navy to catch up to them.

"Lookee what we have here," said a crewmen, walking up to Ted. He could see Ted having a hard time with the smell.

"Leave him be," said the two deckhands, escorting him.

Ted followed them down another ladder- well. It was even worse.

"Open the brig."

The key set in, the door opened.

They shoved Ted inside and locked the gate.

"We have a long journey, so settle in," one said.

Ted stared at them through the bars. The two smiled showing off their yellow rotten teeth, then left.

Placing his hand over his mouth and nose, he turned and looked at the filthy cot. *It has to be covered in parasites or, even worse; rat droppings. I'd rather lie in a coffin.* He decided to sit in the corner on the floor. As he did, the ship rose up then came down, making him hold tight to himself.

A giant rat scurried past his boots trying to escape the brig for a better place to hide from the devilish seas outside. He kicked at it. It ran through the bars. *Disgusting,* he thought, looking out into the passageway. He could see the glow from the guard's candle dancing on the walls down from him. The ship rose up; he hunkered tight keeping his nose and mouth and against his sleeve.

In his state of anger something bore up from the pit of his stomach. He wanted this quest but, knew now that he was ill prepared to take it on. It made him think back over his life.

While drifting in the past, he realized that he never had to work; everything was handed to him, along with his father's hotel empire.

In a filthy brig aboard a ship, Ted Barrington finally came face to face with reality. He was not the man he thought he was. Sure he was rich, had whatever he wanted but, that doesn't make you a man.

Feeling disgusted sitting there, he rubbed his rough hands upon his face. He looked at them; dirty and chapped - his clothing filthy as well. In that moment, the little man inside his head was torn from his soul. He gritted his teeth, spitting him out. *I took on this quest and I will finish it,* he thought, looking out of the bars.

While staring at the glow of the candle dancing on the floor and walls, he made a promise to himself. *I will become her knight,* he thought, thinking of the most beautiful woman in all the land. Her image sat there within his mind's eye. Her sensual lips parted as if saying something. He knew now what it was. He heard it in his dreams a thousand times. *I swear my beloved Juliette; I will save you from the horrors of evil. I'll bring you out of the depth of sleep and care for you all the days of my life.*

"Barrington, Barrington, I beg of you … save me… save me… please save me," her words echoed inside his head. They sunk deep into his soul. He reached up and pulled back his hair, he wanted to pull it all out. "I'm coming my beloved and nothing will stand in my way," he angrily whispered. As he looked out the bars once again he wished he had brought his sword. It did not matter. *From this day forward, whatever it takes, I will kill the Twins.*

With that swirling inside his head, he knew it was going to be a long night, a very long night; maybe the longest night of his life. He could only hope they'd put him to work on deck in the morning to relieve him of the foulness below. There he could start forming a plan.

Up on deck, Howler had Mr. Allen oversee the helm while he proceeded to his quarters below. Upon opening the door, he saw Shana sitting on his bed.

"Stand up. Let me get a good look at you."

"Yes, my Lord."

"What is your name," he asked, taking her in. She was a fine little thing with supple curves, long brown hair and beautiful eyes.

"My name is Shana but you can call me whatever you like, my Lord."

"I like Shana. Remove your clothing," he said, turning to pull off his boots.

Shana waited until his back was to her before reaching down and taking out a small dagger strapped to her leg. She silently crept up and drove the knife deep into his back then quickly put the blade between his legs slicing upward; cutting the main artery in his thigh.

"You little whooore…" he groaned, falling to the floor.

Lying there in pain, she jumped on top of him; stabbing him repeatedly in the chest until he was dead.

With blood soaked hands she stood up staring down at the fool.

"I want securing lines fore and aft," she heard the Bos'n on deck calling out.

Without a thought, she quickly removed her clothing. Inside his closet she put on a pair of his pants and shirt. As she slowly turned around, the Shadow, Alexus Arteria transformed; becoming Captain *Howler* – the dead man on the floor.

Alexus had changed into Shana while searching for cotton. Shana, the lovely maiden, was lying unconscious in a linen closet inside Lyon Head Castle. Alexus had it all planned out; he was going with Ted, not her. A little white powder on a rag over Shana's mouth and nose was all it took.

Alexus now *Howler* pulled off the dead captain's boots and put them on. After he did, he lifted the captain onto his bunk; where he bound his legs and hands then rolled him tightly inside the blanket.

At midnight, Alexus 'now appearing as *Howler*' opened the door and strolled into the crew's birthing. He awoke two crewmen, placed a finger to his lips and whispered, "Take the woman from my quarters and throw her overboard back aft."

"Aye, Captain," they said, looking at one another confused.

"Do you honestly think I could have kept her onboard with these men who haven't seen a woman in months?" he asked, glancing from one to the other.

"No, Captain," they whispered; knowing every sailor would lust over her.

"She's dead. I wrapped her in my blanket. Now, do as I asked."

As they went to leave, he put out his hand. "Remember, dead bodies weigh more, so be very careful not to drop her."

"Yes, Captain." One hesitated. "Yes?"

"What will you tell the crew, Sir?"

"She escaped by jumping overboard while I was asleep."

The two nodded.

"Now Go."

"Yes, Captain."

In the morning, Mr. Pickens, Mr. Allen and Bos'n Teller sat down for breakfast. Howler walked in and took his seat. The three looked at the door expecting the woman to stroll in.

"Is there a problem, gentlemen?" "Where's the woman?"

"She escaped while I slept. By the time I got up on deck, she jumped overboard."

"No alarm bell, Sir?" questioned Mr. Allen.

"I ordered none to be sounded. Now, let's eat, shall we," he replied, picking up his fork and knife.

The men sat there watching him.

"Alright," he grunted, putting his silverware down. "I wasn't intending to keep her onboard while sailing to Grim. I'd suspect she'd cause a mutiny, if you get my drift."

The three eyed one another. They agreed with a nod.

After Breakfast, Howler proceeded forward through the crew berthing. He took the ladder down to the brig below. The sailor watching Lord Barrington stood up.

"How's our prisoner?"

"Fine, Captain. He just had breakfast."

Howler peered between the bars.

Ted looked up from the filthy bunk. In an instant, he watched Howler's pupils change into cat-eyes then change back again. *I'll be damned,* he thought; *it's Alexus.*

"Treat him well. I want him healthy when we turn him over to King Bela." "We will, Captain."

"Captain, Captain," a deckhand yelled, hurrying down the ladder-well.

"What is it, Lad?"

"We've spotted sails astern and to starboard, Sir."

"By the Twins' promise of safe sailing," he grunted, heading up.

On deck, he saw Mr. Pickens pointing aft. His eyes took in the sails of not one but two warships.

"Captain," shouted Mr. Allen.

He turned seeing him pointing off the starboard beam. It was another warship; this one much larger.

"What do you want us to do?" asked Mr. Pickens.

"We cannot out run them," he spat. "Lower the sails."

"But, Captain."

"Lower the sails, damn you!" "Yes, Captain."

As they sat adrift, the two naval vessels approached from either side.

"This is the Jarrett of his Majesty Royal Navy. Tell your men to stand down," shouted Captain Burlap.

Howler stared at the captain then glanced over at the other frigate coming abreast; the men armed along the deck. He spun around catching the larger warship crossing his bow.

"We have stood down."

"Prepare to tie off," ordered Burlap.

On deck of the Wicked, Burlap placed Howler, his two officers and Teller under arrest. "Your men can lower the lifeboats. They can take as much provisions as their boats can handle. Where are Lord Barrington and Shana?"

"Lord Barrington is in the brig. Shana escaped by jumping overboard last night," he lied. Alexus wasn't about to tell Captain Burlap who he really was.

Burlap stepped up staring him dead in the eye. "You want me to believe that!"

Howler said nothing.

"Take them across the plank."

The Jarrett sailors came forward seizing them while others went down to release Lord Barrington from the brig.

With Howler and his officers onboard the Jarrett and Howler's crew sitting in lifeboats, Burlap ordered the three warships to fire their cannons at Howler's vessel. The balls hit their mark; the Wicked began to sink.

Howler's officers along with Bos'n Teller sighed seeing their ship going down. They looked over at Howler watching the yardarm and sails disappear.

"Captain," said Mr. Allen.

Howler glanced over at him. In horror, the three watched his eyes change.

"Jump!"

"Who are you," gasped Mr. Pickens. "I said jump," he grunted.

Without a word, the three went over the side.

Burlap ran across the deck. "Stop!" he ordered.

"Let them go," said Howler; staring out over the seas.

"You ordered them?"

Ted hurried alongside seeing the men swimming for their lives.

"Take the captain to the brig," ordered Burlap, spinning around. "I want all our archers to report to the portside."

"What are you doing," questioned Ted.

Burlap angrily stared at him. None of them are going to survive."

Ted looked out at the men swimming and then focused on the men in the lifeboats waving to those in the water.

"Captain Howler will be the only one kneeling before King William," grunted Burlap. Ted watched Burlap's crewmen escorting Howler to the ladder. *How is Alexus going to get out of this mess,* he thought. He'd wait and speak with him later.

He never did get a chance to speak with Alexus. After the Jarrett made port, Captain Burlap requested a lifeboat over the side. The first order of business was transporting Captain Howler to the King's prison on Gull Island; a small island in the bay where no man had ever escaped.

Shackled hand and foot, Howler sat in the middle while the four crewmen rowed. Upon making the seawall, they rowed underneath a wooden gate to a channel under the prison.

Guards were standing at ready.

"This prisoner is Captain Howler who abducted Lord Barrington and Shana. She is dead. The king will announce when he wants him kneeling before him. In the meantime, he'll be placed in your charge."

"Bring that mangy dog up here, we'll see he is treated well," ordered a prison guard.

They manhandled Howler up a flight of steps into a passageway. The stench was enough to knock a man down. Howler paid no mind to the foulness, and or, the prisoners screaming, moaning; begging to be set free.

After making their way through a dimly lit passageway to an empty cell, they tossed him inside.

"Unshackle him," ordered a guard.

Two went in and unlocked the chains; the one that gave the order left to continue his duties.

"Are any of you going ashore today," asked Howler.

"Shut your mouth," one spat. "I'm just asking."

"I am," the other one said. "I can't wait to see my wife."

As soon as they removed the shackles, Howler yanked the chains from them, swung it at one; knocking him out cold.

The other guard, who was going home to see his wife fought back. He was taken out with crippling blow to the head.

Howler quickly grabbed one and dragged him over to a corner. The one going home, he changed clothes with, and then placed him in the bunk; covering him with the blanket. Howler then turned toward the door transforming himself into the *guard*.

After locking it shut, he went back to the tunnel.

"Enjoy your two days with your wife, Sloth," said a guard, turning the capstan to open the gate.

"I will," he replied, getting inside the boat.

Once in port, Sloth secured the boat, walked up the steps and crossed over the cobble stone pier. After entering an alley-way and seeing no one in sight, he changed back into his Nobel self - *Alexus Arteria.*

Looking back toward the water and out to Gull Island, he wondered what the guards would think had happened to Captain Howler. Alexus decided right then that he'd have William tell the captain of his prison that Howler must have escaped and was eaten by sharks; for they searched and he was never found.

23

The evening prior, when *Zesbrew* returned to Black Water, he ordered Egmon to have Greta and Hagar come see him. Not knowing what he wanted, they were nervous standing at the large metal door.

"You do all the talking," whispered Hagar.

Greta stared at her shaking her head; *she always did all the talking.*

When they opened the door and stepped in with their torch, *Zesbrew* crept out of the darkness. "Who so mindful to visit with *Zesbrew*?"

It's your most trusted and loyal servants, my Lord. You wanted to see us?"

"Yes, yes. I have news that does not set well. Come in," he replied, pointing.

They walked over and sat on a large rock.

"I heard from Gloria," he said, watching their expressions.

They both looked stunned. They hadn't heard from her in a while.

"What did she have to say?" asked Greta. "She is one of yours?"

"Yah, she is. She has been for several years now."

He then told them what Gloria had overheard.

Alarmed by that revelation, Greta stood up. "How can that be," she spat. "No one can enter the Realm from outside. He had to come from across the twelve seas."

Zesbrew shook his head. "You must remain wise in your thinking my charming, Greta. Who do you know that has the power that can?"

Greta answered quicker than lightening. "The Shadow," she gasped; almost losing it. "You don't think," she continued, looking from one to the other. "You don't think Alexus is the Shadow. I mean, if Gloria knows that he was the one who slipped Juliette out of the tower, then," she said, spinning in thought.

A devilish grin appeared on *Zesbrew's* face.

Greta and Hagar waited to hear what he had to say.

"I say Alexus is the Shadow, which gives us a great advantage, because he does not know that we know. He can now be easily killed by one of your spies."

"I might have just the right person." "Good."

"What about Lord Barrington?" asked Hagar.

Zesbrew walked up to her. She stood and bowed.

"Lord Barrington will never leave the Realm again. King Bela is a true and trusted servant. I know once Captain Howler hands him over, knowing that I sent him there, Bela will work him like a rabid-dog until his death."

The two smiled.

Shana awoke confused; finding herself lying inside a linen closet. As she sat up, she could not remember what had happened. With her mind adrift, it dawned on her. *Alexus and I were searching for cotton.... and now I'm lying here,* she thought. *It was Alexus. He put me to sleep somehow. Which means... he saved me from Zesbrew. That has to be it... but what happened? What happened to him and Ted?*

Worried of their plight, she ran down the corridor to Ted's quarters. No one was there. *By the Gods I swear, Zesbrew must have taken them,* she angrily thought. At the balcony rail, she gazed out over the water. "What am I going to do?" In that moment, she got an idea. "I'm going back to Black Water with Jasper. We'll find a way to close off the channels and allow the rats to rip that wooden creature apart."

With a charge in her stride, she hurried to her room. There, she gathered her things and then impatiently waited until early evening when the people of the villages left the square after selling their goods.

Getting out of the castle unseen with Jasper was not easy; getting her horse from the stable, even harder. Her excuse; she loved riding just before sunset, and promised to be back soon.

While casually escorting her horse through the bustling crowd toward the main entrance, she kept her head down.

In front of her, several men were pushing carts through the guarded gate. The sentries stepped back for the men, allowing her to fall in right behind and walk out.

After crossing the bridge, she mounted her horse. Jasper poked his head out of her shoulder bag. "Get back inside," she scolded, gently pushing him down. With a steady kick, her horse took off across the open plain toward the forest and trail leading to the rock bridge and Forbidden Land.

Once there, she prodded her horse in a circle; looking across the bridge, allowing her eyes to drift along the formidable plateaus on the other side. *I must make it to the old camp before dark,* she thought, guiding her horse over.

The old camp was where the Twins turned King William's and King Fredrick's soldiers into stone. They were still there along with their horses; some sitting by fires, some standing, while others were resting in tents. No one dared venture into the camp for fear they'd end up like them.

Shana knew otherwise. She stayed there the night after finding herself lying on the ground outside her village; where Tess had left her. She then stole a horse that evening and camped under the tattered remains of the tent before heading to the Northern Kingdom in the morning.

While thinking of the camp, she gazed through the long desolate valley between the steep high ridges adorned in orange, yellow and greyish rock. Years past, it was a splendid sight; today barren.

Trotting along, she wondered after the Twins were killed and *Zesbrew* dispatched, who would take over, who would be king? That was unsettling to her. Would King Fredrick of the Southern Kingdom march in or, would King William demand the region? William, she knew, had a more formidable army. With him taking on the Twins, she suspected the people of the villages under the control of the witches would side with him. She could only hope.

For the next few hours, she sat still in the saddle, prodding her horse along; ever so watchful for the drifters who kept a low profile themselves. They were a breed of men that took whatever they wanted; leaving their victims helpless. A woman alone would be easy prey; most would be raped or left much worse.

Back at the Northern Kingdom, Ted was disembarking the naval ship, Jarrett with Captain Burlap. King William was there along with his soldiers to greet him. He told 'em the sad news of Shana jumping overboard before she was rescued. It was a lie, but with so many ears listening, that is all he could tell the king for her absence.

While William spoke of his heartache of losing her, Ted was wondering where she was and why she hadn't been seen. *What did Alexus do with her?*

He had no clue and neither did the king or his men. If he found her before they did, Shana and he could come-up with a story that she did in fact jump overboard and luckily found an old crate to hang onto until she reached the shore.

Just then, while thinking, Ted spotted three small birds flying in and out of a stable off the pier; Bree, Nera and Mylee. They appeared agitated.

"Come, Lord Barrington," said William.

Ted took his eyes off the hummingbirds and looked at him.

"We have much to plan before we strike forth," continued William, ushering Ted from the pier.

He looked back, the birds were following.

"Before we do, your Grace, I'd like to wash up."

William gazed down at Ted's filthy clothing. "I'm sure you do. We'll see you in an hour."

When Ted got to his room, the hummingbirds flew in; all chattering at once.

"What do you mean, Shana left with Jasper? Please, one at a time."

Bree landed on his hand. "She did. We followed her to the trail leading to the rock bridge. She is going back to Black Water alone."

Ted sighed, shaking his head. "I've got to catch up with her."

"You can't," replied Mylee. "No one can save her now."

"I must try. So here is what I want you to do. While I am sitting with the king and his council this afternoon, I want you three to locate Major and tell him. I don't know what he can do with her now being in the Forbidden Land but, we must try."

"We will," replied Bree, lifting from his hand and flying out.

Mylee and Nera fluttered there for a second staring at him.

"Go, we don't have much time."

Without a word they took flight.

By evening, Shana turned her horse toward a cove; a small inlet within the mesa walls. There were several trees giving it shelter. She could tell why the soldiers had picked the spot to make camp there; somewhat out of sight and protected on three sides by sheer rock-face walls.

She dismounted, tethered her horse and allowed Jasper to come out. After setting him on the ground, she grabbed her blanket. "You stay with me," she said, lifting the tattered flap and walking in.

Near the back where the tent still gave somewhat shelter, she laid out her blanket. Jasper came over and sat on it. "Ya hungry, my friend," she said, pulling out nuts she saw Ted giving him.

As Jasper ate, she walked outside. *A small fire would be nice*, she thought, looking about for wood.

With a fire inside, her stomach filled with jerky, she settled in next to Jasper for the night. With the exception of the ferret to warn her of trouble, all she had was a small dagger to protect her.

In the wee hours, a rider approached. He got down from his saddle and quietly escorted his horse under the trees. Walking in, the scent of smoke was drifting through the air. There at the tattered tent, he hesitated a moment, startled seeing the stone figures; some sitting, some standing, along with their horses. He walked past them, knelt down and slowly pulled up the flap.

Jasper opened his eyes when the man entered. Before Shana awoke, the man took hold of her; covering her mouth.

She tried to fight.

The man grabbed the knife she brought up from her side. "Shh…" he whispered.

Shana's eyes went wide. It was Lord Barrington.

Releasing his grip, she gasped for air.

"What are you doing here?"

"I'd like to ask you that same question."

She slowly sat up, rubbing her mouth. "I thought you were on your way to Grim with Alexus. Believing you were, I decided to take on *Zesbrew* myself, well… not by myself but with Jasper."

Ted nodded, knowing he would have done the same thing. "Look," he said, "what I am about to tell you stays between us."

Shana nodded.

"Alexus is the Shadow. He put you to sleep and went with me as *you*. I thought it was *you* until he came down as Captain *Howler* to see how I was doing in the ship's brig."

Shana's mouth dropped open. "Tell me everything!"

"If you ever say a word, I'm a dead man." "I promise, I'll never tell a soul; I swear."

Hesitant to say more, Ted stared at her for a moment.

Shana's expression opened his mouth.

"Alright, when you returned to my living quarters, I mean, when Alexus returned as *you*, we confronted *Zesbrew*. We were taken aboard the Wicked; a vessel so foul you'd lose your stomach.

Shana sighed shaking her head.

When he told her the rest of what had happened, Shana sat back; stunned. "You're saying *Zesbrew* gave me to Captain Howler?"

"Yes."

"Then Alexus killed the captain and then had him tossed overboard?"

"Yes."

Shana sat there drifting over his story. It seemed so surreal now knowing that Alexus Arteria was the Shadow and he saved her from the hands of Howler.

"Shana."

She blinked, still drifting.

"Shana."

"Do you think if I get caught by the Twins that I could say," she said then paused, "that I escaped by jumping overboard?"

"Who would be the wiser? Those witches think you and I are on our way to Grim with Captain Howler."

She nodded.

"But let's not get caught."

"That is the last thing I ever want to happen. Now tell me," she replied, "what is the plan for taking on the Twins?"

"They are going by way of ship and by land to surround the castle at Black Water." "Does King William know you're here?" "No."

Shana shook her head. "Maybe we should go back."

"No, we are going on and doing this together. All we have to do is get Jasper inside the castle," he replied, rubbing the ferret's head.

"That will be easy," said Jasper. "You think?" questioned Ted.

"Are you talking to that ferret?"

"You may not understand Jasper's chatter, but I do. The three of us are going on. Together, we will set this all in motion and kill those witches."

She gazed into his eyes. They were lifeless, dead; a look one would give when they were beyond convincing. "Alright, we'll go on," she said, dropping her eyes on Jasper sitting there.

He looked up at her as if he knew what she was saying.

"I'll never get used to this," she said.

"Let's get some sleep, shall we," replied Ted, getting up.

She watched him walk out to get his gear. *After hearing all this, I hope I can sleep,* she thought, lying down.

At first light, Shana awoke. She sat up seeing Ted sleeping near the entrance. She patted Jasper's head, stood up; stretching her body. Ted opened his eyes hearing her. He got to his feet and stretched himself. "I don't think my body will get used to this."

"It better get used to it, we have a long way to go and many nights of sleeping on the ground," she replied. "Are you hungry?"

"Yes."

After their meal, Ted asked her what was ahead.

"First," she said, "we must try and stay out of sight and ever alert. There are bands of drifters and wanton criminals traveling the land. Once we exit the valley, we'll have to slip past the village of Nimrod. The stone people live there. That's what we call them anyways. Once we do, we'll have miles of forest to travel before entering the village of Bissell, then onward to Tribow and Orbed – my village. That will be hard with all the wild beasts that see us as an easy prey."

Ted knew all about the wild animals. He wanted to know more about the stone people.

Shana mounted her horse and turned toward him. "In its day, Nimrod was the jewel of the eastern section of Ur; as you know it is now called the Forbidden Land.

"The rocky cliffs around the village are beauty beyond one's imagination. In years past, before the beginning of the Realm, giant landslides of rocks and boulders carved out the area. Some boulders are as big as huts and the sandstone colors; well… are mesmerizing to say the least.

"When the Twins took over, the village wanted no part of their evil doings. To make a fine example of them the sisters cast a spell over the people; turning them into stone. I suppose they got the idea from the boulders and rocks that surround the village."

"Stone people walking, talking and…"

"Yes, they're still alive – not like these fools, however…" she interrupted, pointing at the soldiers and horses standing there.

Ted glanced back remembering seeing them within his dream. "Let's go," he said, getting into the saddle with Jasper on his shoulder.

When they came to the end of the valley there was a slight climb. Above the ridge, Ted could see the forest.

"We'll dismount and escort the horses up," she said, getting down. "Don't want 'em to break a leg."

"Right."

Making level ground, Ted looked about.

"Not much grows here."

"Sadly, no; it's more like a tinderbox.

We'll have to watch our fires if we have any."

"How the heck did you get through this," he asked, taking in the rugged terrain filled with debris, embedded rocks and dead fall.

"Not easy. We'll just go slowly. There are many gullies we can take shelter in to rest."

Ten miles on, the sun descending, Shana picked out a large gulley with an overhanging ledge on the other side. There, they could shelter underneath for the night.

"Just follow my lead going down," she warned.

Ted dismounted. "Are you sure you want to camp here?" he asked, taking in the sandstone colored rocks, large boulders jutting up from the ground and dead trees that had fallen in.

"Trust me, I slept here before."

"I think you should get down," he said to Jasper.

"I don't like this."

"You don't like what?" he asked him.

"Are you talking to that ferret again?" asked Shana, gently escorting her horse.

Ted looked at her then focused on his friend.

"I sense danger," said Jasper.

Ted looked about. "Danger coming?" he asked, thinking of the wolves and hyenas.

"No, but this place will not protect us."

"We have no other choice. It's getting dark."

Jasper gave him a worried expression and headed down.

Mindful of his horse, Ted cautiously followed behind.

Under the overhanging rocks, Shana tethered her horse and turned around. "Did you bring any food?"

"Just the fruit in my room is all."

"You really planned well," she sarcastically replied.

He tied off his horse and went over to her. "I really had no time to gather baskets of food. I had to find you before you blew the king's plan."

"As like I said, Lord Barrington, I thought you two were on your way to Grim. No one can get into that castle except me. You can give me that much for at least trying."

Ted leaned on his sword handle staring at her.

"Let's find some wood, shall we," she said to his stare.

With evening, came the stars. The gulley and tree line above disappeared within the darkness. Just the glow from the fire was all that could be seen all around them.

Jasper, who had fallen asleep on a blanket quickly sat up; sniffing the air. Ted looked at him. Just then, the horses began tugging on the tethering line.

Shana knew the horses had picked up a scent. She quickly got up and pulled out her knife.

"What is it?" asked Ted, getting to his feet.

Before Shana answered, Jasper called out, "Hyenas." With that, he took off scrambling under rocks and dead fall.

Silver Eye and her pack of ten hyenas gained the ridgeline looking down at the pair.

The horses reared; frantic by the sight of them.

The foul things came down from every side. Silver Eye made the bottom and then leaped up onto a boulder glaring at them in the light of the fire.

She was wicked, terrifying; her eyes like daggers. Ted watched the drool from her mouth hanging from her canines like syrup. In that moment, from the pit of his stomach he wanted to scream. It came out as a roar while drawing his sword. "I'll kill every one of you," he shouted, standing his ground. To his surprise, the blade began to glow, turning red hot. Was it his anger or something else that made it work. He had not a clue but remembered what Patch had said. *Become one with the sword.* It felt like that within his hands.

Silver Eye stood back feeling the heat.

Others crept up snarling but kept clear of the sword.

Shana then screamed.

Ted turned just in time catching one trying to come up from behind him. He stepped toward it, swinging the sword with all his might. It caught the hyena at the side of its head; slicing right through its snout.

The thing leaped backwards; spilling blood from the gaping hole. Its legs buckled then it keeled over dead.

Shana quickly gathered next to him keeping the rest at bay until Ted turned back staring at Silver Eye. "You're next," he grunted, pointing the glowing hot blade up at her.

She glared at him; her torment apparent.

Without warning from above, rocks and tree limbs began raining down inside the gulley.

Ted held fast not giving an inch. His time in the ship's brig, feeling sorry for himself was gone. No longer was he going to be that weak, timid, little man.

Silver Eye kept her stare until several of her pack were hit; crushed by the weight of heavy rocks and tree limbs. She took one last look at Ted and raced out of the gulley.

Ted and Shana watched them trying to escape the barrage of things raining down on them. Once the rest made it out and ran back into the forest, all went quiet.

"It's the stone people," whispered Shana.

Ted glanced up allowing his eyes to scan the ridgeline; as much as he could see. Seconds later, a stone man walked up and looked down.

It was Hons… the ruler of Nimrod; standing six-foot five, weighing two hundred and ninety pounds. He stood there eyeing the soldier with the sword. A sword the likes he had never seen before. "Drop that sword," he ordered.

"Come and take it from me," shouted Ted in return.

"Lord Barrington," said Shana.

Ted looked at her.

"We are outnumbered. What can you do with that sword against so many?"

"You hear what the lady just said," yelled Hons. "I have fifty men with me."

After he said that, the stone men of Nimrod took up the entire ridgeline. Carson walked up to Hons and whispered, "Did you catch his name."

"Yes."

"It's Lord Barrington, the same Lord Barrington the witches are after."

Hons took his eyes off Carson and stared at Ted. "Well, we might get out of this mess sooner than I thought," he said more to himself. He waved his hand. The men followed him down into the gulley.

Shana fell to the ground.

Ted glanced down at her feebleness. He stood defiant, holding his flaming sword out before him.

"Drop it, Lord Barrington," said Shana. "Listen to the woman," grunted Hons.

Mesmerized, he was beyond disbelief; a man made of stone with the exception of his eyes; which were normal, standing there talking to him.

The rest came up. He looked at them. He knew the sword could have split the leader in half, but there were too many to defend against. He dropped the sword. The flame went out. "We want no trouble."

"Trouble," repeated Hons, picking up the sword. Nothing happened; no glow, no flame. "What is this? How did you do that?" he asked, studying the thing.

"It only works for Lord Barrington," said Shana, hoping when they heard his title they'd step back. They did not.

"Those who cross our land are trouble, but you," he said then paused, "you may be a blessing in disguise."

"A blessing," questioned Ted. "Seize them," shouted Hons.

The men came forward grabbing Ted and Shana.

Hons stepped up to her. "Who are you?" "My name is Shana."

"Shana, the peasant girl from Orbed who works for the Twins?" he questioned.

"Yes, I did work for them, but not anymore. I hate 'em as much as you do. Him too," she replied, pointing at Ted.

Hons glanced back at his friends; making Ted stand at ease. Then without warning, he quickly came forward striking Ted with his stone fist. Ted fell to the ground; out cold.

Shana screamed.

"Bring 'em!" ordered Hons.

As Ted drifted in and out of darkness, everything was a blur. His jaw felt numb, he went to rub it but could not move. His arms were tied to a cross beam, his legs bound together on an upright pole. Through his blurred vision, all he could see were mud huts, fires, and people walking about. They looked strange, odd; *the stone people*, he thought, glancing to either side. Shana was not there. *Where is she? Where is Jasper?*

Just then, two kids walked up and kicked him. When they saw Ted's eyes open, they ran off shouting; *he's awake.*

Seconds later, he was surrounded by the village.

Hons pulled back his hair to look at him.

"You sleep well?"

Ted said nothing; gazing over the people. Every one of them made of stone, even the children; as like statues come alive.

"Speak up!" shouted Hons. "Where am I?"

Laughter erupted.

"Nimrod," said a woman. "Shut up," scolded Hons. "Where is Shana?"

"She's cooking."

She's cooking, Ted panicked. *Did they burn her alive.*

"She is now our slave," said Hons.

Ted sighed hearing that. "Why did you hit me and why am I tied to this pole? We both want the same thing; the Twins dead."

"We have other ideas."

"And what would that be?"

"We hand you over to the Twins, and in return, we request they make us normal again. If you kill those witches, we'll never get that chance."

Disheartened by that, he knew Hons was right. While trying to think his way out of this mess, a hawk flew over and landed in a tree.

Hons looked up; so did the rest.

Ted deeply sighed. It was Major. He could only hope he brought reinforcements. "I think you better let me go."

Laughter again erupted.

"Take him to the wagon," said Hons.

They untied Ted, dragged him over to a wagon with a metal cage on the back. After opening the gate, they tossed him inside.

"Lock it," ordered Hons.

Shana stepped out of one of the huts to see what was happening.

"Get back in here," ordered Fran, the village cook.

Shana sighed, turned and walked in.

"Those pots; bring 'em over here and start boiling them vegetables."

"Alright, OK," she angrily replied, picking them up.

Fran stormed over to her, grabbed her by the cheek and squeezed it. "You do as I say without any lip. You hear me?"

Shana presented a frown. "I'm sorry," she said; lowering her eyes to the floor.

Fran let go of her cheek, turned and went back to the woodstove. "Next time," she said over her shoulder, "I'll have you whipped." Shana tightened her grip on the pot handles as she was walking behind her. "It will never happen again, I swear."

Just as Fran went to turn and face her, Shana lifted the metal pots and slammed them against Fran's head. She dropped to the floor; out cold.

Shana then boldly stood over her. "You see, I was telling you the truth… it will never happen again - you wretched woman," she spat. With that, she quickly set the pots down and headed for the door. Before leaving, she looked back at Fran lying there. "I gotta find Jasper and get out of here."

With the village occupied tormenting Ted in the cage, she slipped around the corner and made a mad dash to Hons' hut. She wasn't leaving without Ted's sword. Not knowing how he made the blade light up, she knew they would need it when facing the Twins.

That thought drove into her, while opening the door. To her luck, stupid Hons placed the sword over the fireplace. She walked over, took it down and then climbed out the back window.

There, she headed for the stable; Ted's and her horses were inside. Her problem however was crossing the street. Hunkering against the ironwork shop, she peered out. She was disgusted seeing the kids pelting Ted with rocks; at least the ones that flew between the bars; hitting him.

Now, she thought, racing across the street.

The door was slightly ajar. She slipped inside and hurried down the stable. The horses were in the last stalls. To her surprise, so was Jasper.

She beamed with delight seeing him. "You," she gushed. "I was so worried about you. We are leaving," she continued, picking him up.

With both horses ready, she quietly exited the rear doors and escorted the horses on foot into the forest. A quarter mile away, she mounted and rode off through the woods.

Battered, bruised, and covered in filth, Ted sat in the cage while the village prepared for his ride to Black Water. Before long, he heard a woman shouting. The commotion brought everyone out.

Hons rushed over seeing the women escorting Fran out of the kitchen. She looked hurt; distressed.

"What happened?"

"It's Shana," one replied.

"She has escaped," another spoke up.

Hons spun around. He glared at the men standing there. "I want five of you to go after her. She can't have gotten too far."

The men ran off, gathered their horses and set out after her. They picked up her tracks within the forest and took off like the wind down the trail.

"Woman, go get that sword," ordered Hons.

His wife, Derma, walked over to their hut. Moments later, she came out yelling it's gone.

Hons' stone-face stare drew down on Ted. He saw delight in Ted's eyes; his lips slanted upward. He knew by nightfall, those telling signs of joy would disappear. In its place would be a face filled with pain and agony. That thought made him smile. "Alright, men," he shouted. "Let us set out for Black Water. I'm sure the Twins will be dancing and singing with joy when we show 'em what we have for them."

"Yes," one man said. "By tomorrow, we'll all be back to normal."

The village cheered, believing it would come true; their nightmare over.

"Norwell, take the wagon," said Hons. "The rest split up. I want men out front and men in the rear. For those I have picked to stay, treat Shana well when she is brought back."

"We will," they said.

Let's ride, gentlemen," shouted Hons.

Shana was making good time through the forest. She pushed the horses until the sun was going down. Before her visibility was gone, the rugged landscape disappearing into darkness, she turned north off the trail to hide within a rocky outcrop.

Settled in amongst the rocks, she fed Jasper, had a bite to eat and then waited. Tonight their only company she hoped would be the moon. She watched it come up and hover above the canopy.

While drifting back on the day; her hitting Fran, seeing Ted being tormented in that filthy cage, she heard horses; lots of them. "They're coming," she whispered to Jasper. She quickly glanced back at the horses; both well hidden within the pine grove and brush.

When she turned back looking toward the trail, she saw the glow of torches, heard the sound of heavy hooves. Her heart stopped seeing the stone man out front halting his horse on the trail. The rest rode up.

"Her tracks are gone," the man said; holding out his torch over the ground.

"Find them," shouted Hons.

Two men separated; one headed south, another headed north through the forest on either side.

Shana froze watching the one searching north near to her. She could only pray that she hid the horses' tracks well. After picking out the spot to hide, she went back on foot to cover them up using a long pine branch over the ground.

With her heart pounding, she watched the man on horseback coming closer. *Don't get down… don't get down,* her thoughts raced.

He cantered his horse and headed back toward the trail.

"We're not going to find her tracks with just our torches," she heard him say to the others.

Hons spat on the ground. He looked north then south. "We know where she is going."

"Where?" asked one.

"Bissell, you fool. We'll catch her there," he grunted, kicking his horse and riding down the trail.

Shana closed her eyes and let out a long winded sigh. Rolling over, she looked up at the full moon between the branches. "Bissell would be the last place I'd go with you fools on my tail." That outspoken thought made her realize that she'd have to make a wide birth around the village to reach Black Water.

24

The following morning, back at Lyon Head, the wide double doors opened to the Great Hall. A Royal Guard in his impeccable uniform stepped forward. "Your Majesty, King Fredrick Lennard of the Southern Kingdom."

William casually sat back watching him enter.

Victoria contentedly smiled knowing why the unlawful king was there. She believed he had heard word through *his* trusted spies that someone had come.

As Fredrick walked up, she took in his splendid red and white outfit with high black shoes adorned with red and white lacing; his escorts smartly following behind.

"Your Grace, M'lady," he greeted, slightly bowing.

"Fredrick," beamed William. "How's your family?"

"Good, your Grace." "Your son?"

"He is watching the throne."

"Are you worried someone is going to take it," William lightheartedly replied.

Fredrick glanced at Victoria. *She is still as beautiful as ever.* "No, but I've heard word…"

"Go on," said William with a smirk.

We all have spies, thought Fredrick to William's expression. "I've heard word," he repeated, "that you are preparing to go to war with the Twins."

Besides Lord Nelson, who else is a spy within my kingdom? Before he could answer, Fredrick continued, "I would have thought that after they killed your daughter you would have done this long ago."

Not even his spies know our daughter is still alive, well incapacitated right now. He sat up and replied, "Seeing they killed five of your best soldiers, I'm surprised you haven't gone to war yourself."

"Now, William."

William raised his brow.

"I do not have the power to go to war with them, but I did hear someone had paid you a visit and will be assisting you in your endeavor."

Someone did, but I haven't a clue to where he went, thought William. Right after he dismissed the war council, Ted simply disappeared. It did not set well with him. His gut instinct had him believing Ted went to Black Water. His reasoning for thinking so; Jasper was also gone. "Your spies have done well my friend," he piped up.

"If it pleases you to hear… Lord Nelson or his cousin Ben Gillum worked for me."

William nodded. "So… what do I owe this pleasure of your visit?"

"I would like to sit a spell and talk." "Talk about what?"

"Lending men to assist you."

William glanced at his wife then at his council men sitting there. "Alone?" he asked. "Yes."

William stood up, turned toward his wife while extending his hand.

She got up. "Your Majesty," she said, graciously bowing.

As Victoria exited the Hall, Fredrick stepped aside and bowed. So did his escorts.

William walked with Fredrick to his private setting, Alexus entered from a rear door. "Your Grace," he said, pulling William aside. Out of earshot he whispered to him.

"My instincts were right?" grunted William. "You believe he went to Black Water?" "Yes, but there is more to this," replied Alexus. "It was I who went with Ted onboard that ship. I left Shana inside a linen closet asleep."

William stood back remembering Lord Barrington telling him she had jumped overboard. He knew right then why he lied; there were too many standing there.

"I spoke to the stable hand. He said Shana went for a ride yesterday. She has not returned. He also said that Lord Barrington had come in and escorted his horse out of the stable."

"When was that?" asked William.

"Right after your war council meeting, your Majesty."

William stood there a moment. It was easy to figure out. Ted somehow discovered that Shana had left and went after her into the Forbidden Land. It made him sick. He lost five good men; Fredrick lost five good men himself. *What were the odds of Ted and Shana making it to Black Water?* He let it go. "What are we going to do?" he asked.

Alexus shifted his focus on Fredrick standing a few meters away. He looked at William. "I'll go and hopefully catch up to them."

"What about our plans by sea and by land?"

"This will work. Just make sure Captain Torres kills those crocodiles. With them out of the way, you can take the castle from land and sea while the three of us are inside the walls."

"Go, and by the Gods catch up to them."

Alexus nodded then left.

William turned and walked with Fredrick to his private setting to talk.

As Alexus hurried to get his things and ride out, Hons and his men of stone were on the march; their precious gift for the Twins loathing inside that filthy cage. By nightfall, they had made good time.

With guards out front and in the rear; torches lighting their path, deep within the forest, eyes appeared like fireflies in the night. They were high in the trees, clinging to tree trunks; ever watchful.

Dewclaw, the Guardian of the Redwood Forest stood there eyeing Ted inside the cage. "We'll follow until they make camp."

"The birds of the sky will stay the night. We'll catch up in the morning," replied Major above him on a branch.

The big grizzly bear looked up at him.

"Make sure no harm comes to him, Dewclaw."

"Not a hair on his head will be touched."

Major watched him silently slip away into the night. He glanced back at the stone men on horseback. His thoughts drifted on Grandfather and the promise he had made to him. "We'll save the *Promise*, be sure of that, Grandfather," he whispered to himself.

Behind Major, deep within the forest, large silhouettes appeared. The moss covered ancient one stood there watching the stone men escorting Lord Barrington inside the cage. His eyes locked onto the leader of Nimrod. *He'll be ground into dust before morning,* he thought. With a flap of his enormous ears, he doubled back around the outcrop of boulders. His comrades followed.

Two hours on, Hons stopped his horse. "We'll camp here and enter Bissell at day break."

Carson rode up to him. "Do you want the village to see us?"

"Why not… word travels fast. If the Twins hear we have Lord Barrington before we get to Black Water, they may come to us."

Carson nodded, turned his horse and shouted, "Dismount."

The procession of stone men got down from their horses. After gathering their gear, they set up camp with the wagon holding Ted smack in the middle.

Hons walked up to the cage and tossed a deer-hide canteen at Ted. "Drink!"

"What about some food."

"You'll get some as soon as it's cooked. We don't want you to wither away before handing you over. The Twins love nice strong men to torture; they last longer," he laughed.

Ted could have spit; that's if he had any saliva to do so. It had been a grueling ride for him; one he'd never forget. He drank all he could and handed it back.

After Hons walked away, he leaned against the metal bars. *Where is Major, where are the birds… the bees? Without them, I'll be handed over to the wretched witches of Black Water.* That thought tightened his jaw muscles. It sat there in the pit of his stomach. *Not even with that sword could I get out of this.*

As the night wore on, the air became colder. Ted hunkered down, knees up, his arms wrapped around them keeping him warm. Most of the men had settled in while some remained awake sitting by fires. He glanced at the ones standing guard.

Just as he was falling asleep, he heard a bird call, or thought he did. Sitting there half awake, his ears listening to the sounds in the night – he again heard the call.

The men at the camp paid no mind; they had heard such calls before from owls and others that hunt in the dead of night. Before Ted realized what it was, Dewclaw came charging in.

Those asleep quickly stood up. Seeing the danger, the men by the fires started to scream. Ted's eyes went wide watching the giant bear stand on its hind legs and let out a mighty roar. He then came down on all fours and charged the men. He barreled one over, swiped off the head of another and continued toward the cage.

Hons awoke hearing the horrific cries. When he got to his feet, his heart stopped seeing the bear attacking his men. Swords were pulled, spears came out. Before they struck the bear, the ground began to tremble; trees all around started crashing down.

Ted stood up wrapping his fingers around the bars. When he heard Shoeshon's mighty trumpet, he let out a sigh.

Hons spun around seeing the enormous elephant charging in. The guard standing there was reduced to dust as Shoeshon crushed him into the ground.

Two more bull elephants rushed in; ears flared out and trumpeting.

The stone men scattered in every direction, screaming for their lives.

Hons fell to his knees.

Shoeshon shook his massive head walking up to him.

"Shoeshon," said Ted.

The mighty elephant stopped and kicked the ground; wanting to crush Hons.

"Shoeshon," again said Ted.

"Please, please don't hurt me," begged Hons, cowering like a helpless child.

Shoeshon placed his trunk on him and started pushing Hons toward the cage.

Dewclaw bounded over placing his snout against Hons' cheek. He could feel his warm breath; feel the bear's anger within his growl.

"Shoeshon."

He looked over at Ted.

"Get me out of here."

Shoeshon and his bull friends walked over. With their trunks wrapped around the cage they began pulling it apart. Ted slipped out and fell to the ground. With his face in the dirt, he glanced over at Hons in the fetal position; Dewclaw standing right over him.

Slowly getting up, Ted brushed off the dirt. "I," he angrily said, walking over to Hons. He knelt next to him. "I, command the animals. I can order them to kill every one of you," he angrily shouted, looking about the men lying there scared.

"Please, I beg. We have wives and children at home."

Ted stared him dead in the eye. Dewclaw did not budge. He kept his wet snout against Hons' face. "I could have your village destroyed – your women and children killed. All I have to do is tell them to do so and…" he said, getting evening closer to his face, "and they would."

"Please no. Tell me what you want… anything?"

Ted already had what he wanted; Hons crying for mercy. With him begging for his life, he thought he could win them over. But first, he wanted to drive a fear so great into Hons. "I want your head removed," he snarled, shifting his attention on Dewclaw.

Hons watched Ted's eye shift on the bear. Utter terror swept over him.

Without another word, Ted stood up. Hons froze believing his life soon over.

"Call your men," ordered Ted. "Every one of them better come back here right now!"

Hons heavily sighed. He wasn't dying tonight. He quickly called out.

The men came back.

"Gather in a circle," ordered Ted.

The men gathered.

"Kneel."

They did as he ordered.

"Shoeshon," said Ted.

Shoeshon and his bull friends circled around the men. Dewclaw walked up next to Ted.

"Who are you," a man asked.

Ted stood erect, chest out – shoulders up. "I am, Lord Barrington, Knight of the Redwood Forest" he replied, slowly looking over the group. His eyes then shifted on Shoeshon, his male bull friends and then at Dewclaw. "These are my friends. Together, we are going to save the Countess of Lyon Head."

Shoeshon stared at Ted. *Grandfather was right, Lord Barrington is the Promise.* He lifted his trunk over the stone men. His two bull friends did as well. Together they all trumpeted.

Witnessing this spectacle, men were beside themselves.

"But my Lord," one nervously spoke up. "The Countess of Lyon Head is dead."

"No, she is not dead. The evil Twins have placed a spell on her. She is well kept, but needs our help."

The men looked at one another.

"Is there any man here who would assist us in killing the witches?"

"You kill the Twins – what about us?" worried Hons.

"I believe with all my heart that when the Twins are gone, this place," replied Ted, waving his hand, "this place will return to its former glory, and you, you will all return to normal as well."

"I'll fight," shouted one, standing up.

The rest stared at him, looked at one another and then… they all stood up.

Ted gazed down at the leader of Nimrod.

He knew the man was beat.

"Tonight, I could have been ground to dust and you let me live," said Hons.

Ted nodded.

Hons slowly got to his feet. "We'll join you."

The men all cheered.

Dewclaw stood up and growled. The Elephants trumpeted.

As the men began resetting camp, rolling the wagon upright, Hons walked over to those who had died. Just their heads and portions of their legs and arms remained; crushed into dust by the elephants.

Ted walked over to him.

Hons turned and faced the Knight of the Redwood Forest. "They all had wives."

Ted thought of that. It made him think of his own son, Gabe. He mentioned it to Hons. Hons slowly nodded knowing he never took that into account; Lord Barrington having family of his own. "I pray you are right," he said. "We do not want to be stone people forever."

Ted prayed as well that his vision would come to be. The one thing he did not want to mention to Hons was *Zesbrew;* the real terror behind the Twins' power.

At day break, the party Hons ordered to go after Shana returned to the forest. They had laid low in Bissell for her to show up. She never entered the village.

When they came upon Hons, they were mystified; seeing the busted cage on the ground, the wagon being mended, Ted walking about and... and… three large elephants and a giant grizzly bear.

It took some explaining to what had happened, but each man returning swore an oath to Ted. They would fight alongside him.

Ted's only question to Hons was….

Shana.

Hons informed him that she had escaped with both horses and his sword.

Suddenly, without warning, an immense sound of birds was heard. All looked up to see a hawk flying overhead and then dozens upon dozens of Grassland Pipers. They landed in the trees around the camp.

If that wasn't enough to strike fear into the heart of each man standing there, deep within the forest the sound of thousands of bees heading their way.

The men scattered; believing they would be attacked. To their utter disbelief, they watched Ted lift his arms skyward. The bees swarmed around him; hundreds landing; as if they were his pets.

Hons and his men slowly walked back shaking with fear seeing this. Without an order, without a word, they knelt before the Knight of the Redwood Forest.

From within the swarm, Ted shouted, "Juliette, my darling… I'm coming, I will save you. I will save you my love."

"We are all coming," whispered Hons; now knowing the Knight of the Redwood Forest was madly in love with the Countess of Lyon Head.

25

Shana, wise and true, slipped past the village of Bissell unnoticed by the stone men. She was tired and feeling apprehensive without Ted. She may have been comfortable in her saddle, but within her heart sat an awful sadness knowing when Ted reached the castle of Black Water, he'd face a cruel death.

Frustrated with that thought she felt the weight of the Realm upon her shoulders. *What can a young girl do with a ferret and a sword against the Twins?* That thought crippled her strength believing she could take on *Zesbrew* and the Twins all on her own now.

She knew King William was getting ready to march and his navy preparing to sail. She also knew she'd reach the castle before that happened. With her thoughts dampening her spirits, she thought of the hound's keeper, Bulmen. The last time she saw him, they spent the night prior to her leaving up in the hayloft. *What will he tell me when we secretly meet again? That the witches found out about William preparing for war? If so, what were they up to?*

Little did Shana know that her assumptions were right. Black Water was already a buzz of activity. Within the castle, the courtyard and on the outer walls, the witches' soldiers were on high alert for any invasion.

"Egmon," said Greta. "Yes, Madam."

"Bring me the Raven."

"As you wish."

Greta took it and stepped out onto the balcony. "Now, my little pet," she said, waving her hand over the bird. "Tell me what you see far and wide," she continued, opening the cage. The bird came out and stood on the rail. "Fly, fly and report back to me," she continued, lifting her arms skyward.

The Raven took flight, flapping its large wings out over the Drake.

Hagar and Egmon watched the bird until it flew high above heading west and out of sight.

"Now, we'll see for ourselves," cackled Greta, rubbing her hands.

"Are you sure you feel the enemy coming?" asked Egmon.

"Now, Egmon… are you questioning my abilities?"

"No Madam Greta."

"Then allow me to inform you that the boils in my stomach swell when trouble be near."

Egmon felt sick hearing that. "Yes, Madam Greta. Is there anything else you want of me?" he asked, feeling his own stomach lurch.

"No," she replied, thinking. "Oh, yes, there is," she continued. "Inform the hound's keeper to let the dogs out day and night."

"What about the men who are afraid of them?"

"Men afraid of 'em," she questioned, leaning over and raising one brow.

"Yes, Madam Greta."

"Why, Egmon, do we really need children wearing armor."

Egmon looked at her confused.

"Tell the captain of the guards, I want every soldier who is afraid of the hounds, locked up inside the dungeon."

"The dungeon?" he questioned, raising a brow as well.

"Yes, they will be their next meal." Egmon's eyes went wide.

"You tell him that also, you hear me," she shouted.

"I will, I will," he replied, running off. "Now Greta," spoke Hagar.

"Yes, sweet sister."

"Why do you always frighten the little man?"

"He scares so easy."

Hagar shook her head. "You're not really going to feed them to the hounds. We need every soldier we have."

"No, that would be stupid. But mind me now, you know it will work."

Hagar sat on the bed not at all amused with her sister's antics. In that moment her stomach tightened. The pain was instant. She fell to the floor.

"Hagar," screamed Greta, running to her. "What's wrong?"

"I don't know," she moaned.

"Has someone else entered the Realm?

Who is it, who is it," she begged.

"I don't know, last time it was Lord Barrington."

Greta's face went flush then back to green. "You're not saying," she gasped, thinking Lord Barrington was back. That was nonsense. She looked at her sister slumped over. She got a suspicion. "You've been eating those rats again, haven't you?"

"Just one," she again moaned.

"Oh you," hissed Greta, pinching her sister's cheek.

"Ouch," spat Hagar.

Greta let her go, stood up and headed for the door. "If my calculations are right, Lord Barrington is probably kneeling before King Bela of Grim by now. Captain Howler should be arriving back within the week," she continued, walking out.

Hagar sat up holding her stomach. She looked out the door watching Greta taking the circular stairs back to the Gable. "I hope it is the rat I ate this morning. If not," she paused, thinking. She did not like what came to mind; *What if... what if it wasn't the rat that made my stomach ache; that it was in fact Lord Barrington? How could that be?* she thought, drifting on what her sister had just said; Lord Barrington should already be kneeling before King Bela of Grim by now.

She got up, walked over to the caldron. Holding onto the rim she gazed down at her reflection in the still water. She decided right then that it was the rat she had eaten and swore she'd never eat another one.

It was late when Shana reached her village of Orbed. She was exhausted and wanted to sleep in a bed instead of the hard ground. Going to her mother's house was out of the question. Everyone in the village had to have known that she escaped from the Twins.

She also believed that the witches probably had placed a bounty on her head. If that were true, she knew there would be many who'd gladly turn her in for a few precious coins.

While lying low in the forest on the outskirts, she decided to steal away up in the stable loft for the night. With no moon in the sky, slipping in alone with Jasper would be easy; with the horses would be slightly harder.

When the last village light went out and all was still, she quietly escorted the horses through the forest until she came to the backside of the stable. Behind a grove of pines she tethered them off and walked up to the rear double doors. Placing her ear to them she listened; nothing, not a sound.

Jasper looked up at her within her hands. She smiled then set him down. "Shh…" she whispered, placing a finger to her lips. With that, she slowly opened one of the doors.

Inside was dark; not even the opening in the roof for the owls gave any light. Knowing the layout, she walked in and headed straight for the ladder. As she started up, someone hurried over and grabbed her shoulder.

She went to scream. The man cupped her mouth and tossed her on the floor with him on top. The foulness of his breath and smell of sweat, she knew he was a drifter.

With the little strength she had she fought for her life.

"Stop fighting and give it up," he grunted.

"I'll give you nothing," she spat through his fingers crushing her head into the floor.

Just then Jasper jumped on his back and bit the man's ear and neck. He screamed, letting her head go trying to grab the ferret.

It gave Shana a second to reach down and pull out her knife. She drove it into his side and twisted it.

"You little bitch," he cursed, reaching back to pull it out.

With one hand gone, Shana clawed at his eyes with her nails. He pulled her hair, while taking the knife out and placing it to her cheek.

Shana froze feeling the cold wet blade pressed against her skin.

"Lie still and let me have some fun. I swear when I'm done – I'll let you go," he said, trying to remove her pants.

Jasper quickly looked about. He spotted bundles of hay in the loft. He quickly climbed up and began pushing one this way and that trying to get it to fall on top of the man. A chain with a heavy weight was in the way. He grabbed it with his teeth and dragged it to the edge.

Looking down, the man was right below. Using his back legs he pushed the chain until the weight of it pulled the rest crashing down. The chain and weight smashed into the man's head, sending him reeling off Shana. He laid there bleeding, moaning in pain.

Shana quickly got up ready to fight. When she saw the man lying there half out of it, she spotted shovels and pitchforks on the wall. She walked over, grabbed a pitchfork and walked back to the man.

His eyes went wide seeing her lifting it upward over him.

"No, pleas…"

That was all he got out as she drove it down into his chest then pushed with all her might to sink it in deep. She watched his legs and arms twitch then go still. His head slowly rolled to the side; blood oozing from his mouth.

Gritting her teeth, she slowly pulled it out, walked over and hung it back on the wall. Seeing Jasper sitting there, she asked, "Are you alright?" She checked his fur, checked his head. He was OK.

"Now we have this mess to clean up," she said, letting him down. She opened an empty stall door, grabbed the man's leg and dragged him inside. After covering him with hay she strolled out and shut the door. With an exhausting sigh, she leaned against the door. "C' mon, let's get some sleep," she whispered, heading for the loft above.

In the morning, Shana and Jasper came down. She went over to a barrel and picked out several apples for the horses. With her dry bloody hands she placed one on the floor for Jasper and then took several more.

Outside, she looked down upon herself. A bath and a change of clothing would have to wait. She hurried for the horses and untied the lines. As she mounted with Jasper, she heard the stable hand yelling. "Damn, he found the guy already," she said, turning the horse and heading into the forest toward Black Water.

26

"Raven overhead," shouted Carson, pointing skyward.

Ted and Hons walked over seeing the bird.

"It's the Twins," said Hons.

"The Twins," questioned Ted.

"Yes, they use Ravens to spy on us."

As soon as he heard that, he called out to Major, "Kill that Raven!"

Major took flight, the Grassland Pipers followed.

The Raven tried to circle back. The Pipers caught up, swooping and diving at the bird in midair.

"Someone is coming," shouted one of Hons' men.

Ted looked back at the trail. A smile grew across his face seeing Alexus Arteria riding up on a majestic white horse; his black and red cape fluttering in the breeze. To his surprise so were Bree, Mylee and Nera; his hummingbird friends. They flew up, chirping away.

"Please one at time," said Ted to their excitement.

"We located Alexus and followed him," said Bree.

"I see that," he replied, watching Alexus dismount.

"You can talk to all the animals?" asked Hons; stunned.

"Yes," he said, patting his shoulder. The hummingbirds landed on him; their beaks raised high with delight.

"Who is that?" asked Hons, watching Alexus tethering his horse and walking over.

"He's the Hand of The King," he lied, hoping the title would serve Alexus well.

"Look, the Pipers have the Raven," someone shouted.

Ted looked up. The Pipers were bringing it to the ground. He watched them pluck out its eyes and tear off its feathers.

The bees came next; swarming the Raven.

"Lord Barrington," greeted Alexus.

Ted turned around. They laughed, shook hands and then hugged one another as like brothers. After letting go, Ted introduced Hons and his men to Alexus.

"I'm a bit confused," said Alexus, looking about the stone men and then seeing Shoeshon, his bull companions and Dewclaw; the giant grizzly bear.

"We are now one force," said Hons, wrapping his arm around Ted. "The Knight of the Redwood Forest and me, along with my men will take on the Twins together."

Alexus stood back eyeing Ted. *The Knight of the Redwood Forest*, he thought. *What a splendid title.*

"I'll explain later," said Ted to his expression. "Come, let us talk," he continued, heading toward the main tent.

Hons and Carson followed.

Inside, they gathered around the table where Hons had laid out a map.

"Before we start," said Ted, "what is happening back at the Northern Kingdom?"

"For starters, King Fredrick of the Southern Kingdom has given ten of his best soldiers to assist us. They will be going aboard the Jarrett to help in killing the crocodiles."

"Crocodiles?" questioned Hons. "The water beast," said Ted.

"So that's what they call them," spoke Carson.

"Yes," replied Ted.

"How are they going to kill 'em?" questioned Hons.

"Crossbow, an arrow right between the eyes," replied Ted. "That is their weak spot."

The two nodded.

"What else?" asked Ted.

"The Jarrett and La Bell are loading up as we speak. Once they set sail, King William will march his army across the rock bridge. What plans have you made?"

"I am going to find Shana," replied Ted. "Hons and his men along with my friends will wait deep within the forest. They will hole up until William arrives. Now that you are here, you can bring these forces together."

"What about Shoeshon and his comrades?"

"I want nothing to happen to them, but they will become useful once the main entrance is opened."

"And the Pipers?"

"They will cause havoc from the sky. I'm taking the Zenith Bees with me inside the castle."

Alexus nodded. "I was thinking that both you and I along with Shana could breach the walls before all this happens. You know who I am after."

"Greta and Hagar?" asked Hons.

Alexus looked at Ted. He could tell Lord Barrington hadn't mentioned *Zesbrew*. It was probably better he hadn't. Hons might turn and run knowing what they were facing. "Yes, they will be hard to defeat."

"You two go," said Hons. "Leave it to us to gather within striking distance of Black Water. My men and I will form ranks with King William's army when they arrive."

Alexus nodded.

"I best speak to my friends," said Ted, walking out. After confiding with Shoeshon, Dewclaw and Major, he gathered his gear to ride out with Alexus.

If Ted and Alexus were going to catch up to Shana, they better hurry. After leaving Orbed, she made good time through the forest. Her only fear was Silver Eye. She knew the matriarch would be out there somewhere waiting with her pack.

Two days out from Black Water, on a cold windy night, Shana saw Jasper lift his head sniffing the air. She glanced back at the horses. Both had their ears forward; listening.

She quickly tossed more wood on the fire then stood there holding Ted's sword. Something was coming, but it wasn't the sound of hyenas. It was a covered wagon being pulled by two horses. An old woman was sitting up on the bench. It was Tess!

Shana lowered the sword as Tess rode up. "You," she said, amazed seeing her.

"I," replied Tess, pulling the break. "I had a suspicion you'd be out here."

"How?" she questioned, helping her down.

"Let an old woman sit by the fire, please."

As they walked over, Tess continued, "The Realm is a magical place filled with many mysteries. I had a feeling you'd be out here in the forest."

"Magical place," she repeated. "Before you get into that, how did I end up lying on the ground outside my village after speaking to you in your hut?"

Tess sat down. "You have something to drink?" she asked, side stepping her question.

"Yes," she replied, getting her deer hide canteen.

Tess took a big sip and handed it back. "I no longer have that hut. The rain brought the side of the hill down. Lost everything except my chickens and goat," she said, nodding toward the wagon.

"I'm sorry for your loss. Now tell me what happened."

"Happened?"

"Yes, how did I end up outside my village of Orbed, after speaking to you?" "I'd say you walked there." Shana wrinkled her brow.

"Do you think a frail ol' woman like me could carry you?"

"No, I suppose not. All I remember was… you gave me something to drink and then…" she said, staring at her.

Tess smiled.

Shana saw the gleam in her eyes. "Who are you?"

"Let's say, I am like the wind. Something you cannot see but only feel."

"But I do see you. You're sitting right there."

"Yes, my child. You do see me but many cannot."

"Really? Are you a spirit," she asked, reaching out and touching her.

"Oh don't be silly, child," she replied, looking down at Ted's sword. "That," she said, pointing at it.

"Yes, what about it."

"The marking on the blade is Tykakian; a people long ago when Dragon's ruled the sky. Formidable things they were. Where did you get it?"

"It's Lord Barrington's sword. I' don't know where he got it from."

"I see."

"What happened to the Tykakian people?" asked Shana.

Tess gazed into the young girl's eyes. "It was a time like this when good and evil clashed."

Shana nodded.

"During the time of the dragons, they belonged to an evil king named Athenian Boar; another word for pig. His kingdom sat within the 10th Sea; the Sea of Hasbro. He wanted to rule all the twelve seas."

Shana raised her brow to Tess's description of the king's name.

"Athenian was the most evil of kings. He is the one who stole the dragon's eggs and raised them as pets. Once he had them, he built giant crossbows with five-foot arrows. They were pulled by horses. It took several men to set the arrows. That is how they killed the dragons, leaving him with the only ones in the sky; the ones he hatched from those eggs."

"I see, and I guess he used them to go after the Tykakians."

"Yes, not many survived."

"Is *Zesbrew* from that time?"

"*Zesbrew* is the remanence of those times. He is the one who brought forth the evil from King Athenian's heart."

Shana sat drifting on that revelation. "Tell me," she said. "You mentioned that the Realm is a magical place filled with many mysteries."

"Mysteries I am telling you now." "You mean the past?"

"Yes, to defeat the Twins and *Zesbrew* you must know the past."

Shana sighed hearing that. "*Zesbrew* is the darkness," she whispered to herself; staring into the fire.

"That he is," agreed Tess, "and Lord Barrington is the light."

Shana looked at her.

"No one can be enticed if they do not want to be. You see, lust and greed sits in every man's heart. Some know how to control the evils within themselves. Some don't. *Zesbrew* seeks those that don't. He entices them with flattery to bring forth the evil within their soul."

Shana thought of that. She knew Lord Barrington and Alexus were not enticed by *Zesbrew*. If they had been, they would be kneeling before King Bela of Grim right now.

While thinking of that, something washed over her. It was Hagar; the weaker of the two witches. The years she had spent as their servant she knew deep down that Hagar hated *Zesbrew*. She never heard Hagar say it outright, but she heard it in her voice.

"Something on your mind, dear child?" "Yes, Hagar."

"Hagar is of two minds. They are constantly fighting one another," said Tess. "What do you mean by that?"

"As I said, there is good and evil in every person. Those emotions within Hagar clash with one another. I'm afraid that the evil within her heart prevails due to her sister Greta."

"Do you think if I got Hagar alone and spoke to her on giving up being a witch that she'd forgo her wicked ways and turn on *Zesbrew*?"

"She might," replied Tess, "but, be awful careful if you do try and confront her alone. Her sister Greta is the greater evil. If she discovers you, you'll not see the light of day."

Shana knew all about that. She had seen many tortured and killed by Greta. With a brave face she simply nodded.

"Right now my dear child, it is time for you to sleep… tomorrow is another day," said Tess, waving her hand over Shana. Before she could say a word, she slumped over and fell fast asleep within Tess's arms.

The morning sunlight warmed Shana's face. She awoke looking up into the lush green canopy seeing the break of day. In that still moment while lying there, she couldn't remember falling asleep or even going to bed.

She sat up, rubbed her eyes and looked about. A light smoke was drifting upward from the fire pit. Jasper was sound asleep near her saddle. Then it dawned on her; where is Tess.

Getting to her feet, she searched the trail for wagon tracks. They were there but then… they simply disappeared further down.

She comes and goes as like the wind, she thought, picking up her canteen. Standing in that beautiful morning sunlight, she wondered if Tess was a remanence of the past herself. Without another thought, she headed over to wake up Jasper. When he opened his eyes, Lord Barrington came to mind. "You and I have a mission, my friend. First we must slip inside the castle walls and then," she said, rubbing his furry little head, "we save Lord Barrington when that fool Hons shows up with him inside that filthy cage."

Heading to the horses, she could only pray that they would in fact save Lord Barrington.

27

"Alright, let's get the last of the provisions aboard and stowed away," Captain Burlap shouted to his crew.

"You're all set," said William beside his trusted friend; one of the finest captains that sailed the twelve seas.

"Yes, your Grace. My first mate, Henry Banisher and I, along with King Fredrick's soldiers should reach the eastern side of the ancient volcano in four days."

"Good luck, Captain. I hope to meet up with you after you dispatch the crocodiles and sail into the Drake alongside the La Bell."

Burlap saluted his king and charged up the gangway. "Mr. Banisher, haul up the anchor."

"Aye, Captain."

"Mr. Gannon, lower the jib, half the main."

"Aye, aye, Captain.

"This is a fine day to be setting to sea, Captain Burlap," said Torres – Captain of the fortress guards and the best archer King William had. His job was to kill the crocodiles.

"That it is. That it is. Once we sail out of the harbor, I'll be holding our first meeting in the Officer's dining mess."

Torres nodded. "I'll leave it to you, Sir."

As the Jarrett transited through the harbor, the crew onboard stayed clear of King Fredrick's soldiers. They were viewed with contempt; not pleased with the order from their king to fight alongside them. Their own captain, Captain Burlap reissued that order before the soldiers embarked. It was apparent that the crew had to forgo their grudge against these men now sitting about the main deck; with no job to do but wait until they reached the shores of the ancient volcano.

Three nautical miles outside the harbor, Captain Burlap struck below to the Officer's mess. Mr. Banisher, Mr. Gannon, Captain Torres and the leader of King Fredrick's soldiers, Captain Reinstead followed.

Torres knew what was coming. He had sailed with Burlap before. After the door closed, the men sat down.

"Gentlemen," said Burlap. "There is only one captain aboard this ship and that is I. Your rank onshore is where it belongs, onshore. Once we breach the waters of the western sea and send our boats to the volcanic island, Captain Torres will be in charge of those going ashore with him. Is that understood?"

The men looked at one another. They all nodded, but within the eyes of Reinstead sat distain.

"Captain Reinstead," said Burlap, "that order was agreed upon by both kings."

"I know that. I will follow those orders but understand one thing."

"What is that?"

"I'm still in charge of my men."

"That you are, Captain… and I'll hold you to that while onboard my ship. That is all, gentlemen."

The men got up.

"Captain Reinstead," said Burlap.

He turned at the door.

"Stay."

Reinstead sat down.

"Wine?"

"Sure."

Burlap poured two glasses and handed him one. "Captain Torres is the captain of the king's walls. He too must swallow his pride in this endeavor to finally rid ourselves of the evil that resides in the Forbidden Land. So let's not forget our main objective – killing the Twins. That is why we are here."

Reinstead pondered that. It was true; they all wanted the witches dead.

"Captain Torres is one of our finest archers. His only job, as you know is to be lowered down by rope to kill those beasts. You and your men will be in charge of seeing that through. That is something you can take back to the Southern Kingdom with pride."

"Truly, as you say, Sir."

"And let's not forget. Once they're killed, you and your men will then sail into the Drake onboard the Jarrett. There, you'll be lowered into our lifeboats to go ashore near the castle. Remember what I said…. your distinguished rank as Captain starts there. That will be the time you take charge of your men; for no one will be giving you orders inside those walls."

"Truly impressive, Captain."

Burlap stared at him.

Reinstead stood up. "I bid you a good day, Sir."

When the door closed, Burlap sat back rubbing his chin. *And I hope for many good days ahead.* With that, he stood up and walked over to his bay window. Over the fast rolling seas, he thought of Alexus. Word got out that he was heading into the Forbidden Land to catch up with Lord Barrington. It was something he'd never wish upon any man; facing the witches of Black Water. *By the Gods, I pray this all comes to an end and victory lies at our feet.*

28

Back at Black Water, Greta was leaning out over the tower balcony truly beside herself. "Now where do you think that Raven went?"

"Maybe it got lost," replied Egmon.

"That could be the reason," agreed Hagar.

"Who needs enemies when I got you two you lamebrains," spewed Greta, over her shoulder.

"Now, Greta," scolded Hagar. "We're just trying to help?"

Greta slowly turned and faced them. Her expression was of displeasure. "You wanna know where it went?"

Wide eyed, they waited.

"It was shot down, that's where."

"Now who would go and do a thing like that?" spat Hagar.

Greta sighed. *These two,* she thought. *They cause me more warts and boils than them bees giving me those irritating lumps.*

"Let's look into the crystal ball," said Egmon.

Greta dropped her thoughts. "Why my little man," she replied, walking over to him.

Fearful, he took two steps back.

She leaned down and squeezed his cheek. "I should make you captain of the guards," she said, letting him go.

"Really?" he beamed, rubbing his cheeks. "No, but let's have a look, shall we," she replied, hurrying over to the circular object. "From the tower of Black Water, to the sky above," said Greta, rubbing the glass, "show me our Raven."

As the ball began to glow and turn a light blue, they all stood back. Clouds appeared, and then mountains were seen as the vision flew eastward. It stopped over a field then slowly descended. There on the ground was their Raven or, what was left of it; bird feathers scattered about; one wing torn off and the eyes of the bird plucked out.

Horrified, Hagar clasped her hands to her face.

Egmon's mouth dropped open.

Greta stood there, steam pouring out both ears. "Why," she hissed, "our Raven was not shot down, it was torn apart."

"By what?" moaned Hagar.

"Only one thing could have done that, Grassland Pipers," she spat, glaring at the ball. "Pipers," repeated Egmon. "What would they be doing this far west?"

Greta pondered his assumption. "That is the plains just outside Bissell; which is further west than the Valley of the Damned where we turned the king's soldiers into stone?" she said, thinking. "Something tells me the North may be on the move," she murmured, walking to and fro.

Just then, Hagar's stomach went into knots. She began rubbing it while heading for a chair.

"What be with you, sweet sister," she asked. "Was it what I said?"

"I'm not sure," moaned Hagar.

"Hagar," yelled Greta. "The last time you felt this way…" she said then stopped.

"I know, I know."

"Well… answer me. Is the North on the march?"

"I don't know."

"Then what is it?"

Hagar looked up at her.

"Your eyes deceive you, sweet sister," scolded Greta. "You've been eating those rats again."

Hagar lowered her eyes to the floor. Greta sighed then turned and faced Egmon. "I want you to go to Bissell and investigate my suspicions."

"Suspicions?"

"Yes, you fool; find out from the people if William's men have been there and… enquire about the Pipers. Take five soldiers with you."

"Yes, Madam Greta."

As he proceeded to the stairwell, Greta eyed her sister. "Well," she spat, placing her hands on her hips.

From Greta's stance and her awful expression, Hagar knew she'd have to confess. "Well," repeated Greta.

"I only ate one, that's all." "One?"

"Yes."

"Disgusting."

Hagar displeasingly nodded.

"Is that why your poor stomach feels ill?" "I think so."

Greta stormed over to her. "You think so!?" she blasted.

"What else could it be? It can't be Lord Barrington again."

"No, you're right, sweet sister. Lord Barrington is working the mines for King Bela," replied Greta. "I haven't a clue however, why Captain Howler hasn't returned by now."

"I'm surprised he hasn't," said Hagar. "Go get some sleep," she grumbled.

"I think I will."

Down the flight of stairs went Egmon; through the castle and into the Gable where the sister's thrones sat. He stopped in front of the horrid things; cast from molten iron, sculptured to appear as vultures; wings spread out around the armrests, the seats carved into the belly of the bird, and the head and beak protruding above them when they sat.

"Egmon," said Lord Beetle, the Castle Administrator.

He quickly spun around seeing him.

"Oh, Lord Beetle, you startled me."

"What has you transfixed on the thrones?" he replied, walking up.

"Nothing, nothing, I was just…"

Beetle smiled. "Beautiful aren't they?"

"Why yes," he nervously chimed. "I must be going now. I need to speak with the captain of the guards."

"Your reason?"

"Greta wants me to go to Bissell. She thinks King William is preparing for war."

Beetle raised a brow to her assumption that William was on the march.

"Our Raven is dead," said Egmon to his expression. "I must go and find out how it died," he continued, hurrying toward the entrance.

Lord Beetle stood there watching him leave. *War,* he thought. *Unlikely,* he figured. After dismissing Greta's worry, he turned and looked at the thrones.

They were the center piece within the Gable; along with its black marble flooring, the red velvet runner up the middle, and the high wooden stanchions reaching to the ceiling. Carved into each of the eight, fifty-foot structures were idols depicting figures of half man — half beast.

With no one around, he walked up the steps and sat on one of the thrones. In his relaxed state, leg resting over an arm; he imagined ruling Black Water. His imagination went even further; wishing he had the Twins' power as well. "Power to seize whatever I wanted," he whispered, thinking of all the fine maidens throughout the Forbidden Land.

"Lord Beetle," chimed Greta, coming into the Gable from the tower stairwell.

Beetle froze hearing her voice. He quickly got down.

"Are you enjoying yourself; pretending to be me?"

His knees quickly hit the floor. "Why no, Madam Greta, I was just…."

"Relaxing on my throne?" she interrupted, looking down at him; his eyes glued to the floor. She smiled seeing him quivering like a child. It made her feel good knowing that all her subjects feared her, and they should. She made it quite clear that he better, too. "You know what happened to the last person I caught sitting on one of our thrones."

"Yes, Madam Greta. They were boiled alive."

"They were *slowly* boiled alive," she repeated, strolling past him.

"Yes, Madam Greta," he said, suddenly feeling warm.

She turned and faced him. "Rise, Lord Beetle."

He stood and faced her.

"Look into my eyes," she said, leaning toward him.

He watched her pupils turn yellow in the center. "Could you just imagine being escorted to the outer courtyard and placed inside the caldron?" she continued as if studying him.

"No, Madam Greta," he nervously replied.

"Neither could I," she confessed, walking toward the staircase leading up to her bedroom. "Goodnight, Lord Beetle."

"Goodnight, Madam Greta."

When she was gone, he sighed with relief. "I'll never sit on that throne again," he whispered through his quivering lips.

Outside, Egmon was looking for Captain Storm.

"He's up there," a soldier said, pointing.

Egmon looked up. Their trusted Captain was on the walkway looking out over the castle.

He hurried up the steps. When he reached the walkway, Storm turned seeing him. "Egmon," he beamed, smiling. He loved the little man now wearing his shiny black cape. "Where are your servants?"

"They're in the dungeon, that's where I keep 'em."

Storm laughed. "What can I do for you?"

Before he answered, he took in the captain's dazzling uniform. He was a very tall man, with an impressive outfit made of black leather adorned with a gold breast plate, and a white wolf pelt draped over one shoulder. His black boots rode up just below his kneecaps; his black pants snug tight with a shiny gold buckle. Ingrained into his breast plate was the symbol of a vulture's head.

"Our Raven was killed just outside of Bissell. I need five soldiers to come with me to speak to the village and see if they had seen any Grassland Pipers and… if any of King William's men have been there."

"You suspect it was Pipers?"

"Yes, our Raven was torn apart."

Storm turned and gazed out over the wall; allowing his eyes to study the Dead Forest and then the sky above. None of his soldiers had reported anything unusual or had the Twins' spies within the villages. To him something was amiss. *Grassland Pipers this far west?* he thought, turning and facing Egmon.

The little man could see Strom deep in thought. "You think we have trouble coming, Captain?"

"Yes, I will speak with Madam Greta. Go see Dorn. He'll assign you five men."

"Thank you, Captain. I'll get word back as soon as I can."

"Do that."

As Egmon gathered the five assigned and was getting ready to leave, two hundred yards away within the forest, Shana dismounted. From her position she could see the torches perched on the castle walls. She glanced up into the canopy. *It's just my luck … no moon tonight,* she thought, grabbing her canteen and settling in next to a large tree trunk.

Several minutes later, she heard guards shouting. Slightly getting up, she spotted Egmon and five soldiers leaving the castle. As she watched Egmon riding away; his cape flying in the breeze, she felt sorry for him. *He has been abused as much as I living inside those awful walls.*

That thought made her think of Greta and Hagar. Her real objective was Hager – she was the weaker of the two. If she could get Hagar alone and speak with her, she just might convince her to give up the life as a witch. She knew it was a risk; one she'd gladly take.

She waited until the forest went pitch- black before slipping through the trees and coming out on the side of the castle near the Isle of Drake.

The air felt moist; chilly near the water's edge. She caressed Jasper within her coat while casting her eyes out along the large rocky embankment. *Keep moving,* she thought, nervously continuing onward. *The tunnel is up here somewhere.* As she felt her way in the dark, her hand came upon the bricks slightly sticking out. Kneeling, she set Jasper down.

Heart pounding and frightened, she glanced at the front of the castle; the torch light bathing the area out front. With a heavy sigh, she quickly began removing the bricks. When the opening was big enough for her to enter, she stood and wiped the sweat from her brow. Out of nowhere, two men rushed up and grabbed her from behind; one covering her mouth.

Terrified, she fought with all her strength. In the struggle, they spun her around. Her fate was sealed, her death was near; her body instantly went limp.

"Shh… it's us, Shana."

Hearing Ted's voice, her knees went weak to the point of melting. Collapsing in his arms, she could have stayed there forever while thanking the heavens it was he and Alexus.

"I'm lost for words," she gasped. "I thought you two were the Twins' soldiers," she continued, stepping away from Ted. "How did you escape from Hons?"

"I had friends come and rescue me," he replied, opening his jacket. Shana could not see what they were, but from the soft buzzing sound she knew what is was; Zenith Bees.

"Thank the Gods," she gasped. "Where is Hons? I hope he's dead."

"It would have been foolish to kill Hons. Instead, I turned him and his men. They are now on our side."

"Really," she replied, looking at Alexus; now knowing he was the Shadow. It was like standing next to Royalty or more so a legend. It gave her strength having not only him there but also Lord Barrington, whom she thought was going to die a wicked death.

"You ride fast, Shana. We discovered your tracks outside of Orbed. Followed them here," he said. "We were waiting for you to set off toward the castle before we left our position."

"No kidding?" she questioned, looking from one to the other. "You got that close without me seeing you."

"Yes, now let's get inside before someone does see us," replied Alexus.

"Do you smell that?" she asked. "Yes, it's awful," replied Ted.

"It gets much worse inside," she warned, handing Ted his sword.

He gripped it feeling its weight then placed it in his sheath.

"Let's get this over with," said Alexus, kneeling and removing more bricks.

Jasper stood up on Ted's leg. He picked him up and rubbed his head. "I missed you," he whispered.

"I missed you, too."

Shana shook her head. How he had the power to communicate with the animals was beyond her reasoning.

Once the small opening to the tunnel was fully exposed the foul air came rushing out. The two men shirked from the stench.

"I told you," said Shana, getting down and entering.

The two looked at one another then hesitantly followed her in.

When they were inside, Shana whispered, "The dungeon is forty or so feet down on the right. The way I used to escape is up here a bit. I dug it out months ago. We can stand there and talk, and then we need to get inside the dungeon so we can let Jasper go down inside the channel."

"OK, but let's make it quick, the stench is overwhelming," replied Ted.

"Hold onto me and don't let go," she warned.

As Shana moved out, the pungent smell was even worse; like walking through a sewer. The sound of trickling water was all they could hear.

At the end, they could see a bit of light seeping through the brickwork on the right hand side. "That's the dungeon. We can talk over here," she whispered.

Shana told them of her time getting there. The man who tried to rape her was not easy to hear. Ted and Alexus were glad she escaped that fate.

Ted then explained how he got Hons to come in with them.

"I would have paid to see that," she said. "Anything else?"

"Yes, the Jarrett and La Bell have set sail. King William's army should be on the march into the Forbidden Land," said Alexus.

Shana sighed knowing William was on his way. "Now that the three of us are here, what is *our* plan?"

"After Jasper is inside the channel, you two stay together," said Alexus. I'll make my way to the catacomb below the castle and wait there until Jasper shows up before barricading the metal door holding *Zesbrew*. Please convey that to him."

After Ted told Jasper, Jasper looked up at Alexus.

"OK, right now we need to get inside the dungeon. We'll have to kill the guards."

"No problem," said Alexus.

"I'd suspect there will be prisoners in there also – maybe even Mani, Fons, and Drew," said Shana.

Alexus knew all three. He also knew they were great warriors. "Let's hope they are," he replied. "We could use 'em."

"Alright, let's go, but keep quiet," said Shana.

They walked down to the end and knelt near the dim light. Shana slowly pulled a brick out far enough to see inside. From the light of the dungeon torches, she observed two guards down at the end sitting by a table. There were ten men behind bars. To her luck, so were Mani, Drew, and Fons. She conveyed that to Ted and Alexus; who in turned leaned forward to take a look.

The layout was a straight passageway with five prison cells on each side. After the last cell there was a huge column attached to one wall. At the other end, they could see a stairwell leading up. The guard's table sat in front of the steps. Two guards were talking while rolling dice. The darkest point was where they were entering.

Alexus pulled the two together and whispered. "I'll take them both out."

Shana patted his arm then began removing the bricks.

As she did, Mani opened his eyes lying in his bunk. The slight scraping sound was not rats. He slowly sat up listening. To his utter relief he saw the bricks being slowly removed.

Who was it? He did not care, for whomever it was, they were sneaking into the castle. Only one kind of person sneaks into a castle – saviors.

He picked up a pebble and tossed it across to where Drew and Fons were being held. They looked at him. He touched his ear and then pointed toward the wall. Smiles appeared on each of their faces.

Alexus slowly crawled through the hole and knelt there looking at the men. He placed a finger to his lips then quietly stood up. Gathering himself tight to the wall, he inched his way down the cells. When he was ten feet away from the guards he coughed.

The two jerked back in their chairs. When they saw Alexus, they stood; drawing their swords.

"What are your names?" he asked.

"Names," grunted one. "We'll need yours to carve on your grave."

"Before you do give us your name, how did you get in here?" asked the other.

"I just appeared, now – what are your names?"

"Torrance," one said, charging at him.

Alexus quickly reached back over his shoulder drawing two knives. He threw both. One drove into Torrance's forehead, dropping him like a fly. The other sunk deep into the chest of the other. He grabbed the handle, looked at Alexus then fell over dead.

While Alexus pulled the bloody knives out, Shana and Ted entered the dungeon.

Alexus tossed the keys to Ted. The men being held cheered. "Quiet," whispered Shana.

Mani, Drew, and Fons stepped out and hugged Shana; so did the rest.

"Alright, you guys," said Alexus. "Go through the hole and out the tunnel. Make your way into the forest and hide. Once this is over, go home to your wives and children."

That is all they wanted; just to go home to their families. They clamored to be the first through the hole to escape.

Egmon's servants stayed to hear what Alexus had to say to them. It was simple, it was quick. "You want your revenge?"

"Yes," they grunted in unison.

"Two of you change into the guard's uniforms – take their weapons."

Drew and Fons hurried over, stripped the pair then dragged them into a cell.

"Where is the channel to set Jasper in?" he asked.

"Over here," replied Shana.

The men looked at the square hole near the floor.

"OK, tell me what he has to do," said Ted.

"Alright," she said, looking at Ted. "The water system is rather easy. Once he enters into this air vent, he'll go though it until he comes to the main water channel. He needs to drop down and run through the channel until he is on the other side of the castle where the water is going back out into the Drake.

"There is a large square block which is held open by two large ropes. He must chew through them so the block falls, closing off the water from leaving the castle. Once he does, he must run as fast as he can back to the air vent and take it down into the Catacomb before the water raises high enough to start entering the air vents.

"If I can remember, I think there are about ten air vents in the ceiling of the catacomb. It's the only way to breathe down there. Once the water enters the air vent system it will be a straight shot down to the catacomb.

"I'd keep that in mind Alexus, you won't have much time down there before it is completed flooded."

Alexus nodded.

"OK, let me explain it to Jasper," said Ted.

When Ted finished, Jasper looked up at Shana.

"You have the worst job," she said to his expression. "But it's the only way we can trap *Zesbrew.*"

Ted told him what she said.

"Don't worry; if it saves the Realm and breaks that evil spell over Juliette, I'll do it," he replied, darting inside the vent.

Ted stood up.

The expression on each of their faces said it all; *disgusting.*

As Jasper started his mission, Egmon entered the village of Bissell to investigate the Grassland Pipers and find out if King William's men had been there.

29

The ride to Bissell was hard fought through the dark of night. Egmon and his men halted at the stable and dismounted.

"Let's try the Inn," suggested Egmon.

The men walked over and opened the door. The place appeared deserted, not a soul in sight.

Egmon rang the bell.

A man stepped out in his nightgown. "May I help you?" he nervously asked, looking at the soldiers and then down at the ugly dwarf that worked directly for the Twins.

"I'm here to enquire if anyone in the village has seen Grassland Pipers in the area of late," said Egmon, pushing back his black shiny cape.

"Pipers?" questioned the owner.

"Yes. You know the big white birds? Also," he replied, "have any of King William's men been here?"

The man looked at Egmon thinking; *yes* they had been here along with the Pipers and stone men. They had come and surrounded the village and spoke to the people, who in turn wanted what they wanted, freedom from the witches of Black Water. *But I am not telling this little man that.*

"Have you lost your tongue," shouted Egmon. "Speak up!"

"Yes, yes, I've seen the Pipers."

Egmon glanced at the soldiers. A big one stepped up and leaned on the counter.

Fearful, the owner stepped back.

"How many?" he asked. "A dozen or so… why?"

"Are they still here?" asked Egmon.

"No, they seemed to have left. I haven't seen one in days."

Egmon rubbed his chin while staring at the man. "Have you seen any of King William's men?"

"King William?" he replied, raising his brow.

Egmon noticed the quiver in the man's voice. "Seize him!" he shouted.

"Wait, wait," the owner pleaded.

Two soldiers rounded the desk, grabbed the man then dragged him out in front of Egmon, pushing him to the ground.

Egmon pulled out his knife and introduced it to the man's throat. "Would you like your tongue cut out? Hagar would be pleased using it in one of her potions."

"No, please, I beg. I have a wife and children."

Before he could answer, a loud thunderous noise was heard.

The soldiers quickly spun around toward the door.

"What is that?" shouted Egmon, listening. His mind went numb when he heard the trumpeting sound of elephants. "Lord Barrington," he gasped.

"Lord Barrington?" a soldier questioned. "It can't be. He's in Grim serving King Bela."

Egmon looked at him then at the door fearing what was coming. To his horror, a massive grizzly bear came charging in; with it, a dozen stone men.

Wide-eyed and scared, Egmon bolted around the desk. He ran into a room and tossed himself out the back window. Lying there, he heard the soldiers screaming, being torn apart by the bear; others dying by the sword.

He quickly got up, tossed off his cape and made a mad-dash down the back of the building. Out front, he could hear the elephants and men shouting.

Looking this way and that, he spotted some hay bales next to a wagon. Cautiously, he slipped over and crawled underneath.

From under the hay and wagon he peered out into the night. The main street was full of people along with three large elephants. He froze when the bear came out dragging one of his soldiers. A stone man walked up and lopped off the man's head. The bear stood up and gave a mighty roar.

I've got to get out of here, he thought, glancing at their horses tethered near the stable corral.

"Where is that little man, Egmon?" he heard one shouting.

"He went out the back window," someone yelled.

"Find him! Don't let him get away!"

I'm doomed, thought Egmon. He slowly crawled over to the other side of the wagon and listened. People were running this way and that. He knew there was no way he'd get to his horse and ride off. *What am I going to do?* With that thought causing him panic, he looked into the forest near the stable. Then the stable came to mind. *The loft…*

Closing his eyes, he made a wish, a promise to himself if he got out of this alive. When he opened his eyes, he took in a deep breath and started crawling, crawling toward the forest and trees. Once at the edge, he rolled into the brush. From there, he slithered over to some dead fall and crawled underneath.

Shaking to death, he looked at the distance to the stable. He then checked the people all in the street. They had formed into a group. One was barking orders; while others were searching the village for him. *Now…* he thought, crawling along the ground to the rear of the stable.

Quietly… he opened one door. Inside, he sighed looking about. To his surprise there were several horses in pens. *The loft or… take one?* He decided right then to take one and escort it out on foot.

He quickly grabbed a harness, opened a stall and then got up on the rail and placed it over the horse's head. After getting down, he escorted it out of the stall and opened the back door.

The forest was so dark; he knew just one fool step would bring his demise. He cautiously escorted the horse into the woods. The farther he went; the shouting and yelling got fainter. It did not matter, he wasn't going to get on and ride. Not tonight. He walked until day break then rested.

In that time while traveling on foot, Egmon knew war was near, it was coming. The Twins may have thought it was coming and put the castle on alert but, that was all. They should have marched all the way to the Valley of the Damned.

With his little head spinning he thought of their spies. None of them had reported anything out of the ordinary. Heck, none of them had even been to Black Water in a while. *Maybe they're all dead!!*

Images began appearing in his mind's- eye of the Twins' spies being captured by King William's henchmen. Heart stricken while thinking of that, something else then floated inside his head, *Lord Barrington.*

I never asked the Inn Keeper if he had seen Lord Barrington. It sounded foolish when it came up. How could he have escaped from Howler's vessel, the Wicked? The thought was ridiculous and he dropped it right there.

As Egmon journeyed onward through the forest, thankful to be alive, he had no clue himself how close war was coming. At that time, King William's schooners, the Jarrett and La Bell were sailing to the ancient volcanic island.

30

"We are two nautical miles out from Dragon Bay, Captain," said Mr. Banisher; in charge of the Jarrett's helm and sails.

"Aye," he replied, gazing out over the water. He turned and faced him. "Before crossing the bay, douse all lanterns. From there, we'll set a new course west by northwest. I want plenty of water between us and the Isle of Drake before we make our turn south toward the ancient volcano."

"Aye, aye, Sir."

"Give word when we near the Drake," he said, taking the ladder to the main deck.

"Aye, Sir."

Crossing the deck, Captain Reinstead approached him. "Evening, Captain." "Evening, are your men ready?" "As ready as can be, Captain."

Burlap glanced down the portside rail at Reinstead's men sitting there in a row. "In an hour, I'd have them get up and stretch. They'll have a fit of a climb this evening," he replied, walking toward his cabin.

"Good advice, Sir," said Reinstead to the back of Burlap's head. He watched the Captain strut toward the ladder and go below. *The Captain has the temperament as like the sea.* It was a life not for him; too much water, too much time away. *That would harden any man's soul.*

As Dragon Bay came into view, first mate Banisher ordered darken-ship.

The lanterns went out.

Mr. Gannon walked up to him. "I think it best we place securing lines fore and aft. The seas will be getting rough as we change course and head for deeper waters."

"See to it," replied Banisher.

Captain Reinstead looked about at the men running to and fore, and those going aloft. *Not one word from the crew,* he thought. *They do their duties as like tying their shoes; each man knowing his job.*

He took a seat next to his men. They too were in awe watching the crew going about their task.

"Remember men," he said, getting their attention. "This is how a crew of a ship operates. It's called team work. They all know their roles and get busy doing them when orders are issued. This is how we'll strike forth from this ship and assist Captain Torres in killing the crocodiles."

The men nodded ready to do their part.

As the Jarrett headed for deeper waters, back at Black Water, Ted, Shana and Alexus were making plans as well.

Inside the dungeon Mani asked to go with Alexus to dispatch *Zesbrew.*

"You might need him," suggested Ted.

"I may at that," agreed Alexus, "now what about the other guards?"

"We'll have to take them out," replied Shana. "There are three two-man teams that watch the prisoners on a nightly basis down here. The ones that will be relieving these two are upstairs. I don't know how many are up there right now, though."

"I'll go up and do it," said Ted.

"By yourself?" questioned Mani.

"No," he replied, "with these," he continued, opening his jacket.

Mani, Fons and Drew stepped back seeing the bees; hundreds of them covering Ted's body.

"I am the Knight of the Redwood Forest; I command all things living within. I'm here for Juliette Tyrus. She is all that matters to me."

"The Countess of Lyon Head," questioned Drew. "We heard she was dead."

"Juliette is not dead. The Twins placed a spell on her. In order to break it they must be killed."

The expression on Ted's face and the tone in his voice, not one soul standing there saw Lord Barrington. They saw an angry Knight; one who'd kill a thousand men to rescue the Countess.

Alexus slowly nodded; it pleased him to hear such words.

"Hold these, Shana," said Ted, pulling out Bree, Nera and Mylee.

"Awe… they are so cute," she gushed, taking 'em.

"They may be cute but actually they're spies."

"Spies," she repeated, looking at him then down at the birds in her cupped hands.

"Are you sure you want us to stay?" asked Bree.

"Yes, the Zenith Bees will be all I need."

Mani, Drew and Fons, glanced at one another. They heard the hummingbird chirping and Ted answering.

Without another word, Ted headed for the stairs.

At the top, he stopped and listened. Guards were talking not far from him. Taking a deep breath, he took the remaining steps and walked out into the room.

The men turned seeing him.

"How did you get in here," one asked.

"I just appeared," replied Ted, thinking of what Alexus had said below. They drew their swords.

"That was a foolish mistake," he said with a smile.

"Foolish?" one belted. "We're going to cut you into little pieces and feed ya to the hounds."

"Come try," replied Ted, opening his jacket.

The guards panicked seeing the man covered in bees.

"Attack," he shouted, drawing his sword. The bees took flight; swarming mercilessly all over the four guards. As they tried to defend themselves, Ted walked up and drove his sword through one. The other three tried to escape. One fell; his face and arms covered in bees. Two made it to the door. Overwhelmed with hundreds of bees upon them, they fell until they were overcome themselves.

When it was through, Ted placed his sword inside its sheath then opened his coat. The bees circled then landed. Before walking down the stairs he looked at the dead men lying there; their faces unrecognizable from the poisonous stings.

In that moment, it was something he never thought he'd do; kill another person. It crippled him for a second.

"Lord Barrington."

He slowly turned seeing Alexus standing there. The flush expression on Ted's face was understandable. He too, felt sick killing someone for the first time. "Are you alright?"

"Yes, I think so. Let's go."

Back in the dungeon, Alexus ordered Drew and Fons to stay. "Kill anyone coming down. We can't afford someone to get the word out that we are here."

They nodded.

"Alright, let's get back to the tunnel," said Shana.

As the four entered the tunnel, the Jarrett along with the La Bell, were nearing their positions. The La Bell was to transit to the northern point and drift, while the Jarrett's crew sailed onward toward their destination.

As Captain Burlap prepared for the night ahead, there was a knock on his stateroom door.

"Come in."

It was a young seaman. "Mr. Banisher is about to make our turn and head toward the volcanic island, Captain."

"Aye, I'll be right up," he replied, strapping on his sword.

The young lad bolted out the door.

Burlap stood there watching him race up the ladder. He would have loved to be going with Captain Torres but knew that was out of the question. He walked out the door and made his way up to the main deck.

In the dark, without the ships lanterns, he proceeded to the helm. On his way, he told the crew to maintain silence about the deck.

The stillness crawled up each man's spine knowing they were in dangerous waters. The Twins' vessels, the Caldron and Dark Fin were out there somewhere.

"Evening, Captain," said Banisher. "Evening, what is our position?"

"We made our turn southward and should be in striking distance of the island within the hour, Sir."

"Thank you," he replied, glancing down the deck. He spotted Captain Torres and Captain Reinstead gathered with Reinstead's men. Burlap knew this was not going to be easy for them. The volcanic island was hard enough to just make it to shore, much less climbing to the top. He knew that feat would drain every man's strength. He could only pray they would have enough to kill the crocodiles and return to the ship soon after.

Gazing up at the stars, his mind set adrift. He quickly flashed back to when they first heard of such menacing things in the water.

It was when the beautiful schooner the Victoria disappeared. She was a fine vessel named after the queen. Little did King William know back then of the Twins having such protection guarding the Isle of Drake.

William's spies had discovered it much later; after the Victoria was sunk; crew dead – possibly eaten. William found it hard to believe when they told him what had happened, especially their learning of a halfwit dwarf by the name of Egmon somehow taming the creatures by feeding them. When the Twins happened upon Egmon and his pets, they in turn, offered him a lavish lifestyle at Black Water; if he would move his pets into the Drake.

Pets, thought Burlap.

"Something on your mind, Captain?" asked Banisher.

Burlap stared at him still in thought.

"No, just reminiscing on the Victoria."

"Tonight, Sir, we'll get our revenge for her sinking."

"That we will, that we will," he replied.

Thirty minutes later, the crow's nest lookout shouted down, "Island in sight."

"How far?" Burlap called up.

"Two nautical miles, maybe less."

"Alright, gentlemen, let's ready the lifeboats," ordered Burlap.

Captain Torres and Captain Reinstead took to the forward rail. Reinstead's men did as well.

"As soon as we come abreast, grab your gear gentlemen," said Reinstead.

Out over the water, all eyes were fixed on the dark shape coming into view; a barren land of molten rocks, massive boulders and high cliffs. It looked like a mammoth beast itself, jutting up from the sea.

"There she be," said Torres.

"The devil himself," remarked Reinstead. "I've seen it in daylight. There are many ravines running up between the boulders." "Big enough for us to go up through?" "Yes, but it will be a climb."

"Mr. Gannon, lower the main and take down the jib," ordered Burlap. "Aye, aye, Captain."

"Mr. Banisher, come right and let the current bring us in closer."

"Aye, Captain."

Burlap walked down the ladder and headed toward the bow; the lifeboat crew had the boats over the side on J-davits. He stepped up to Torres and Reinstead. "On this moonless night, you'll have to find a place to come ashore. That will be hard without torches."

The two nodded.

"I'll let the Jarrett drift south then circle back to the northern point and allow her to drift south again until you return."

They again nodded.

"Are you ready?"

"Yes, Captain," they said. "Let's go."

At the J-davits, the boat crew and deckhands waited for the order.

"We'll not be anchoring. Lower the boats but keep the davit lines taunt until the men are in. They'll cast away all lines when ready and head for shore."

"Aye, Captain."

"Lower the netting," said Burlap.

Once down, he looked at Reinstead and Torres. "Good luck, and may the Gods be with you."

They shook Burlaps hand and then Reinstead ordered his men over the side.

Once in the lifeboats, the lines were cast.

The boat crew pulled away from the ship.

The waves and current were hard fought; the crew straining over each and every wave. Once close to shore, Torres and Reinstead studied the shoreline.

"There," shouted Torres, pointing.

The crew heaved on the oars bringing the boat left.

"Take her in hard," said Torres.

"Brace yourself, men," one man yelled out.

The life boat rose up on the incoming wave then slipped past two large boulders into a small inlet. The boat drove up onto the dark gravelly sand. The men jumped and pulled her further out of the water. There, they waited for Reinstead's boat to come ashore.

With the two boats secured, the men grabbed their gear; swords, grappling hooks, torches dipped in grease, and the line Torres would use to repel down.

Torres secured his crossbow and the four iron tipped arrows, especially crafted for this one mission.

The climb was more than the men thought it would be. The rocks and hard lava was not easy getting a footing. From boulder to boulder they climbed over and through the small openings. Once at the cliff, a ten foot steep wall, two men tossed grappling hooks up and over. It took three tries to finally sink the hooks into something that would hold each man's weight.

At the top, men sat and waited until all were up. From there, they had more to climb. What gave them the strength to continue was seeing the peak, a circular opening fifty feet across.

Each man crawled up the last remaining part out of breath.

When Torres finally made it to the top and stood before the men, he whispered, "We'll take a break and gather our strength before I go down."

The men agreed and took a seat wherever they could.

They sat for nearly twenty minutes, not talking much. Every man just wanted to get this over with and get back to the ship.

Torres stood up, stretched his legs and arms and said, "OK, as quiet as mice, let's secure the rappelling line."

A large jagged rock sticking up was chosen. Secured tight, Torres slipped the line around his body, setting the knots to hold him firmly to the rope.

"Alright now, here is the plan," said Torres.

The men gathered around.

"If I tap the line once, stop the line. If I tap the line twice, let it go down."

They all nodded.

"Now, we have no idea what is down there. When I get far enough and see a ledge or something I can swing myself over and stand on, I'll shoot them from there. I may need a bit more line to accomplish that. I'll tug twice to have you lower me more then start my swing. If I make a ledge, I'll pull the line three times."

"OK."

"Torch," said Torres.

A man stepped up and handed it to him.

"Alright, take hold of the line," he said, gathering himself at the opening.

The men took hold and braced themselves.

Torres slowly went over the top and clung to the ledge. "I'm ready, he said, letting go.

The men strained from his weight being lowered.

Ten feet, twenty feet, then at thirty feet - Torres tapped the line once; stopping him in mid-air. He tucked the torch into his belt then pulled out his flint. Several sparks flew off. He struck it again; the thing lit.

Hanging there, he allowed his eyes to roam across the large cove. It was a maze of steep walls, jagged rocks, and water as black as coal below him. He reached out the torch to see all he could. When his eyes landed on the large flat rock and seeing what was sleeping there, crawled right up his spine. Shana's description did not even come close; they were the most terrifying things he had ever seen. Forty-feet long, weighing more than twenty men and a mouth full of razor sharp teeth.

He tapped the line twice.

The line took him further down. Reinstead watched the rope going, going, and then he felt one tap. The line halted.

Hanging in the center of the cove, Torres spotted a nice flat section on one side where he could get a foot-hold and shoot the crocodiles. He tugged on the line. As it free fell, he swung out then back, and then out then back; just inches from the ledge. One more try his foot took hold. He quickly tugged the line three times.

"He made it," said Reinstead, glancing back at his men.

They heavily sighed, allowing the line to relax in their hands.

Standing on the rock, Torres reached back, grabbed an arrow. With a steady aim, he lined up on the closest beast.

The crocodile's eyes opened.

He pulled the trigger.

The arrow left the crossbow in a flash. With immense speed, it flew through the air, spinning toward its target. The sound of it slamming into the monster's head was deafening.

Its head jerked back from the impact; the tip sunk deep between its eyes. The thing tossed this way and that, flipped over twice waking the other crocodile.

Hurry, hurry, Torres panicked, setting another arrow. The arrow missed its mark and slammed into the second crocodile's back; sending the reptile scurrying into the water.

He quickly tapped the line twice and swung out over the water. While swinging back and forth scanning the surface for the second one to come up, without warning and without realizing how far a crocodile could leap out of the water, the monstrous beast shot up right underneath him. Mouth open, it grabbed Torres at mid-section.

He never had time to scream. He was cut in half before the crocodile splashed back into the water and went under. What remained of Torres dropped from the line and floated at the surface. Seconds later, the croc's head appeared and took the rest.

At the top of the volcanic mountain, the line pulled all ten men toward the opening.

Two went over. Their terrorizing scream ended when they hit the water below.

Reinstead quickly started pulling the line. When the bitter end came out of the hole, he knew Torres was gone. They all stood there numb; not having a clue to what had happened down there.

Some took a guess.

"Maybe he fell in," one soldier said.

"Or, he is still down there on the ledge," another suggested.

Reinstead dangled the ripped line out in front of him. "Does that look like he fell or, is still down there?"

"What are we going to do," a soldier asked.

Reinstead looked at him then cast his eyes across the group. "We're going back."

"Don't you think we should at least take a look," another soldier suggested.

As Reinstead hesitated to answer, one got to his feet, picked up a torch and lit it.

"What are you doing," shouted Reinstead.

Without a word he walked over and lowered the torch in the opening. He could only see the top half of the cove. "Come," he said.

The group walked over and looked down into the darkness below.

The one with the torch let it go.

All eyes watched it free fall toward the water. As it did, the bottom half of the cove lit up.

"There, you see it," one shouted.

"Yes," replied Reinstead. "One is dead on the flat rocks, but where is the other one." "Maybe it sunk after he killed it."

Reinstead turned staring at the soldier.

"They are both dead," another soldier spoke up.

"Is that what we're going to tell Captain Burlap?" asked Reinstead. The men all stood there.

"OK," he said. "That is what we will report. We lost Torres, two of our men and both crocodiles are dead."

The men agreed with a nod.

"Let's get back to the ship."

On their return, Burlap was disheartened not seeing Captain Torres in the boat. He conveyed his worries. "Where is Torres?"

"He was taken by the crocodiles," said Reinstead, climbing the netting.

Burlap glanced at Banisher. He too looked ill hearing that.

They waited for all to get up on deck. "What do you mean," asked Burlap. "I lost two also," he replied.

Burlap shifted his attention on the men that went; they all appeared drained as well.

"Are they dead?" "Yes."

"You sure?"

Yes, we even tossed a torch down into the cove. Both were lying there dead," he lied.

"So how did they take Torres if they are both dead?" questioned Burlap, sensing Reinstead wasn't telling him the truth.

Before Reinstead could answer, the crow's nest shouted down, "Muzzle flash off the northern point."

The entire crew raced toward the bow. Captain Burlap glared out into the night.

Another flash was seen. "The La Bell is under attack. Haul up the boats; prepare to sail."

"Bos'n," shouted Mr. Gannon, "have some men go down and bring up the weapons."

"Aye, Mr. Gannon."

With the Jarrett in full sail, the crew at the ready, Burlap came up behind the Twins' warships advancing on the La Bell out in front of them.

Onboard the Twins' ship the Caldron, a crew member shouted, "Sail astern, Captain."

"I'll be. So that's where the Jarrett is," he said. "Helmsmen come right," he ordered. "We'll circle back and engage the Jarrett at her stern."

Onboard the Jarrett, Burlap watched the Caldron making her turn. "Helmsmen, hard left to port, we'll out run the Caldron trying to come about and overtake us and sail swiftly to engage the Dark Fin."

"Aye, Captain."

"With this course, Captain, you'll put the Caldron right behind us." said Banisher, worried. "She does have a formidable forward battery."

Burlap smugly grinned at him. "I see you doubt my abilities."

"No, Captain, he replied, "I…

Burlap did not wait for Banisher to finish his remark. He spun around to the crew. "Every man to the starboard side; hang off the rigging lines. We'll use this foul wind to sail up on the Dark Fin before the Caldron has a chance to advance our stern."

As the men raced across the deck, Banisher came abreast of Burlap. Burlap looked at him. Banisher smiled his approval then took off to find and place along the starboard side.

As the Jarrett came left, the wind hit her sails full force, lifting the starboard side up. Each man took hold of the rigging lines; some hanging way out over the ship.

Before the Dark Fin realized that His Majesties ship, the Jarrett had entered the fray; the Dark Fin's crew spotted her sails. The only thing they had going for them was her lower batteries were manned and ready. The order was given, *prepare for battle.*

As Jarrett came abreast of her, the two ships fired their cannons.

The Dark Fin's mid-section was hit; taking out two batteries below. Her main deck was torn apart; bodies lay everywhere.

The Jarrett lost an entire battery crew and a massive hole near her stern. Both ships were on fire. The blast from the cannons echoed across the sea; smoke blanketing the ships like fog, leaving only their top sails to be seen.

From the stern of the La Bell, a quarter mile out front of the two ships, Captain Stuart focused on the battle. He saw the Jarrett, her stern on fire, come hard right across the bow of the Dark Fin; her cannons once again striking their target. The Dark Fin's bow exploded, her jib came crashing down upon the deck; the sails hanging over the side.

"Mr. Peggly, have the helmsmen come right. We'll circle back and engage the Caldron," ordered Stuart.

"Aye, Captain."

As the La Bell made her turn to take on the Caldron coming up behind the Jarrett, the Caldron hesitantly made a turn herself; to safer waters. The Caldron's captain, Captain Fields, seeing the Dark Fin out of commission, he ordered his helmsmen to tuck-tail and run.

Onboard the La Bell, Captain Stuart stood there eyeing the Caldron's retreat. First Mate, Mr. Peggly came abreast of him. The two men looked at one another. "Are you thinking of following her, Sir?"

Stuart glanced back at his crew gathered along the rails watching the Caldron themselves. They were itching for a fight. "Yes, we'll follow them to the ends of the twelve seas if we have to."

"What about the Jarrett?" asked Peggly.

"We'll sail past her and see if she is in need of help. If not, we'll take the La bell into the wind."

"Aye, Captain.

As the La Bell sailed toward the Jarrett, she came alongside the Dark Fin, sitting dead in the water. Some of her remaining crew was staggering about the main deck. Captain Stuart ordered all four of the La Bell's cannons fired. After the massive explosion from her four cannons, the Dark Fin started taking on water. Those that survived jumped overboard, to drown instead of being burnt alive.

"Captain Burlap," shouted Stuart; his ship the La Bell coming alongside. He walked over and waved. "How's your ship, Sir?"

"We'll make repairs and sail on home, and you?"

"We'll continue sailing onward and make sure the Caldron never returns to these waters."

"See to it," Burlap shouted. "I'll report this battle to King William."

After the La Bell departed, and the Jarrett's crew put out the fires - Burlap yanked Captain Reinstead aside. "As Captain of this ship, I am like a king. You are aware of that?"

Reinstead stood back eyeing the captain.

"I'll ask you again and if you lie to me, I'll have you hung along with your men and there isn't a damn thing King Fredrick can do about it."

Reinstead waited to hear his question; a question he knew was coming.

"Did Torres kill both crocodiles?" Reinstead slowly shook his head *no*. Burlap, grabbed him by the collar. Reinstead's men walked over.

The crew of the Jarrett brandished their swords. They hated them, hated them even more now that Captain Torres was dead.

"Sit down," ordered the Bos'n.

The men took to the deck, surrounded by angry sailors.

Burlap let Reinstead go. "I'll be setting you and your men ashore near the Drake. You can walk home and or make your way to the battle at Black Water. I hope I never see you again, Captain Reinstead. It would be your last day on earth," he grunted, walking away.

Reinstead stood there still feeling Burlap's words or, more so, his threats. He walked through the sailors and took a seat alongside his men.

<h1 style="text-align:center">31</h1>

"Someone is coming," a guard shouted.

Captain Storm rushed over to the outer wall.

"Let me in, let me in," cried Egmon, riding hard toward the gate.

"Hurry, open it," ordered Storm.

Egmon rode in, dismounted and fell to the ground completely exhausted.

Soldiers rushed over shouting questions at him.

"They're coming, they're coming." "Who is coming?" they asked.

"Get out of my way!" ordered Storm.

The men stood aside.

Storm knelt beside Egmon; sucking in air as fast as he could.

"What is coming?"

"All of them, including the animals," he gasped between breaths.

Storm yanked Egmon up by his collar.

"Start making sense," he scolded.

Still panting, he glanced up at the men standing there. "We were over-taken in Bissell," he said, shaking his head. "A giant grizzly bear, elephants and the stone men," he continued, reliving the nightmare; the nightmare of the bear busting down the door at the Inn. In those thoughts, a faint memory washed over him. He remembered soiling his pants seeing it all. He kept that to himself.

"What are you talking about? Where would King William get a bear and elephants to do his bidding?"

"Should we sound the alarm," a soldier interrupted.

Storm looked up at him then down at Egmon. The fear in his eyes was evident enough that the dwarf was telling the truth. "Yes, sound the alarm. Every man to his position," he shouted.

Hearing the commotion, the hound's keeper, Bulmen stepped out of the holding pens. His ears heard every word. Within his mind he thought of Shana and their last night spent up in the loft together. *Where is she now?* He drifted on that, and then a smile appeared. *Is she here? Had she come back? If so… did she bring others?*

He quickly wiped his hands on his apron, turned and headed back inside the pens to wait for the right moment to slip away and find out.

Meanwhile, up in the castle, Hagar was sitting on the privy. In her relaxed state she felt something funny on her bottom. She got up to look. Rats started pouring out of the opening; then lots of water started gushing out. She screamed seeing the sight. As she hurried to leave, her stomach suddenly went into knots.

Greta heard the scream. She ran across their bedroom to a private hallway. Hagar was on the floor moaning. The next thing she saw caused her to stop dead in her tracks. Rats began scurrying out of the latrine along with water from the channel. *Jasper was on the move closing the gate.*

"Hagar," she shouted, racing toward her. She knelt, pushing the rats aside. "Get up," she scolded.

"I can't!"

"You can't?" she repeated, seeing the pain etched in her face. "What is it this time?"

Just then, Greta heard the castle alarm. Her eyes grew dark and menacing knowing something terrible was wrong.

"Lord Barrington," whispered Hagar, lying in a fetal position and holding her belly.

"Lord Barrington," spat Greta, getting up. "Lord Barrington," she angrily repeated. "The man is dead. We are under attack by King William's army. That is what has your stomach upset," she huffed, lifting her hands and quickly vanishing.

A swirling dust devil kicked up in the courtyard.

The soldiers stood back.

Greta appeared within the haze.

The soldier's all knelt, so did Captain Storm.

When the vicious hounds saw Greta, they ran toward her, barking and yelping. As they rubbed against her for attention, her eyes landed on Egmon lying there in the dirt. She stomped over to him.

He looked up at her.

She slowly placed her hands upon her hips.

She is in a fit of rage, thought Egmon.

"Get up!" she belted.

Egmon slowly got to his knees then to his feet.

She looked down at the pitiful sight; his clothes in tatters. "Where is your cape?" she shouted.

"Madam Greta," he said in a tone of sadness.

"I'm waiting."

"We were attacked in Bissell."

"By whom?" she asked, already knowing or, thought she did.

Captain Storm knew she would fly right off the handle once Egmon told her.

When he did, she went off like fireworks. "Bears, elephants and stone men," she angrily repeated.

"Just one bear," corrected Egmon. "It was…"

"You," she grunted, dismissing his foolishness. Then suddenly she stopped talking. *Our Raven,* she thought. *Grassland Pipers* then washed over her. She looked down at Egmon. It was all there within his expression; scared stiff.

"Did you see Lord Barrington?"

"No, we asked the Inn keeper. All he said was…"

Greta again waved her hand interrupting him. "Captain Storm," she barked. "Yes, Madam Greta."

"Are your men ready?" "Yes, they are."

"Good," she said, training her attention on Egmon.

He stood there nervous knowing she was going to have him do something.

"I want you to row across the Drake and wake up your pets, we'll need them tonight.

"Yes, Madam Greta," he sullenly replied. "Now, I must be off to gather my sister," she said, hurrying toward the steps.

By this time, Ted, Alexus, Shana and Mani had gone deeper inside the castle using the secret passageways. When they came to the stairwell leading down to the catacomb, Shana reminded them where to find the key to the gate.

The four stood there a moment looking at one another. It was time. It was time for revenge and to finally end this nightmare.

"Good luck," each said, hugging one another.

With a sigh, Shana turned and continued onward with Ted to the tower.

Alexus and Mani slowly descended the stairs below.

Greta ran down the corridor toward the Gable. Hearing an odd noise, she stopped in full-flight. "What was that?" she whispered, looking this way and that. She could not tell and carried on.

Bree, the hummingbird was flying then she quickly landed, hearing someone running toward them. Her two friends, Mylee and Nera were perched across from her on one of the stone vultures overhead. The three froze like statues themselves gazing down at Greta coming through the corridor.

This was their first time seeing the witch. She was awful looking; wearing all black, her dark green face, supporting a long crooked nose and pointed chin.

As Greta entered the Gable, her eyes locked onto someone, someone she thought was gone; escaped more like it. It was Shana.

She and Ted had made it that far and were heading up to the Tower. Ted was still in the side entrance.

"Why my pretty," spew Greta.

Hearing her voice, Shana's heart stopped. She quickly turned around. "Oh my word," she gasped. "Thank the Gods I'm back," she continued, walking casually toward her.

"Thank the God's" replied Greta, confused. "Last I heard you were on the Wicked bound for Grim with Captain Howler."

Trying desperately to look thrilled that she was back at Black Water; Shana started her long winded story. "Well, let me tell you. Before I was placed onboard that ship, *Zesbrew* came to the Northern Kingdom. I told him that I had been captured by spies while visiting with my mother in Orbed. When they brought me back, tied and bound to a horse no-less, they gave me to that wretched fool Lord Barrington as his..." she said then stopped speaking, thinking of a polite word.

"Whore," spat Greta.

"Well, yes. I guess you could say I was now his whore," she replied. "*Zesbrew* did not believe me and handed me over to Captain Howler as a trinket."

"Trinket," repeated Greta, eyeing the young thing.

"Yes, it was awful," she said, looking down at the floor as if she were reliving it all. "I waited until he had fallen asleep then I snuck up on deck and jumped overboard."

"Way out at sea," questioned Greta, smelling a rat.

"No, the ship hadn't gone that far. I was lucky to have found a plank of wood drifting and took hold of it. From there, I used it to get back to shore."

"Then what?" asked Greta, coming closer to her. "Tell me my sweet servant," she continued, placing her arm around Shana's shoulder.

Shana quivered having her so close. Greta's face was hard enough to look at from across a room; up close, with all those grieving lumps, made her stomach heave.

"It took me days and days to walk back.

When I finally got to Bissell, I stole a horse." "You stole a horse," she laughed Shana laughed, hiding her fear.

Greta suddenly stopped laughing. Her expression instantly changed; her eyes now glaring at Shana. "There are two kinds of people that crawl up my neck like leeches," she started.

Shana knew from the tone in her voice and stern expression, she was in serious trouble. "I know oh – so, well, Madam Greta."

"You do?" she oozed, lifting one brow. "And what kind of people gives me boils?"

"Ones that lie or steal from you?"

Greta took her arm from around Shana's shoulder and stood in front of her. "You have that right. And for some reason," she said, "I believe you are lying to me."

"Madam Greta, I…" she started to say, stepping backward.

"Do you remember Clara Brown, that pretty little thing?" she interrupted, stepping toward her.

"Yes."

"You know I could have been her forever?"

"No, I…"

"Well I could have," she angrily interrupted.

Shana fearfully again stepped back.

"You know why I never wanted to be her forever?"

"No."

"Well," said Greta, casually getting closer, "because I've always wanted to be you," she gleamed. "You are the essence of beauty, beauty I've always admired," she continued, grabbing the back of Shana's head and pushing her mouth over hers'.

Shana screamed, desperately trying to pull away.

"Let her go," a man's voice suddenly sounded.

Greta's eyes grew wide hearing the stranger. She quickly released Shana. With a wave of her hand, she sent the girl flying across the room.

Shana landed on her back and continued sliding until she slammed up against the steps to the thrones.

Greta quickly turned facing the man walking out from the corridor. She knew instantly who he was. "By the God's of darkness," she hissed, glaring at him.

"There is only but one God," replied Ted, drawing his sword.

She watched it begin to glow red hot.

"I have waited a long time to finally have you in my clutches, Lord Barrington," she grunted. "Before I kill you, tell me… How did you escape my beautiful ship, the *Wicked*?"

"She was overtaken by King William's navy," he replied, leaving the Shadow out.

"I see," she spat, "and Captain Howler?" "He and his crew were put to death."

Greta's face turned into an angry mess. "I have only one more thing to ask before putting you in a boiling hot caldron. Why did you enter the Realm? Was it to seek revenge for your poor cousin, Sheppard, who was a fool for trying to rescue Juliette all on his own," she said, already knowing his reasoning – to kill Hagar and her. She'd never give that away, for she was going to kill him.

With that, she kept up her rant. "That poor fool was discovered torn apart by," she continued, glancing back at the staircase leading up to her bedroom. "Rye my darling," she called.

Her pet hyena came out from the steps. "He was torn apart by a pack of these," she grunted. "Lovely aren't they?" she harped.

Ted glanced at the mangy thing coming across the marble floor toward Greta. It gathered next to her leg snarling at him.

"Speak up," ordered Greta, "or shall I have Rye attack Shana. That would make you squeal wanting to tell me everything."

Shana sat there scared out of her mind.

Do something Lord Barrington!

"You," said Ted. "You are the essence of pure evil. I am here to break the spell you've placed on Juliette."

"Oh, I see," laughed Greta. "Well… just like your cousin, you too are a fool. No one can break that spell," she replied, pointing her hand toward Shana.

Shana started to rise off the floor. "By just closing my fist, she'll feel as if she is being strangled," she said, turning her attention back on Ted. "Kneel before me and I'll let her live."

"I think you have it wrong. You kneel before me and I'll let you live," he grunted, gripping his sword. A flame appeared around the edge.

"Do you honestly think you can come against me with just a silly sword?"

"I come with more than a sword. I come with the immense power of the natural world," he boasted, opening his coat.

Her eyes locked on the horde of bees attached to him.

Bree, Mylee and Nera flew into the Gable.

Greta looked up seeing them darting this way and that. She glared across the room at Ted.

Without warning, several of the witches' soldiers rushed in.

When they saw Ted they drew their swords.

Greta smiled. "Seize him," she ordered.

As they rushed toward Ted, he opened his coat. "ATTACK," he shouted.

The bees took flight creating a black angry swarm. The buzzing sound was terrifying as they flew though the Gable toward the soldiers and Greta.

Greta's fright seeing the bees coming caused her to release her grip on Shana. She fell to the floor.

"Run…. Get to the tower," yelled Ted.

Shana took off.

The soldiers were instantly overwhelmed with bees, they fought back desperately swinging at the air.

"Sic him Rye," ordered Greta. "Devour him until there is nothing left," she continued then quickly vanished.

Rye charged at Ted. As she leaped up to sink her canines into him, Ted sidestepped her in mid-air while swinging his sword. The hot blade sliced deep across Rye's stomach. She yelped in pain falling to the ground; blood and guts pouring out her gaping wound.

With the hyena dead, Ted readied his stance to continue fighting. He looked up at the bees going this way and that, attacking something in the air.

Little did Greta know – bees do not see as human's see. Their vision is in yellow and red, detecting Greta's visible outline. She flew up the stairs trying to escape the angry horde.

The bees followed.

When she made it to her room and shut the door, the bees that remained on her she pulled off and crushed with her shoe.

After the last one hit the floor, the pain was instant. Her face began swelling up like a rotten green tomato.

Storming across the room, her torment was apparent. "Hagar," she shouted, going through her sister's ointments. She tossed bottle after bottle looking for the right one. PIG'S INTESTINES / CRUSHED MONKEY

BRAINS; *used for removing poisonous barbs* "Hagar," she again shouted, opening the jar and rubbing the awful stuff all over her face and arms.

Nothing but silence came back to her.

"Now where did she go?" she murmured.

Shana crept up the last remaining stairs toward the tower. She stood there listening. Hagar was inside talking to herself. She knew Hagar did that most of the time. Hagar was crazy; crazy with anger for becoming a witch.

She slightly opened the door, seeing her standing at the balcony rail looking out over the Drake.

Opening the door fully, she heard Hagar yelling, "Row, Egmon, row."

Shana coughed.

It was quick; Hagar spun around seeing her standing there. Her eyes became like black marbles glaring at the young girl.

"Are you surprised to see me," she said, not knowing what Hagar was going to do.

Hagar said nothing.

"I know everything," continued Shana, hoping her words would sink into the witches' heart. "I know all about the ship of fools, the Bestow - your father and his friends. I know all about the treasure, *Zesbrew* and about poor Pristina…"

"Silence, you foolish woman," she barked.

Shana stepped toward her knowing full well Hagar could kill her in an instant.

"How did you return?" grunted Hagar.

"I never went aboard that ship. The Shadow went as *me*. From what I heard, Captain Howler never made it to Grim, nor did his crew."

That struck Hagar.

"What is coming is beyond your power, even *Zesbrew's,*" she lied.

"Tell me," said Hagar. "Is it King William?"

"It's the entire Realm; the animals of the Redwood Forest, every village in the Northern and Southern Kingdoms. Even the villages within the Forbidden Land are on the march to Black Water," she again lied.

Hagar turned, seemingly gazing out over the Drake.

Shana knew she had the witch; the weaker one she knew just might turn. She stood there watching Hagar drifting on all that she had said.

Just then, Ted entered the room.

Hagar casually glanced back at him. *Lord Barrington,* she thought. *As handsome as the day is long.*

"She knows everything," said Shana. Seeing the expression on Hagar's face,

Ted placed his sword inside its sheath.

"The Shadow?" said Hagar, facing him. "I can feel his presence."

"He is here," replied Shana, "and as you can see, so is Lord Barrington. You know now that I have not lied to you."

Ted stood there calculating the situation. Hagar seemed more adrift than wanting to fight.

"I heard your words at the caldron with your sister, Hagar."

Hagar's eyes went soft. "You were spying on us, Shana?"

"Yes, all the time."

She nodded glancing at Ted. "No words?"

He took two steps toward her. "I want the secret to breaking the spell over Juliette. If you give it to me, we'll let you live."

"Do it Hagar," pleaded Shana. "You will return to normal along with your beauty."

Hagar looked from one to the other. "I have waited for this day forever. I have always hated being a witch and just want to be normal again; but my sister… you know," she replied as if thinking.

Shana and Ted slowly nodded agreeing with her.

"The spell is rather simple." "Simple," repeated Ted.

"We all know… well girls at least do. You never get a doll wet. It will ruin them."

Ted wrinkled his brow.

"Water, just plain ol' water," she giggled. "I created that spell. A spell *so* simple that no one would have ever guessed that just by placing Juliette in a tub of water would have broken the spell."

Ted slowly nodded. Inside however, he was sick to his stomach; sick that Hagar would do such a thing to a beautiful woman. "I want to thank you," he said. "We will let you live," he continued, turning to leave.

Hagar sighed; knowing her life was spared and she could return to her normal self. While her heart danced with joy believing it was all over, Ted quickly pulled out his sword, violently turned and chopped off her head. It hit the floor and rolled across the room. Her body dropped into a heap.

"Lord Barrington," shouted Shana, dismayed.

He slowly faced her.

His angry expression was so… she could barely look into his eyes.

"We are not done," he spat, walking past her to the door.

"My Lord," she softly spoke.

He stopped; keeping his back to her.

Shana looked down at Hagar. A part of her felt sorry for the witch but, she knew it was the right thing to do for all the wickedness Hager had done to others. "Where to now?" she asked.

"We must find Greta and end this once and for all."

32

When the sun rose up in the east, on the morning of the great battle, King William's army was on the march. By columns of hundreds on horseback and on foot, they crossed over the rock bridge into the Forbidden Land.

King William, wearing an impressive white uniform, gold breast plate and silver helmet, surrounded by Royal Guards, rode across first.

In the rear of the columns, came the catapults, pulled by horses; under the escort of William's gladiators. A unit of strong men specialized in the art of hand-to-hand combat. Their mission was to reduce the fortress wall, weaken their defenses and smash open the gates.

They marched all day and made good time entering the village of Orbed. The people all clamored about to witness such a sight. They waved and shook hands with soldiers as the army went through.

On the outskirts of the village, a stone man rode out of the forest. When he dismounted in front of the columns, soldier's immediately surrounded him.

William halted; stunned. It was the first time he had seen a stone man. When he learned of this evil spell by the Twins over the people of Nimrod made him angry. Seeing one up close was truly heart wrenching to witness.

"My name is Hons, ruler of Nimrod. I have met Alexus Arteria and Lord Barrington."

"Let him pass," ordered William.

Hons walked up to the king on horseback. He bowed then relayed what Alexus and Ted wanted him to say.

William was beside himself. "You have elephants?"

"Yes, your Grace. The Knight of the Redwood Forest has instructed his animals to wait here with my men for your arrival. Along with them there are dozens of Grassland Pipers, Zenith Bees which he took with him to Black Water and," he said, glancing at the men around him, "one giant grizzly bear he calls Dewclaw."

William waved him closer.

Hons stepped up to the king's horse.

"Did you say the Knight of the Redwood Forest?"

"Yes, your Majesty. Lord Barrington is that Knight. My men and I were mystified, dumbfounded actually to see him with these animals; as if they were his pets. They themselves are a formidable army to reckon with. I saw it first-hand."

William sat up in his saddle gazing down the road into the night; mystified himself.

"He also professed his love for your daughter and pledged his life to break the spell," added Hons.

Those tender words washed over William. *Once this is over, my daughter Juliette will marry Lord Barrington, the Knight of the Redwood Forest.* It was an impressive title, which sat well within his heart. He knew Ted would love Juliette more than a princess; he'd love her as if she were his queen.

"What can my men and I do for you?" asked Hons.

"I will have my archers and catapults weaken their forward defenses and outer wall. When that is accomplished, we'll have Lord Barrington's elephants smash through the gate. You and your men along with my gladiators will then go in and secure the courtyard. The rest of his animals can come in as they please, as long as they do not attack my men."

"You have my word, or more so, Lord Barrington's that none of your army will be harmed. I'd suspect the Grassland Pipers will wait until day break – that's if, there is anything left to attack."

William nodded. "Have your men fall in with the columns, the animals can move on their own."

"Yes, your Majesty.

While the procession of torches lit-up the way for William's army to continue onward to Black Water, high in the air, the Pipers and Major were following, as well. They would risk all to protect the *Promise*; even flying at night to do so.

Back at Black Water, the castle was fortifying their stronghold.

Captain Storm had every post manned; his archers standing ready at the wall.

To lessen the king's advances, he ordered the Twins' soldiers to meet William's army on the battlefield. By the hundreds they marched through the night with Commander Vanstone in charge.

At the edge of the forest they halted. Before them was open grassland stretching five hundred yards long; three hundred yards wide. The field was surrounded by forest, a good place to set-up an ambush.

Vanstone ordered his columns to separate. Two columns varied left and right to the sides of the field; while he held the front line with the major portion of the Twins' army.

It wasn't long after that they saw the forest on the other side glowing with torches. Vanstone and his soldiers hunkered down and waited.

William halted at the edge.

Commander Phelps and Hons rode up to him. "I don't like this, your Majesty," said Phelps.

Hons agreed.

"Send two riders out, one with a torch," ordered William.

"Yes, your Grace," replied Phelps, waving his hand.

Two soldiers rode up.

"Go half way and wait in the middle." "Yes, Sir," they replied.

As King William and his men watched, Shoeshon and his mighty comrades along with Dewclaw walked through the columns.

The men on foot and on horseback moved aside.

They came abreast of William and his Royal Guards.

The three massive elephants lifted their trunks; Dewclaw stood up on his hind legs.

"What are they doing?" asked William.

"They're sniffing the air. It's a telling sign that something is out there, your Grace," said Hons William sat back, watching his men riding out to the middle. Their horses then stopped and circled.

Dewclaw growled.

"The bear has detected something," said Hons.

"Douse the torches," ordered William.

From man to man the order was sent down the line. The torches went out. The forest went pitch black.

Dewclaw dropped down on all fours and headed left with one elephant. Shoeshon and another bull elephant went right.

Just then, an arrow went soaring through the air. It struck one of William's riders. He fell off his horse dead.

The one holding the torch dropped it and bolted back.

Vanstone rushed across his line and grabbed the soldiers who had fired that arrow. "You bastard, we just lost our advantage!"

Before letting him go, a horrific scream was heard then more screaming and yelling along with men running wildly through the dark.

Dewclaw had silently crept up to Vanstone's column on the left hiding within the brush along the tree line. He charged the group, tearing men apart. His mighty friend trumpeted charging in as well; crushing men as he ran through the ranks of Vanstone's soldiers. By the time Shoeshon joined in on the other side of the field, Vanstone's men were riding and running on foot back to Black Water.

Vanstone drove his sword into the ground; his anger apparent. The king of the north has animals. It did not set well with him. *Only one man has the power to command the animals… that is Lord Barrington. He's now working the mines for King Bela of Grim, so how can this be?*

With his army in disarray, he needed to get back to Black Water and inform the Twins that Egmon was right; they were coming with elephants no less. As he was about to give the order to retreat, a grunting sound came from behind. His column of soldiers began screaming and running.

He quickly turned facing the menace. Dewclaw was just meters away glaring at him. Vanstone desperately tried to pull out his sword from the ground. Before he could, the angry bear was upon him. He prayed it would be over quick; it was. Dewclaw raked his face with his giant paw; removing Vanstone's nose and tearing the facial skin down to the bone.

The brutal bite to his throat sent Vanstone into total darkness; darkness he'd never escape from. As his blood poured out, Dewclaw let go and went after others.

"Do we hold our line, your Majesty?" asked Phelps.

"No, we'll march through the night. Light the torches and let's be on our way," said William.

33

Inside the small boat, Egmon was upset. *All that I have done for them has never been enough.* "Row across the Drake, Egmon and gather your pets," he sarcastically repeated Greta saying. "I'll gather them alright."

When he came abreast of the tunnel leading into the cove he stayed clear of the massive rocks jutting up out of the water. After rowing around them, he allowed the incoming waves to push him inside.

Setting his ores down, he lit the lantern and placed it on a pole secured to the bow. Slowly paddling through the cold, damp tunnel, he sat there watching the flickering light dancing upon the rock walls and ceiling.

At the end, the lantern disbursed the darkness within; the massive cove came to life. He continued toward the pile of small rocks he used to tie off the boat and get out. With the boat secure, he grabbed the cloth bag of venison, the lantern and then carefully climbed up onto the large flat ledge.

He instantly froze. The cloth bag dropped from his hand. His little body began to shake; tears welling up in his eyes. "Jewel," he sniffled, seeing one of his pet crocodiles lying there with an arrow stuck in its head.

Emotionally distressed, he slowly walked over. One of its eyes was open, blood streaming down its snout; pooling on the rock.

He crumbled next to it, hugging the creature's head. The sadness in his heart, tossed him back to when he came upon the pair. They were just small then and were looking for food along the bank of the

Mead. He felt sorry for they too had been abandoned by their mother, as he was.

Over time, they would be waiting for him. Deer, lizard, whatever he could kill or capture, he'd toss out to them. It wasn't long that they grew in size and became his protectors.

Coming back to the present, he lifted his head off the croc and glanced down its twisted body. He knew his pet had died an awful death. With a heavy sigh, he got off his knees, walked over to the edge, looking for Brat, the male crocodile in the dark still water.

Raising the lantern high in the air, he called out to him. There was no answer. With his mind adrift on losing them both he glanced up at the large hole in the cove ceiling. His little jaw tightened suspecting what had happened.

The King of the North, he angrily thought. *My beautiful pet was killed by soldiers aboard a ship. It's the only way they could have made to the cove.*

"Brat," he again cried out, watching the surface.

It remained calm.

He went back to the bag, grabbed some meat and tossed it in.

Nothing; the meat just floated there. He called out to Brat again and again. Nothing but silence.

"He left me," sniffled Egmon, looking toward the tunnel leading out to the Drake. "I can't blame him," he murmured, wiping his tears. "Brat's companion is dead," he said, glancing back at the massive beast lying there dead.

With a slump of his shoulders he walked back to the boat. Before casting off, he thought of Greta. *What will I tell her? It doesn't matter. My whole life has been ruined.*

34

As Ted and Shana searched for Greta, way below in the bowel of the castle, Alexus and Mani descended the stairs. Near the bottom, they heard a wretched voice.

"Oh, my sweet, Pristina," said *Zesbrew,* waving his hand over her face.

Her head became unfrozen. She blinked a few times then tried to move; her body was as stiff as a board.

"How is my lovely servant?" asked *Zesbrew.*

"What is going on," she replied confused. "Don't you remember," he said, standing in front of her.

She turned her head then looked down at herself. "What have you done to me?" she gasped, gazing into his eyes. They were as dark as night.

"I have kept you all this time here with me in the catacomb. I wanted someone to keep me company."

She looked at the closed gate. In a flash, she remembered slipping down there to steal from the crypts. Rings, necklaces, anything she could find that would help her to escape.

"You do want to talk to *Zesbrew,* don't you?" he asked, reaching up and touching her soft cheek.

Before she could answer, Jasper poked his head out of one of the air-vent holes in the ceiling. He jumped down onto a tomb, then to the floor and made a mad dash toward the gate.

Stunned, *Zesbrew's* eyes locked onto the critter. When it ran through the bars, he heard this awful sound. Quickly turning back, he saw rats pouring out of all the holes; then water, lots of water came pouring down into the catacomb.

"Oh my," he said. "*Zesbrew* does not like water or rats," he panicked, knowing his wooden frame would not hold well in water; along with hundreds of rats desperately trying to escape, themselves. He hurried through the rats and water to his cave like structure.

"Where are you going?" yelled Pristina, fearing for her own life.

"*Zesbrew*!" shouted Alexus, stepping down on the cold damp floor. "Hurry, Mani. Get the key," he continued at the gate.

Zesbrew spun around hearing the ancient one's voice; a voice he'd never forget. "Alexus Arteria," he replied, looking down at the rats climbing his wooden frame to escape the water. He brushed them off and kept going. "You have a date with destiny, *Zesbrew*," shouted Alexus.

"I am and will always be," he yelled. "We will meet again one day, until then," he continued, looking about. His eyes fell upon the crypts. A devilish grin appeared. Raising his hands he called the dead. "Come out of the depth of darkness… awaken, and defend me." With that, he glanced back at the men opening the gate then hurried toward the metal door.

Mani set the key in. Alexus pushed it open.

"Get me out of here," cried Pristina; standing there frozen in place.

"We'll be right back," said Alexus, drawing his sword.

Mani drew his.

"You'll be right back," she spat, looking down at the water rising. "You fools… I'm going to drown if you don't get me out of here!"

Zesbrew opened the metal door and walked in. Water and rats came in with him. He quickly closed it; locking it shut. Within the darkness, he could feel the water still rushing in. Through holes at the bottom of the walls rats frantically came in; desperately climbing and holding onto anything to escape from drowning.

Zesbrew panicked fighting the rats clinging onto him. They were fighting and biting one another. He climbed up a rock in the back, pushing them away.

As Alexus and Mani headed to the end of the catacomb to ensure *Zesbrew* could not escape; an awful scraping sound was heard. They halted, ankle deep in water. To their utter disbelief, the crypts started opening. Skeletal hands came out pushing the large stone lids away.

Mani's eyes grew wide watching the dead crawling out of their graves. Some skeletal; some mummified. They were a ghastly sight.

Alexus stood back, sword ready. "Slice them to pieces," he shouted, swinging wildly at the dead men and women staggering toward them.

Mani watched Alexus cut off the head of one – then slice a skeletal body in half. Scared out of his mind, he let out a howling scream rushing toward the dead.

One after another, they fought their way through the sickening scene; skeletal and mummified body parts lying everywhere. At the end they looked for something to hold the door shut.

"The statues and bust next to the crypts," shouted Mani.

Alexus placed his sword in its sheath and headed back. "Come on," he said.

The two picked up one after another and placed them in front of the large metal door.

When they felt the door was securely blocked, Alexus yelled, "Let's get out of here."

As they ran through the water, rats and dead body parts to the gate. To their surprise, the hound's keeper, Bulmen was standing with Pristina.

"I'll carry her up. You two find Shana."

They nodded then took off for the stairs.

As the two made their way out of the catacomb, William's army was positioning their catapults fifty yards out from the castle wall.

Captain Storm ordered his archers to fire.

The battle commenced; the flaming tarred rocks from the catapults began raining down on Black Water; smashing through the wall and into the courtyard; setting fires throughout.

Arrows by the hundreds rained down on William's soldiers. Many took hits; many used their shields.

From out of the sky Grassland Pipers using the castle torches to see, came swooping through the air to attack the archers on the wall. The archers now in peril were unable to fire their arrows while defending themselves from the vicious attack from above.

William, gallantly sitting on his horse, saw his chance. He ordered the elephants to break down the gate.

The massive bulls charged. One after another, they tore into the wooden fortified gates until they burst open.

Seeing the raging elephants rushing in, the Twins' soldiers ran this way and that to escape being crushed. Many took to the lofts that were on fire; others ran back inside the castle.

The hounds attacked but were trampled; or ripped apart by Dewclaw.

William's gladiators rushed into the battle along with Hons and his stone men.

Swords, arrows, knives and axes were used on both sides.

The blood bath continued from the courtyard into the castle itself. Lord Barrington's animals were gaining the advantage; his elephants destroying everything in their path, the Pipers causing havoc from the sky, and Dewclaw ripping men apart.

Hearing the awful sounds outside, Greta had to find her sister. She waved her hand and disappeared. When she materialized in the tower, she instantly froze. Trembling, she walked over to Hagar's decapitated body; her precious blood pooling on the floor.

"Hagar," she moaned, seeing her head laying there. Her mouth dropped opened, her hands came up pressing against her chest. She staggered over and picked it up.

Greta's mind began shutting down; her reality slipping. "Hagar, stop this now," she scolded, carrying her head back to her body. She knelt next to it and placed it where it belonged.

It rolled away. "Now you listen to me, you put your head back on. I need you, sweet sister," she cried.

Sitting alongside her dead sister, she lifted her head and placed it within her lap. Hagar's eyes were open, her lips slightly parted. Greta caught her breath taking in her beautiful complexion. She touched her soft cheeks and began playing with her hair; all the while staring into Hagar's lifeless dead eyes.

"You look so, so, beautiful," she sniffled. "Just as beautiful as when you were a child," she continued, flashing back in time.

"Do you remember all the fun we had as children," she said. "Silly girls we were, putting on mother's make up, her jewelry and wearing her shoes," she laughed, pausing to look about the room.

"We had it all, sweet sister. Spoiled to the core we were. We could have anything we wanted," she sighed, curling her finger around Hagar's hair. "I can still remember our seamstress making those dresses for us. Yours blue, mine yellow and we pretended to be flowers dancing on the wind inside the courtyard," she whispered. "Do you remember that," she continued, looking down at her.

While sitting there in an emotional state of shock, she heard Egmon screaming. It brought her back from the darkness. She placed Hagar's head on the floor and got up.

At the balcony rail, her eyes locked onto him in the boat; rowing like a mad man. Behind him she saw the forty foot crocodile.

"Row, Egmon, row," she yelled through her cupped hands.

Desperately paddling, he looked up at Greta. He knew he was in serious trouble.

"Row, Egmon, row," again shouted Greta.

Egmon looked back. Terror filled his eyes seeing the monstrous beast with an arrow sticking out of its spine.

Ten feet.... Five feet... the boat hit the rocks near the castle.

Before Egmon could scramble out, the crocodile took hold of the backend; violently shaking it, tossing him out of the boat. He landed on the rocks up against the castle wall. Terrified, he watched the angry reptile shaking the boat within his teeth; banging it against the wall near him. He scooted away just in time.

Seeing Egmon, the crocodile let go of the boat and tried to grab him. Egmon ducked; its massive head hit the wall. The wall began to buckle.

Brat came up again trying to grab him. The force of its leap drove its head through the wall making a large gaping hole at the base.

The water began pouring in taking Egmon with it. Not being able to swim, he panicked. While desperately fighting to stay afloat, Egmon took hold of something. It felt like a statue until the thing wrapped its arms around him.

"You my gallant servant… carry *Zesbrew* out of here and I'll give you riches set for a king," he heard the wretched thing speaking.

Egmon screamed, realizing he was in the cave like structure with *Zesbrew*. The place now completely flooded; he let go of *Zesbrew* and pushed him away. As he did, the huge crocodile came into the hole. It opened its large jaws trying to grab Egmon. Instead, it grabbed *Zesbrew* almost biting him in half.

Scared out of his little mind, Egmon watched the beast take *Zesbrew* out of the cave and pull him back into the Drake; where he quickly went under. As the crocodile descended to the murky bottom below, it died due to the arrow sunk deep in its back. *Zesbrew,* trapped within his jaws, its teeth like a cage, the Relic, the Entity would remain in Brats' grip for all eternity; forever ending his reign of evil throughout the Realm.

Just then, Ted and Shana reentered the tower.

Greta turned glaring at them. "What have you done to my sweet sister?" she hissed, pointing down at Hagar's dead body.

Shana's mouth dropped open. "Look at you," gasped Shana.

Greta's eyes took in her hand pointing at Hagar. It was normal. She felt her face. Her long crooked nose was gone; her power fading.

"*Zesbrew* is dead," grunted Ted.

This can't be true, this can't be true.

Zesbrew is my power, thought Greta

"Your time is over!" shouted Shana, drawing her knife.

Ted drew his sword.

Furious, Greta did not want to believe it was over, but had to accept her fate. "My sweet evilness. My joy of darkness is ending," she helplessly moaned.

As Ted walked over ready to end her life, the tower violently shifted. The entire back wall was giving way due to the gaping hole at the bottom.

"We must get out of here," said Greta.

"You're not going anywhere," replied Ted.

Scared the tower was going to collapse, Shana headed for the door.

"Please, I beg of you," sighed Greta. "Let me go and I will leave this place forever. I swear I will."

"Many had begged you to spare their lives like Clara Brown, and you paid them no mind," reminded Ted, backing up.

The tower again shook.

"Please, I'll never harm another soul. I promise," replied Greta with soft caring eyes.

"You can promise me one thing," said Ted.

"Anything…. what, please tell me."

"You can die a quick death," he replied, pushing Shana out the door. He quickly shut it behind them. "Run," he yelled, taking the stairs down with her.

Greta desperately hurried to the door.

The tower began crumbling, making her fall. As she slid toward the outer balcony, she frantically took hold of one of the table legs. The table started sliding too. The back half of the castle let go, taking the tower with it.

Greta's terrifying scream went unanswered. She plunged into the water along with tons of bricks and debris; crushing her to the bottom, imprisoning her forever.

<h1 style="text-align:center">35</h1>

By the time Ted and Shana entered the Gable to leave, the place was on fire; dead bodies lay everywhere. The ceiling structure started to give-way, raining down on the black marble flooring below.

"We have to get out of here," shouted Ted, tucking her within his arms. They hurried through the heat and the thick smoke to the corridor.

Outside, they collapsed against a pillar, inhaling the fresh air. Before them was a horrific scene; there were gaping holes in the fortress wall, the entrance gates torn off. The courtyard had been completely destroyed; thick black smoke was billowing up into the sky, fires were still burning and the ghastly sight of mutilated bodies sprawled out all over the ground.

What was left of the Twins' army was sitting in a small group in the middle of the courtyard guarded by soldiers.

Ted sighed holding Shana within his arms.

She looked at him. Upon her filthy face sat the relief he felt deep inside. The war was over, the Twins were dead and hopefully *Zesbrew*.

As they stood there numb taking it all in, Shana gasped seeing Bulmen on the ground and Pristina, the chambermaid, kneeling next to him. She let go of Ted and rushed over.

Bulmen had taken an arrow to his shoulder.

"Are you alright," she asked, taking a knee.

""It hurts but I'll be OK," he replied, looking up at Pristina.

Shana picked up a piece of wood. "Bite down on this," she said.

It took her several turns to pull the arrow out.

He screamed.

"Bulmen," gasped Pristina, caressing his face.

"I'll be fine," he said, gazing up at her.

Shana saw something within his expression. She shifted her attention on Pristina gazing at him as well. *Did I miss something,* she thought. *These two… I would have never guessed.* To her it did not matter. She used Bulmen while at Black Water. *I guess he was using me as well.* She slowly stood up. "Take care of him," she said.

"I plan on it," replied Pristina.

"By the way, how did you get free?"

"Bulmen came down and carried me out."

"I see," she replied, glancing at Bulmen.

"You knew she was down there?" "Yes."

Shana nodded. Her assumptions were right. "I wish you both the very best," she replied, turning toward Lord Barrington.

As she met Ted's eyes, his warm smile – then suddenly, without warning - everything from then on seemed to go in slow motion.

Behind Ted, Shana saw Alexus and Mani come running out of the front entrance. "RUN!!!" they shouted. "The place is coming down!"

She watched Ted turn hearing Alexus screaming. She looked up just in time to see the outer castle walls giving way. Bree, Mylee and Nera flew out a smoke filled upper window.

As everyone in the courtyard started running for their lives, she stood there watching Mani pick up Bulmen and carry him toward the fortress entrance.

"Shana, Shana," she heard Ted calling. Before her mind engaged, he grabbed her and half carried her to safety.

Behind her, she could hear the elephants trumpeting, they and Dewclaw escaped through a hole in the fortress wall.

At the entrance, Ted looked back.

"Where is Jasper?" he shouted, panicking.

He was nowhere to be seen.

Ted fell to his knees watching the castle come crashing down in the courtyard. His heart sank as well. He couldn't imagine losing his friend; the one who set the whole thing in motion.

Shana walked up and fell to the ground alongside him. She couldn't bear losing Jasper too.

As they knelt there believing Jasper had no chance of escaping the castle, someone screamed. "There, there he is!"

Ted looked up from the ground. He spotted Jasper staggering out from the flames and the debris falling.

"Jasper," he yelled, quickly getting up and running toward him. "Jasper," he again shouted, ducking falling debris and fires.

"Ted!" yelled Shana, worried.

Jasper fell. He weakly got up and staggered a bit more then fell again.

Ted raced up, grabbed his ferret within his arms and took off for the gate.

As he ran through the smoke, burning debris, bricks, and wood flying through the air, all eyes were on him.

When he made it to safety and fell to his knees; his clothing smoldering, Shana, Alexus, and Mani raced up to him.

Shana quickly took Jasper. He looked dead.

Ted knelt there, out of breath staring up at her.

King William hurried over along with Commander Phelps and Hons.

They stood there heart-stricken watching Shana blowing air into the small creature's lungs.

Tears rolled down Ted's face, believing his beloved ferret was dead.

Shana would not give up. Through her tears she blew into his mouth, pushed on his stomach and did it again and again.

Jasper's tail finally moved, then his legs. She blew into him again.

Jasper coughed.

A heavenly sigh washed over the group. Ted got up and staggered over.

Shana placed Jasper within his hands. Jasper opened his little eyes.

"Jasper," gushed Ted.

"I didn't think I'd make it," he weakly replied.

Bree, Nera and Mylee, landed on Ted's shoulder.

Jasper looked at them and then saw Shoeshon, his big friends and Dewclaw standing there. To his surprise, Major flew down and landed on Shoeshon's tusk.

"You had us worried," said Major.

"I was worrying myself," he said then coughed. "I tried several passageways without any luck."

Major nodded.

"I then just followed the rats."

They held their laughter, but deep inside they were delighted to hear that; for a rat will do anything to survive.

The humans standing there saw something they would have never dreamed of seeing in their life time. The Knight of the Redwood Forest surrounded by his friends, worried about Jasper.

King William walked through the group. The elephants and Dewclaw moved aside. He too was beside himself taking in all the animals.

Ted glanced up at him; the king's outfit dirty and tattered. He too, had fought.

"Since you are on the ground, Lord Barrington, will you please kneel before me?"

The animals moved back – the humans did also, giving the king room.

Both looking tattered themselves, Ted knelt before the king while holding Jasper.

"Lord Barrington, Lord Jasper," he said, placing his sword on Ted's shoulder. "On this day, after the great battle and finally ridding our land of the Twins and the evil Relic, *Zesbrew* – for your gallantry, I hereby pronounce you Knights of the Northern Kingdom."

Cheers and shouts resounded from the group. The elephants trumpeted; Dewclaw stood on his hind legs and roared.

King William stepped sideways. "Shana, come forward."

Shana's face went flush; she was shocked standing there.

"Come," said William.

She walked over.

"Kneel."

Shana took a knee.

"What is your last name?"

"Cambridge, Shana Cambridge."

William nodded. He placed his sword on her shoulder. "Shana Cambridge, you now hold the title of Lady Cambridge. You will always have a seat in the Great Hall and can call upon the king whenever you so desire. Stand, Lady Cambridge."

With tears of joy rolling down her cheek she stood in front of the king. "Thank you my Lord. I will serve you in all endeavors."

He nodded.

"Hons, Mani – step forward."

The two looked at one another surprised.

They walked over.

"Kneel before me."

"They did as he asked.

"I, along with the rest of the kingdom – are glad you and your men along with your people are normal again."

"We are pleased as well, your Grace," replied Hons.

William then placed his sword on each of their shoulders and pronounced the pair Knights of the Northern Kingdom, and… he gave them an added title; Lords over their villages.

When the ceremony was over, Shana looked about, several were missing; *Drew and Fons?* She asked about them.

Mani shook his head. "We went down to try and get them out. Sadly, they did not make it."

It broke her heart hearing that.

Ted wrapped his arm around her. He too was disheartened.

She looked up and gave him a sad smile.

"Lord Barrington," said William. "Yes your Grace."

"I believe you have some unfinished business," he replied, raising a brow.

"That I have, your Majesty, and I," he said, looking about the group, "I will cherish your beloved daughter for the rest of my life; until the end of time – until the day after eternity."

Shana's heart melted hearing that. It made her pause for a moment. In the stillness of her mind she thought of Egmon. Why, she had not a clue, but then realized – he too was abused by those evil witches. She slowly turned toward Ted.

"I'll see you back to your village," he said to her expression.

He was surprised to hear her reply. "I'm not leaving."

"You're not?"

"No, I must find Egmon." "Why?"

"Because, Lord Barrington, I just realized…. he's been abused as much as I have while living here. He deserves a better life."

"You think you can find him?" replied Ted, glancing back at the castle, or what was left of it.

"She looked that way."

"Excuse me," they heard a voice.

The both turned.

It was one of the Twins' soldiers. "The last I heard, Egmon was going to the tunnel to get his pets."

Shana stood back staring at him. "I may know where he is."

"Where?"

"The bank of the river." "I'm leaving, Shana."

She had a question within her eyes.

"Where… to Juliette?"

"Yes, back to the Beginning."

That was puzzling to hear. "I'll catch up." Ted smiled, leaned in and kissed her cheek; knowing he'd never see her again. "You are one hell of a woman, Shana. You do that." She left his side and headed to the Isle of Drake.

As the groups began disbursing, Shoeshon, his bull comrades and Declaw walked up.

"How can I ever repay any of you?" he asked, rubbing Shoeshon's trunk.

"There is only one way to repay us, Lord Barrington," replied Major.

Ted raised his brow wanting to hear.

"Go to Juliette and make her well again."

Ted was so overwhelmed he had no words. He stepped up and rubbed Major's head. "I will, you can count on that. You can ALL count on that."

"We'll see Jasper makes it back to the Redwood Forest," said Shoeshon.

"No," replied Ted, looking down at Jasper's dirty face. "He's coming with me. I will never forget any of you, and will always cherish our time together."

The animals nodded.

"I must say goodbye to Alexus and Mani.

Walking over, he knew their moment together would be an emotional one as well.

"Your war is over," said Ted. "It's time to repair, to rebuild, and to make things right here in the Realm. And, as our noble king had said, I do have business to attend to elsewhere."

"That you do, Lord Barrington" replied Alexus. "You have the key to return. Go to her," he continued with a gleam in his eye.

Ted had all forgotten all about the key around his neck. He reached up and rubbed it within his shirt. "It's what I came here for and I cannot wait to be by her side."

Saying goodbye is one thing. Saying goodbye forever is another. It's not easy walking away knowing you'll never see them again. He tucked that moment deep inside his chest, shook their hands - then went off looking for a horse.

He spotted Commander Phelps and headed over to him.

"I need a horse."

"I suppose you do, Lord Barrington," replied Phelps. "Take mine."

"Yours?"

"That's right. I'll be here for days cleaning up. The king's council will be coming soon. This," he said, waving his hand at what was left of Twins' castle, "and all the land back to the rock bridge is now considered the Northern Kingdom."

From the side, Ted watched William's chin lift as if to say; that's right.

"I could not agree more, your Majesty. The people of this land love you. Look after them and they will gladly serve you."

"No better words spoken, Lord Barrington. Go now, see to Juliette and give her our love."

Ted bowed his head, shook both their hands and headed over to the Commander's horse. "Hang on Jasper," he said, nudging it in the side.

"Lord Barrington," shouted Hons.

Ted cantered the horse.

"I really have no words," he said, reaching out his hand.

Ted took it within his. "You just said enough, my friend. I am glad to see you normal again."

Hons wiped the tear in his eye. "I'll never forget you. Take care, Lord Barrington."

"I'll never forget you either, Hons," he replied, leaving.

As Ted trotted down the road he wanted to look back. In his mind's eye however, Knights do not look back. They sit high in the saddle, faced forward and shoulders up.

That is what King William, Commander Phelps and Hons observed as they watched Ted until the road turned and he was gone.

It was evening on the third day when Ted finally entered the Redwood Forest. While riding through the tall trees, he began drifting. Gabe, Hazel and Juliette sat warmly within his heart. *Home, I just want to go home.* That thought made him realize he had a lot of explaining to do; his time away and Juliette.

How would he explain *her* to them? Gabe saw her, but that was when she was a doll. Hazel on the other hand, well – she just might end up needing a shrink. The other part that tugged on his heart was Juliette herself. He worried that she'd be so confused living in another world that she'd demand to go back. It was something he'd have to contend with.

When he rode up to the path and seeing the beautiful blue haze, he had forgotten all about Grandfather. *If he is asleep, should I just ride past?*

Coming to the clearing he decided *yes,* he'd allow him to sleep and head straight to the ridge. Slowly, he came abreast of Grandfather. He was…. sound asleep. Quietly, he rode on.

Twenty yards away, Grandfather opened his eyes seeing him leaving. He contentedly smiled knowing Lord Barrington had completed his quest; the Twins were dead. The Realm would become anew and he… well… he would always be the Beginning.

Ted ventured out of the forest and up to the ridge line. He slowly dismounted, took off the saddle and gave the Commander's horse a pat on the rear. "You are free my friend."

The horse neighed, then galloped away.

"Are you ready, Jasper?" "Where are we going?"

"Home, we're going home."

"Home?" he replied confused.

"Yes, to the Great Beyond. You do want to go home with me, don't you?"

"To the Great Beyond," he repeated, gazing out over the valley. "Yes, I sure would."

"Hang on," said Ted; he then suddenly remembered something.

"What is it?"

"The sword; I can't take it with me. It belongs in the Realm," he replied looking about to lay it somewhere. He spotted a dead tree trunk and placed it on top. "Now," he said, walking back to the edge. "Are you ready?"

"Yes."

With that, Ted leaped off.

A great flash of light engulfed them. Through the portal they went. When everything stopped, Ted opened his eyes; sitting on the storage room floor. He glanced over at the chair. Juliette was not there. He began to panic thinking it was all a dream. *How could that be with Jasper in my arms?*

"Mr. Barrington!!" he heard Hazel scream.

"Oh no…" gasped Ted. "Juliette," he said, dropping Jasper and racing out of the room.

After running up the stairs and opening the door. Hazel again shouted his name. He ran through the kitchen to the entrance-way.

"Mr. Barrington," she sighed, holding her hands to her chest.

"What is it?"

"I don't know," she gasped, pointing up the staircase. "Someone, something; whatever it was… just ran up the stairs. I lost my breath seeing her or…"

"OK, I'll go check."

"You do that. I'll be out front. I'm about to lose my mind," she replied, hurrying for the front doors.

As Ted proceeded up, everything seemed to go in slow motion. He spotted James walking toward the staircase above. The two said nothing staring at one another. As James went to pass heading down, he whispered, "I told her everything. She is up in your room."

Ted had a million questions to ask him, but right now, was not the time. Heart pounding, he continued up.

When he entered his room, Juliette was standing in front of the bay windows looking out. Ted lost his breath seeing her standing there.

She slowly turned. The moment seemed forever as Ted took in every detail of her beauty. Even though she was still a doll, she was the most exquisite creature he had ever seen.

"M'lady," he said, bowing his head.

"You must be Lord Barrington," she softly spoke. "Sheppard's cousin?"

Her voice was like sweet violins playing in his ear. "Yes M'lady."

"Alexus just told me everything that you have done to remove the evil spell the Twins had placed upon me but, as you can see," she sadly replied, "all your efforts were for naught." Those words caught in her throat; tears welled up within her eyes.

"I prayed with all my heart that upon my return you'd be back to normal like the rest of those in the Realm who were placed under their evil spells."

She cupped her hands to her face and began to cry.

Seeing her distress, saddened his heart; he slowly walked over.

She fell into his arms sobbing.

It startled him having her so close.

"Shh… everything will be alright."

"Everything will be alright," she sniffled, lifting her head and gazing into his eyes. "Even though my parents, King William and my mother,

Queen Victoria have granted you my hand in marriage, you cannot marry a doll. How can I bear you children and raise a family together. I mean… how can we even make….”

Ted placed a finger to her lips. “I know the secret to removing the spell my darling.”

She stood back staring at him.

“Before I killed Hagar, she told me.” “She told you?”

“Yes. It’s quite simple.”

“Simple,” she repeated, hoping beyond hope that it would be.

“Come,” he said, gently picking her up within his arms.

She rested her head on his shoulder.

“Soon, my enchanting Countess, you’ll return to normal,” he whispered, carrying her out of the room.

Down the flight of stairs, through the archway and into the back of the mansion, he carried her through the open patio door.

“Now, just hang onto me.” “I will.”

Crossing the tiles, he took the steps down into the pool. “Together, we’ll go under.” “OK.”

The two slipped under. Ted held her there for a moment then lifted her out and over to the side. There, he laid her down along the edge and got out.

James and Gabe stood at the patio doorway watching.

“I can’t believe what I’m seeing, James.

How did she come alive?”

“All in good time, Gabe… all in good time. Tell me though.” “Yes?”

“How would you feel if Juliette became your step-mother? Not that she could ever replace your real mom. No one could ever do that.”

Gabe looked at his father kneeling next to her. “I think it would be the coolest thing, James. No one would ever believe…”

“That Gabe must always remain a secret,” he interrupted.

“A secret I’ll keep forever, James. I promise you that.”

“Come,” he said, walking to the pool.

The pair watched in amazement as Juliette, Countess of Lyon Head started to transform; her soft velvet skin returning to normal.

She opened her eyes, staring up at the three. She could see it in their expression; something magical had happened.

"Welcome home M'lady," said Ted, with a warm bright smile.

With tears in her eyes, she reached up and touched her face, looked at her hands and arms. "I'm normal. I'm really normal," she gushed.

"I know this isn't a good time to ask," said Ted. "I mean, when you ask a woman such a question; one would want to make it a special occasion."

She raised her brow; listening to him rambling.

"Will you marry me and become my wife?"

More tears rolled down her cheek. "Yes, yes, I'll marry you, Lord Barrington," she happily sobbed, reaching up and touching his face.

"Lord Barrington," mouthed Gabe to James.

James light heartedly smiled. "More like the Knight of the Redwood Forest," he replied.

Ted glanced up at him. *James,* he thought. *The man of many faces as Queen Victoria had stated.* It was beyond his thinking several days ago, but now - it all fell into place with his words stating he was the Knight of the Redwood Forest. *James is the Shadow, and all those he changed into. And now,* his thoughts continued, *he is the guardian of the Barrington family with Juliette, Countess of Lyon Head as Queen.*

"The Knight of the Red Forest," repeated Juliette, looking from James to Ted.

Ted stepped out of his heart-felt thoughts. "We have lots of time to explain," he said, helping her to her feet.

"And you are," she asked Gabe. "I'm his son."

"Well… a handsome one at that," she teased, rubbing his hair. "I saw a woman," she continued, glancing at Ted.

"You mean that one," replied Gabe, pointing at the door.

Hazel stood in the patio doorway shaking her head; awestruck to what she was seeing. One minute the woman looked different, odd — and now… her mind tried to engage what had just happened.

"Hazel," said Ted.

"Yes, Mr. Barrington," she replied, tossing her thoughts aside.

"It's Lord Barrington," corrected Juliette.

Hazel wrinkled her brow. "Am I missing something? I mean, can anyone tell me what in the dickens is going on?"

"Yes, later. Right now, will you please go down to the storage room and see if we have any clothes she could wear."

By his expression, she knew what he was saying. Do we have any of his late wife's clothing still? "Yes, Lord Barrington," she humorously replied.

"Yes your Grace," corrected Juliette.

Ted, James, and Gabe held their laughter.

"Oh, my word," murmured Hazel, turning to leave. As she did, she shrieked cupping her hands to her face seeing a ferret. "Lord Barrington," she shouted.

Ted saw Jasper and smiled. "He won't harm you. Come, Jasper."

Jasper ran out and sat next to his feet.

"I'm losing my mind," gasped Hazel. "After today, you might need to order more liquor," she said, leaving.

The laughter was instant.

"Never in all my life have I ever been corrected with such out dated baloney. Yes, Lord Barrington, yes your Grace," she spewed, heading to the basement door.

EPILOGUE

Shana found Egmon along the bank of the Drake, lying with his face in the mud. He appeared to be dead.

"Egmon," she said worried, rolling him over. She checked his pulse and smiled. "Egmon," she again said, softly tapping his face.

He opened his eyes. "Where am I?" he moaned, half out of it.

"You're safe now. It's over." "What's over?"

"The war. The Twins are dead."

He closed his eyes. In that still moment, he flashed back to hanging onto *Zesbrew* in the cave like structure, and then *Zesbrew* was taken by Brat. "That horrid creature is also dead," he sighed with relief.

Shana sat next to him. "How did he die?" she asked, gazing over the Drake.

"My pet crocodile took him out of his cave. He almost grabbed me."

"It's all over, Egmon. Right now we must catch up to Lord Barrington."

"Lord Barrington," he questioned, believing he was in Grim.

"Yes, Egmon, he was here. He escaped from Captain Howler who now sleeps with the fish."

"Where did he go?"

"He mentioned something about the Beginning to me. Do you know where that is?"

"It's at the beginning of the Redwood Forest."

"Wow, we better hurry then," she replied, yanking him to his feet.

"Why do you want to catch up with him?" he asked, being tugged along.

"Because he is the Knight of the Redwood Forest and will be marrying Juliette Tyrus, Countess of Lyon Head. We would be in good stead working for them," she replied, escorting him to the corner of the castle. "Now let's find two horses, shall we."

They slipped past the soldiers cleaning up and carrying out the dead. Several horses were grazing near the tree line. "We'll borrow those two," she whispered.

The ride through the Realm was long and grueling. By the time they made it to the Redwood Forest, the morning sunlight was bathing the interior.

When they came down the path with the beautiful blue mist, they dismounted, stunned at what they saw; a single white tree, perfectly shaped, surrounding by lush green foliage. Without realizing there was a face carved on the tree, they continued to the ridge.

Lord Barrington was not there.

Looking down into the valley, Shana called out to him.

Nothing, not a sound returned.

"He is not here," spoke a female behind them.

The two turned seeing an ol' woman sitting on a dead tree trunk.

"Tess," beamed Shana, walking over. "How did you get here?"

Tess looked at her then at the dwarf with the disfigured face.

"This is Egmon. He too worked for the Twins."

"She saved me," remarked Egmon, pointing at Shana.

"I did not save him. He was lying in the mud along the Drake," she blushed. "So where is Lord Barrington?"

"He went to the Great Beyond," she replied, nodded toward the ridge. The two glanced that way.

"You mean down in that valley?" asked Shana.

Tess gave a pleasant smile.

Shana leaned on one foot gazing at her.

She had seen that smile before.

"The Realm is where you two belong. Just follow that path, you'll find the place much different."

"Different?" repeated Shana, glancing at Egmon. "Why sure it's different. The Forbidden Land is no longer dead. Everything has come back to life."

"It has," agreed Egmon.

Tess sat there staring at the two. "You'll find so much more has changed once you return," she replied, "and please, take this," she continued, handing Shana the sword.

They both gazed at it.

"I think this belongs to you, Egmon." "Me," he questioned.

"Yes, now come," said Shana, tugging his shirt. "Goodbye, Tess."

"It was nice to meet you," he said.

When they got to the path with the beautiful flowering trees, they looked back. Tess was not there.

"Where did she go?" asked Egmon

"I'm not sure, but she has done that before to me," she replied. "Let's go home," she continued, gathering their horses.

"I have no home," he said with a frown.

"You do now. Orbed is a lovely village. The people there would gladly have you... you'll see."

"Are you sure?"

"Yes, now let's keep moving."

When they came to the top of the hill, they froze seeing the face carved in the tree.

"Was that there before?" asked Egmon; surprised.

"Maybe it was and we did not see it."

"Can we check it out before we ride off?" "Sure."

The two walked down the hill and stood in front of the tree.

"Look," beamed Egmon, seeing the colorful Manta Rays flying through the mist overhead.

"Well, I'll be," gushed Shana.

"Who are you," a deep voice sounded.

The two stepped back holding each other. Their eyes went wide seeing the face on the tree looking at them.

"Did you say something?" asked Shana. "Yes, I asked... who are you?"

"Well, I'll be," she sighed. "I'm Shana and this is Egmon."

Grandfather looked at the dwarf.

"Who are you," she then asked. "I am the Beginning."

"The Beginning," mumbled Egmon, remembering Shana telling him that Lord Barrington was going back to the Beginning.

"Everything starts here in the Realm."

They stared at him wanting to hear more.

"You two are now standing at the Beginning. Your destiny starts down that path," he said, shifting his eyes toward the trail.

"But we already live in the Realm."

"Now that you are here you must start over."

"We must start over," questioned Shana, confused.

"Yes, but this time you have a chance to live a new life; especially you," said Grandfather, staring at Egmon.

"Me?" he replied, surprised hearing that.

Grandfather looked up; spreading his branches.

To their shock, the blue haze began drifting downward; with it, came the Manta Rays. They flew this way and that all around the pair.

Egmon started feeling funny. His body started tingling. "What is happening to me?" he said worried.

Shana stood back watching his face becoming normal; his little body getting bigger. She fell to the ground amazed seeing Egmon changing; changing into a handsome young man. His clothing began tearing; he was getting taller.

The blue haze and Manta Rays drifted upward.

"Get up," said Grandfather.

Shana slowly got to her feet; mouth open - gawking at Egmon.

Egmon stood there in awe looking down at himself. "It's a miracle," he beamed. "I'm normal," he said, smiling at her.

"Egmon," she laughed. "You…"

"Everything becomes anew at the Beginning," interrupted Grandfather.

They looked at him.

"Your beginning starts now for the two of you."

"I could just…" gushed Shana, kissing Grandfather's nose.

He blushed with delight.

"Come, Egmon," she said, taking his hand. "Goodbye, Grandfather and thank you." "Good luck in your quest of finding happiness," he replied with a twinkle in his eye.

Walking hand in hand with their horses following, the two smiled at one another.

Twenty yards down the path, Egmon suddenly stop.

"What is it," she asked, seeing him staring at the ground.

As if in a trance he said nothing.

"Egmon!"

He slowly looked at her. "What is it?" she begged. "The treasure!"

Shana stepped back. Her mind exploded. "By the Gods," she sighed, flashing back to hearing Greta saying the treasure was worth a thousand kingdoms.

"You know," he said, squeezing her hand.

She stepped out of her heavenly thoughts.

"We're the only ones in all the Northern Kingdom that know where that treasure is."

A huge smile slowly appeared upon her face. She looked back to where Grandfather was. *"Good luck in your quest of finding happiness,"* she whispered his words. "I think we just found it, Egmon."

"You're right my sweet Princess. Let's go, we have much to think about and plan." "That we do, that we do."

The *Realm* is a place where dreams come true; that's if you truly believe in your destiny of discovering a lifetime of happiness filled with magical adventure.

THE END

ABOUT JEFF WRIGHT

Jeff's brilliantly crafted novels are a must read. His reading audience expands across 5 countries; they have been enthusiastically waiting for this his tenth book – *The Realm*.

Please check out his prior novels. You just might find yourself becoming one of his fans; like thousands of others.

The Ghost of Sage Grey... A ghostly thriller with one awesome ghost.

The Mysterious Abigail Rose... A magical story for all ages.

The Mr. Bones Trilogy... A fast pace detective thriller that takes you straight into the Twilight Zone.

Whiskers... A magical story about a famous singer.

Yeti – 1 & 2... An Alaskan Thriller like no other.

Catherine Knox; A Rose amongst the Thorns... A brilliantly crafted 1700 sailing adventure.

You may purchase Jeff's books on Amazon, and or – directly from him at www.facebook.com/jeffwrightbooks.

www.ingramcontent.com/pod-product-compliance
Lightning Source LLC
Chambersburg PA
CBHW071250300726

48975CB00002B/629